Praise for the novels of John (J. Edwin) Buja

"Charles De Lint's nastier brother."

Christopher Golden – NYT bestselling author of
THE HOUSE OF LAST RESORT

"J. Edwin Buja is a mesmerizer."

Linda D. Addison – the first African American
recipient of the *HWA Bram Stoker Award®*,
and *HWA Lifetime Achievement Award* winner.

"Buja's prose is crisp and involving. His portrayal of the characters is convincing. It's not often I discover a writer who is so darn good with the mechanics of storytelling."

Tony Tremblay – author of DAMAGE DONE

"…kept my mind spinning with possibilities and left my lungs breathless."

Char's Horror Corner

"…written in spare, swift-moving pellucid prose…the ideal novel in which to lose oneself over the course of a rainy weekend of cozy reading."

Michael Rowe – author of ENTER, NIGHT

"… a wild and woolly novel with a sense of humor and a great sense of mystery."

Alan M. Clark – author of
A PARLIAMENT OF CROWS

"Quiet, isolated and tranquil, Coverdale could be the inspiration for a Norman Rockwell illustration…if it was painted by Gahan Wilson."

P. D. Cacek – author of SECOND LIVES

COVERDALE

John Buja

YAP Books

Haverhill House Publishing LLC

Coverdale © 2024 John Buja
Cover illustration design and setup © 2024 Errick Nunnally

978-1-949140-54-5 Hardcover
978-1-949140-55-2 Trade Paperback

YAP Books is an imprint of Haverhill House Publishing LLC

Haverhill House Publishing LLC
643 E Broadway
Haverhill MA 01830-2420
www.haverhillhouse.com

For Dianne
Forever and a day.

Acknowledgments

Trish Cacek read the first version of this over a weekend at Necon. Her enthusiasm and advocacy were overwhelming. I want to thank her for dragging me to a publisher to make a pitch. It was the kind of experience I needed.

Thank you to my writing group support team; Sal Clemente, Jason Salzarulo, Terry Emery, Carolyn Cooper, and Brian MacDonald. Your advice and critiques are invaluable and make me a better writer.

COVERDALE

Chapter One

"Why should *I* help *you*? *I* didn't ask to move to this stupid town."

Charlie Bowen watched while his sister, Ant, brushed some dust from her shorts then continued to sand her fingernails. He winced when a spasm of pain ran up his leg from his trapped foot.

Working hard to control his anger and frustration, he said, "You're right, Ant. You'd be less than useless anyway." He attempted to shift his position, but the heavy oak desk had him pinned against the banister. "Besides, we wouldn't want to scratch the nice wood floors with your furniture. Better it rests on my foot." The last word came out as a gasp when the desk shifted, and its typing drawer slid into Charlie's stomach.

"Dad! Help me, please," said Charlie in a voice he hoped was loud enough for his dad to hear.

George Bowen appeared at the front door, looked surprised, and said, "Honey, couldn't you give your brother a hand? It is your desk, after all."

"*Daddee!* No way. I don't want to wreck my nails. I just got them perfect."

"Okay, but at least sit somewhere out of the way."

"Like in the middle of the highway," said Charlie quietly.

"What was that, Charlie?" George turned to face his son and grabbed a corner of the desk, realizing Charlie needed immediate help.

Charlie sighed in relief when the weight of the desk left

his foot and he could move freely.

Ant got up from the stairs where she had been attending to her nails. With a loud huff, she stomped to the front door. "I'll just go out and kill myself. As if anyone in this stupid house would notice." She stormed out.

"That's fine, honey," said George.

"Dad, have you ever thought about getting a hearing aid? All those concerts must have affected your ears."

"I'm fine, son. I just don't pay attention as much as I should." George took a deep breath and lifted his end of the desk. "Shall we try to get this thing upstairs without dropping it or punching a hole in the wall?"

Two hours later, Charlie and his father watched the moving van pull away from their house.

"Strange guys," said Charlie. He noted the company logo, a big red circle enclosing a cross, on the side of the van. It had been on the movers' shirts, and both men wore rings that bore the symbol. "Temple Movers. They seem kind of solemn for moving guys. No swearing or rude comments about mom's shorts."

"Can't say as I noticed," said George between sips from his can of soda. "All I cared about was getting everything in the house before dark."

"Dinner," Charlie's mother, Nell, shouted from the kitchen. "We're eating out on the deck."

"And what about the neighbors?" said Charlie. "I saw a lot of them watching us. Not one of them came by to offer a helping hand. I thought small towns were supposed to be friendly."

"Calm down, Charlie," said George. They walked through the kitchen. "Your mother and I met them last week when we came to sign the final papers for the house. They were all very nice and friendly. Besides, ...”

George held the back door open so Charlie could pass through. A crowd was on the deck, silent while all eyes were on Charlie.

He couldn't help but wonder how so many people were able to get here without making any noise. For a moment, Charlie feared he was going deaf like his father. But that was ridiculous.

All thoughts of the neighbors vanished when he beheld the picnic table by the railing. It was covered with food: at least four kinds of salads, several jellies already melting in the late afternoon heat, rolls, cold cuts, and cheese. Someone's drooling dog stood ready to pounce at any stray food. And that looked like, yes, it was, the largest lemon meringue pie Charlie had ever seen.

“What do you think of our neighbors now?” George stood waiting with his arms folded.

Charlie shrugged. He still thought it would have been nice to have had some help. Before he could voice his opinion, his father had joined a small group of men by the deck stairs.

Nell Bowen introduced Charlie to everyone. He promptly forgot their names. The only thing that stuck in his mind was the fact that every man in the crowd wore a red cross ring. None of the women wore them.

He wondered if it was a local school crest or something like that.

Charlie quickly grabbed a large slice of the meringue pie before anyone else could get their claws into it, and then he pigged out on tuna salad and cold cuts. He also went to work on a huge green salad that few people were eating. Ant sat by herself near the sliding door, checking out her reflection to see if a hair was out of place.

While he sat quietly, alone in a corner to eat, Charlie scanned the people in attendance. He realized that he and Ant were the only young people there. Didn't the neighbors have children? When he asked a woman who was filling her plate with tuna salad—Charlie staying close to the meringue in case someone else tried to finish it before he could get more—she assured him that, yes, there were kids in town around his own age. They were off somewhere doing what kids his age do on an August Saturday afternoon. He guessed meeting the new kid on the block certainly wasn't one of them.

The men had gathered in small groups separate from the women. They were busy talking about something, but not work. Definitely not work. Earlier, Charlie heard his father raise the subject with a couple of the other men. He was told brusquely, "That is not something we discuss outside of The Institute, Mr. Bowen." When the speaker, a short, thin man with a tiny, upturned nose and a shining bald head, noticed Charlie listening, he glared at him with such anger and hatred that Charlie nearly lost control of his bladder.

He shivered, wondering how such a small man could instill such a feeling of fear.

Even his father looked uncomfortable and stared at his shoes. No one would make eye contact with the little man. The bald guy kept staring at Charlie with his tiny, weasel eyes until Charlie looked away from the group.

Ant had pulled herself, or been pulled, from admiring her reflection and was now at the center of a large group of women. They cooed about her long, curly brown hair.

Charlie's own hair was long, brown, and naturally curled. No one cooed at him, which made him slightly jealous until he remembered he hated being the center of attention.

Finished with eating, after having a third piece of lemon

meringue pie—if no one's going to eat it, why let it go to waste—Charlie made his excuses and left the deck. He needn't have bothered. No one paid him any attention, least of all his father.

Charlie ran upstairs to his new room, searched the boxes, and found his Walkman and tapes. Selecting a tape that fit his mood—tired and a little hyper—he slapped it in the machine and secured the Walkman to his belt.

Walkman.

Charlie yearned for a smartphone, or at the very least, an old iPod. He still couldn't afford either and wasn't about to settle for something cheap. His father didn't see the need since the old Walkman still worked just fine, and there were plenty of tapes. Despite being a scientist, George Bowen was a Luddite regarding technology. He still preferred vinyl, though Charlie was slowly coming around to that choice. Noticing that his bed hadn't been put together yet, he hesitated. Should he do it now? It would be a drag to do it later when he was even more tired. No, he really wanted to get out and run.

Sleeping on a mattress on the floor wasn't such a bad thing. Anyway, he only ever needed about five hours of sleep a night, so it wouldn't be much of an inconvenience.

The solitude of running gave Charlie plenty of time to think through his problems and sort them out. It was also the perfect way to work off all the food he had scarfed down at the party. He'd been on his high school cross-country team for four years but didn't care about winning. Peer pressure forced him to take up a sport, and long-distance running involved the least amount of teamwork.

Charlie's biggest problem right now was figuring out why his family had moved to the middle of a dense forest. To Coverdale, a town that was so unknown, it didn't even have a page in Wikipedia.

George Bowen had been offered a plum job by The Institute—always spoken of with capital letters—and he had leaped at the opportunity. The money was better, and he was being given the chance to work on some cutting-edge research. That was all that Charlie knew. His father was a biologist, and there had been mention of blood and DNA or something like that. Charlie wasn't interested; he preferred history. On those rare occasions his father talked about science, Charlie zoned out.

One thing that did interest Charlie was his father's attitude after he got the job. He kept going on about how important his position was and that it would be a stepping stone to even greater heights. No more being a grunt in a small lab where no one noticed him. The family would benefit greatly from his newfound prestige. What those benefits and heights were, George Bowen never said. This developing concern about power and prestige was something new. Charlie's mother had listened patiently while her husband droned on but showed little enthusiasm.

Thinking back to the gathering on the deck, Charlie thought that his sister seemed more important to the women of Coverdale than his mother. He couldn't recall whether or not his mother had mentioned her art at all. There was a time when you couldn't shut Nell Bowen up about her passion. Her enthusiasm was contagious, and everyone near her caught the bug. Everyone that is, except her husband. He had never shown the slightest interest in his wife's talent, so Charlie had gone out of his way to be supportive of her.

But that had changed so much. Sometime in the previous year, Nell Bowen had lost some of her zeal. She used to be vibrant and happy all the time; however, she recently stayed in her studio doing little more than staring at a blank canvas.

Charlie decided to get running. Thinking about the change in his mother made him sad, and the last thing he needed was to be dwelling on bad stuff. Running always helped clear that out of his mind.

He ran about a block down his new street before he stopped to consider that he had no idea where he was going. The family hadn't visited Coverdale before the move. He hadn't seen a map of the town. Charlie figured he would run and let his feet take him where they wanted. To some woods and nature trails, he hoped.

Would it be too much to ask for ruins of some sort?

Reaching an intersection and the end of his road, Charlie turned right and followed a wide tree-lined road.

Ant popped into his head. The run was not doing its job of clearing his mind.

Charlie never called his sister her by her proper name. It was always something beginning with "An," and it drove her crazy. This was a good thing. Ant had been a problem for a few days, but both parents had taken her aside and given her a long talking-to. Eventually she shut her mouth. Ant hated the idea of leaving her small circle of devoted friends— devoted to Ant, of course. Plus, there were the boys who followed her around and told her how gorgeous she was and did anything she asked. With no cell service, the poor girl couldn't stay in touch with her crowd.

It made Charlie sick. He could sense the resentment burning off her whenever he got near her, as if she blamed him for everything. Charlie made an easy target for his sister's anger and frustration.

He knew he could do nothing about it, so he might as well get over it and enjoy his own life.

Charlie's mother, Mary, though everyone called her Nell for some unknown reason, was easygoing about the move to the point of oblivion. She still never got worked up over anything, so long as she got to do her painting every day. What seemed to get her most excited was the idea of having a real garden. Their home in the city had been a townhouse, their backyard only thirty feet across. All their neighbors had put up wooden privacy fences, so almost all of their yards were in perpetual shade. It was perfect for a cool place to read during the summer but terrible for a garden. The new house had a huge backyard, and she had already consulted her gardening books and planned where everything would go. She would be in her glory.

In a moment of silence between tunes, Charlie's mind cleared enough for him to note that he was now running on a slope. He looked around to discover that he was moving up the side of the hills that surrounded the town. Looking back through a break in the trees, he could see his house, where the people were all still on the back deck. To the south, he spied most of the rest of the town.

The side of the cassette on his Walkman ended, so Charlie took the opportunity to look over his new hometown. He walked to the edge of the clearing and took in the view of Coverdale.

Located in a valley surrounded by high, wooded hills, the town sat at a bend in the Pannon River atop a steep bank. Streets ran west from the center and were divided evenly by streets running north and south. The town center, which wasn't actually at the center of town but down in the southeast corner of a neatly laid out rectangle, was like a four-spoked wheel. In the hub sat a large round building with a road running around it. Between this road and the wheel lay four large areas divided by the spokes, narrow cobblestone roads. Two of the areas were parks. The third must be the school, Charlie decided, since he could see the oval of a track. The fourth area had a large rectangular building. Charlie's house was at the town's westernmost boundary. Around the whole town ran a loop road called Molay according to the street sign at the end of his street.

Charlie saw flashing red lights along the main road coming into town from the highway. He figured there must be an accident, though he couldn't see any other cars besides the parked police cruiser.

After flipping over the cassette—which he wouldn't have to do if he had a smartphone or iPod—Charlie continued along the road. A high stone fence stood to his left, topped with pointed pieces of shale that looked like they would slice open anyone who dared to attempt to climb over. He reached a gate and paused to look inside.

Far back, behind tall oak trees, stood an old house. It was a mansion, built of stone blocks, grey and weathered. Towers at the front corners and battlements along the roofline made it look like a medieval castle. A couple of cars were parked on a gravel area in front of a bank of garages, and a police cruiser pulled away while Charlie watched.

The heavy metal gate swung open with a hum and Charlie stepped aside to avoid the cruiser when it passed him. Inside sat a large policeman with very short blond hair and sunglasses. When the cop turned to look at Charlie, he did not look at all friendly. Charlie shuddered. He tried to smile and waved at the cop, but the cruiser had passed and was moving down the road quickly.

"Aren't you the pleasant one," he said after the cruiser turned a corner.

He heard the gate swing shut and turned in time to see an angel walk across the lawn in front of the house.

At least she looked like an angel to Charlie.

The girl looked about Charlie's age, eighteen, maybe a year older or younger, and had blonde hair that fell halfway down her back. Her white dress came to just above her knees. On her feet were a pair of those plastic sandal things. Crocs or Craps, as he called them. What especially got Charlie's attention, though, was her height: she had to be at least six feet tall.

"Oh. My. God."

The girl looked up, and Charlie realized that the music had prevented him from hearing how loudly he had spoken. He felt his face flush when she looked at him and something inside Charlie turned to mush.

She was the most beautiful girl he had ever seen. She was the most beautiful anything he had ever seen.

She smiled, and Charlie thought his chest would explode. The angel kept walking and soon disappeared around the corner of the house.

Charlie pulled off his headphones and ran. He didn't want the music distracting his thoughts.

"I've got to meet her; I've got to meet her." He often spoke to himself while running and had earned quite a few strange looks from passers-by. This road seemed deserted, so he felt he wouldn't make a fool of himself. "She'll never know I'm alive, so why even think about it. Because I'm in love. That's stupid. You've never even met her. It doesn't matter."

Without conscious thought, Charlie veered onto a faint path leading into the woods a couple hundred yards up the road. When he was running, his feet often guided him while his mind pondered the mysteries of the universe.

Mysteries like how to meet the angel.

"She's probably got a voice like a horse. Remember Cindy."

Charlie thought about the girl he had had a crush on a few years ago. After pining for her across the classroom for almost a year, he'd found an excuse to talk to her. When he asked her about that day's homework, she had brayed an answer. Taken aback, Charlie had tried to make conversation, but the girl seemed unable to string two intelligent sentences together. His crush had faded rather quickly.

He continued to argue with himself. "Nobody that gorgeous could be that dumb. What about Ant? She's my sister, and all sisters are dumb. Anyway, Ant only thinks she's gorgeous. She's just regular."

"Hey, you! Where do you think you're going? And who's that with you?"

Startled by the voice, Charlie skidded to a halt and looked around. He was next to a chain link fence topped by razor wire. On the other side stretched a vast sea of grass that ended about a mile and a half away. In the center of the sea loomed a large building covered in black glass. It stood three stories tall.

There was no sign of movement anywhere. Not even birds.

"I asked you a question, kid. Where do you think you're going? And what happened to the guy you were talking to?"

Charlie saw the man who was questioning him come out of the woods: a security guard pointing a machine gun straight at Charlie. He didn't look too happy to see him.

Before he could stop himself, Charlie said, "Actually, you just asked me two questions." The guard glared at him and raised the gun slightly. "I was out running. I was just following a trail. I don't know where I am.

"Who were you talking to? Where'd he go?" The guard glanced over to the bushes by the fence.

"No one. I was talking to myself. Do it all the time. Helps clear the mind and I always win the arguments." Charlie wanted to kick himself for being a smartass again.

"You on drugs or something?" The guard grunted. He checked the bushes again and said, "No one else around."

"That's what I said." Charlie shut his eyes and waited for the expected blast of gunfire. When none came, he opened his eyes. He tried to control his nervousness. The gun looked threatening, and the guard appeared ready to use it. Anxious, almost.

"Could you point that thing somewhere else, please? I don't want it to go off accidentally and make me another statistic."

The guard lowered the machine gun a little. "You know you're not supposed to be out here."

"No, I don't. We only moved here today. I don't know anything. Where am I?"

"You must be one of the Bowen kids. That's The Institute," he looked over at the black building, "and you stay well away from it. Now, get the hell out of here. The road's over that way." He pointed away from The Institute, and Charlie could make out a break in the trees.

Charlie ran towards the road and looked back at the guard when he reached it. The man stood watching him from the edge of the trees, machine gun still held at the ready.

"Nice guy." He quickly looked around to make sure there were no other guards who might hear him speak.

Something bothered him about the guard besides the fact that he looked like he was ready to kill him. Something about his uniform.

It was the patch on his sleeve. It was the same circle with a red cross that Charlie had seen on the moving van.

Chapter Two

The neighbors had left by the time Charlie got home. Before he had a chance to take a shower, George Bowen pressed him into helping assemble Ant's bed. Ant stood by and supervised, complaining constantly about how long it was taking and how tired she felt. At least she'd stopped going on about her stupid phone.

Charlie kept his mouth shut and imagined her tied to railroad tracks with a train barrelling down upon her.

As soon as the bed was finished and Ant's bedroom had been rearranged several times according to her instructions, Charlie escaped into the shower.

Feeling so much cleaner, with one foot out of the shower, Charlie heard the front doorbell ring. There were muffled voices, and then his father yelled up the stairs for him to get down in a hurry. Deciding that speed was of the essence, Charlie dried himself quickly and pulled on the dirty clothes he had left piled on the bathroom floor.

When Charlie reached the bottom of the stairs, he could hear his father talking in the living room. He was apologizing for something and promising it would never happen again. George Bowen sounded nervous.

Charlie entered the room, shocked to see the policeman who had passed him in the cruiser at the big house. The man stood up and Charlie was able to get a look at him.

The policeman was less than six feet tall but projected

himself as taller. It was probably the way he stood ramrod straight and seemed to be looking down on Charlie. At six feet two, even Charlie felt short in his presence. He had a barrel chest, and the muscles of his arms rippled through his uniform shirt. His blond hair was cut short and stood straight up from his face.

On the policeman's shirtsleeve was a patch with that same red cross in a circle. Charlie guessed it might be the town coat of arms or something like that.

"Charlie, this is Chief Wycliffe." The Chief grinned, but only his upper lip moved, making the grin more of a sneer. A white chunk of food or plaque between his two front teeth was distracting. "Chief, my son, Charlie."

Charlie smiled and was about to extend his hand, but the withering look the Chief gave him made him pull back.

"The Chief tells me you were trespassing on Institute property."

"No, not really. I was just out running and got lost in the woods. I didn't know where I was."

"Ignorance is no excuse, Charles," said the Chief. His voice was steady and low, almost a whisper. He stared at Charlie, who couldn't take his eyes from that piece of food in the Chief's teeth. "There are dangers at The Institute. Stay away from it. I don't like having to give second warnings."

Charlie looked into the Chief's hooded eyes. He knew instantly that the man hated him and had decided Charlie must die.

"I don't give second warnings." The familiar voice from behind him startled Charlie and he jumped. "Wait in the car, Chief."

The Chief nodded to Charlie, then left the house without another word. His boots never made a sound on the hardwood floor.

Turning to see the skinny bald guy from the party this afternoon, Charlie was surprised at how thin the guy was. His clothes seemed ill-fitting and old. Those beady little eyes were locked on Charlie, and it felt like they were boring into his soul. El Baldo—Charlie had decided that was the guy's name, no matter what it actually was—extended his hand to Charlie. Charlie took it and was immediately repulsed by the wet and clammy feeling. The guy was one of those idiots who liked to show dominance by squeezing the shaken hand as hard as possible. Though not much of an athlete, Charlie had strong hands and squeezed back until El Baldo released his grip.

El Baldo looked furious.

"You will learn the rules of this town immediately, young man. Breaches are not tolerated and will be dealt with severely. Do I make myself clear?"

Charlie was taken aback by the vehemence in the warning. A vein in El Baldo's head pulsed while he spoke as if keeping beat with the rhythm of the words. Like a metronome. No, a metrognome. Concentrating so he wouldn't smile, Charlie nodded.

Apparently, a nod wasn't good enough for El Baldo. "Well? Are you clear? Will you obey the rules, or are we going to have a problem with you? You look like a troublemaker. Your actions could have dire consequences." He looked over at a red-faced George Bowen, who seemed to be shivering. Sweat poured down his forehead.

"Answer the man, Charlie."

"Yes, sir. I will obey all rules. I will be careful, even if I have no idea what the rules are."

El Baldo nodded, glared at George, and then walked towards the front door.

Unable to leave well enough alone, Charlie said, "Sir, you wouldn't happen to have a copy of the rule book handy, would you? Or could you tell me where one might obtain it?"

The little man halted momentarily, then continued out of the house. No one moved until the slam of a car door and the cruiser sped away.

"Who the ..."

George broke in. "I didn't need *that* the first day we're in town. How dare you jeopardize my job like that."

Charlie was taken by surprise by what his father said. "But I didn't do anything. I was just running. How was I supposed to know about The Institute?"

"You ask!" His father's voice rose.

"How am I supposed to ask about something I don't know I have to ask about?"

His father glared at him.

"Mom, tell Dad to lay off, huh." Charlie looked at his mother, but she sat in the corner reading a gardening magazine.

"Your father knows best, Charlie. Listen to him and stay out of trouble."

"Yeah, listen to Daddy, Chucky," said Ant from the kitchen.

Charlie held in his anger. Ant knew he hated being called Chucky, her revenge for being called Ant, and she was simply joining in to make him feel worse. If ever there was a chance to be malicious, Ant took it.

"Dad, I'm sorry, I didn't know," Charlie said.

His father scowled at him and walked into the kitchen without saying another word. Charlie heard the refrigerator open and the pop of a beer bottle open. There would be no further conversation tonight.

Frustrated at not being allowed to defend himself, Charlie decided to go running again. His muscles ached a little, but there was nothing like a good run to get the tension out. Besides, he didn't want to stick around the house after the humiliation of the visit from the Chief and El Baldo, and Ant would be on his case all night.

To avoid any possible trouble, Charlie ran in the opposite direction of the one he had taken earlier. Though the temptation was there to run past the big house and try to catch a glimpse of the angel, Charlie thought better of it.

He ran south along his own street, then turned east onto the loop road and followed the river. Charlie crossed the intersection where the bridge from the highway joined the road and soon came to what he assumed was downtown Coverdale. The town wasn't that big, so he figured any concentration of shops and businesses must be in the downtown area.

This was Charlie's first actual visit to Coverdale.

Across the road from the river was an old theatre with a small diner next door. There appeared to be a row of shops on the other side of a small road, Dalmatian Way. Someone liked dogs.

Charlie ran up Dalmatian Way, between the shops and the diner, and came to the large circular area he had seen earlier from on the hill. To his right was an L-shaped strip mall with a large parking lot. To his left, behind the theatre, was the town library.

The circle was divided into five sections. The two closest to where Charlie stood were parks. The two on the other side held a school, and the rectangular building he now saw was the town hall.

The section at the center of the circle contained a colossal round church surrounded by grass. Around the church was a narrow road that was probably a traffic circle since there were no traffic lights and only a couple of one-way signs.

Charlie was about to resume his run when something on the church caught his attention. It was that cross in a circle again.

"Relax, Charlie, don't dwell on it." He quickly checked to see if there were any angels about when he realized he was talking to himself out loud again. Unfortunately, there were none.

Charlie ran back to the loop road and followed its curve to the north. At an old stone bridge, he was tempted to cross and check out the woods on the other side of the river. He stopped when he noticed that the bridge paused mid-air near the middle of the river. Old bridge pilings rose out of the sand on the far shore.

Charlie surmised that the loop road ran north now towards The Institute, so he decided to swing into the woods to the east. Ducking under low branches and trampling through bushes, he found a path that roughly paralleled the river and followed it.

Charlie kept running, ignoring his surroundings, letting the events of the past few hours percolate through his mind. All he had were lots of questions:

Who was the blonde angel?

Why had the Chief and El Baldo been so adamant about staying away from The Institute?

Who was the blonde?

How quickly had the Chief and El Baldo been informed about his trespass?

Will she be going to the same school as him?

Why would a guard have a machine gun?

Was she wearing those nasty sandals by choice, and if so, why?

How long would it take him to find out what it's all about?

Was that mud he had just stepped in?

Charlie's favorite subject at school was history. He loved pouring through old books to find all the facts about whatever had caught his interest. He wasn't about to let the warnings of some Fascist police chief scare him off. And El Baldo was a joke. He hoped.

He came to a fork in the path. To the right, it kept along the riverbank, while the left branch went deeper into the woods. Estimating he had run about four miles from downtown, Charlie elected to take the left path and see if it curved back towards home.

Feeling that he might be running straight towards The Institute, Charlie paid attention to his route.

Breaking through the trees, Charlie stopped dead and stared ahead in amazement. He stood outside a circle of standing stones. Including several that had fallen over, he counted fifteen stones arrayed in a perfect circle. Eight more stones outlined a cross in the center. They looked quite old and were covered with a deep green moss. He guessed they were approximately fifteen feet tall and had been smoothed by eons of weather. From where he stood, he couldn't see any evidence of carving on them.

"These shouldn't be here," he said to the air.

"But they are," said a voice from behind one of the stones. "I've heard they're sacred or something, but no one talks about it."

Charlie crouched down and looked for a large stick or something to defend himself. Not that sticks or stones would do much against a machine gun if it were another guard.

"Don't worry, I don't bite," said the voice. A figure emerged from behind one of the stones. It was a young man about Charlie's age, quite stout, with red hair and freckles.

"My name's Knox, James Knox. My friends call me Jimmy." He approached Charlie and held out his hand. "You're not one of those hand-crushing assholes, are you?"

Charlie took the hand and said, "Bowen, Charlie Bowen. We just moved in. And no, but I have crossed paths with El Baldo."

"I know. You live three houses up the street from me on Charnay. I watched you moving in." He pointed to a fallen stone where some moss had been scraped away. "That's the cleanest place to sit unless you want to try the mossy stones. That's poison ivy behind them."

Charlie sat on the clean stone.

"So, why didn't you come over and give us a hand?"

"You had the Temple guys already, and besides, I didn't know who you were, and I could see the Chief's car down the road. I figured he was watching you, and you don't want to mess with the Chief."

"Tell me about it."

"No, you tell me."

Charlie told Jimmy about his encounter outside The Institute and the visit from Chief Wycliffe and El Baldo. Jimmy nodded knowingly.

"You've had it now," he said. "Once the Chief gets it into his head that you're trouble, you're marked for life. 'Believe half of what you see, and none of what you hear.'"

"What does that mean?"

"It's something I heard from someone I used to respect. The problem is the Chief believes half of what he hears, and it's always the wrong half. It doesn't matter if someone's made up a lie, the Chief only believes the worst about someone."

"Guy's a creep."

"Maybe, but he's got nothing on Justin LaRennes. El Baldo to you. And I think to me from now on."

"Who is that guy? Everyone seems afraid of him, even the Chief. My dad nearly wet himself when El told me off."

Jimmy shook his head. "No one will say what El does. He seems to be important up at The Institute and around town. Has the ear of the Mayor and is rumored to be after the Mayor's granddaughter even though he's decades older than her." Jimmy quickly looked right and left. He leaned closer to Charlie and said, "I've heard he takes anyone he wants, if you know what I mean."

"You mean ...?"

Jimmy nodded. "Yeah. No one dares stand up to him, and the Mayor and Chief apparently turn a blind eye. The good thing is, he rarely ever takes anyone now. Too hung up about the granddaughter."

"Pig."

"But forget about El Baldo, Charlie. You've gotta tell me, who was the babe that was hanging around your place? Some movie actress, a goddess?"

Charlie was appalled and stared long and hard at Jimmy. "What? My Mother? I admit, she's nice-looking. But ..."

Jimmy looked surprised. "No, no. How could you think that? No." He thought for a second. "Well, she is kinda hot for an older lady. I'd need a closer look to be sure. But, no, not her."

"You can't mean the harpy with the curly hair, can you?"

"Hair like spun gold."

"It's brown."

"Hair like spun ... brown gold ... bronze ... spun bronze."

"That doesn't sound too flattering. 'You have hair like spun bronze, my darling.' It makes you sound cheap."

"Hey, I'm sorry. If a girl's not going to cooperate and have hair like spun gold, what can I do?"

"Yeah, I see what you mean. Anyway, she's no girl, she's my sister, Ant."

"You're a family of insects?"

"No. I just call her that to bug her."

"Ant," said Jimmy, looking to the sky. "So, her name must be Ann, or Annabel, or maybe Angeline. Yeah, Angeline, short for Angel."

"Short for annoying, more like. Forget it, Jimmy, she's bad news."

"She can't be that bad. She's your sister, and you're a nice guy. So, she *must* be okay."

"How do you know I'm a nice guy? I could be a creep."

"Hey, you're talking to me, aren't you? Most people avoid me because the Chief has me marked as a troublemaker."

"What'd you do?"

"I'll explain later when I'm sure I can trust you. No offense, of course."

"None taken, but I'm not going to set you up with my sister."

"Aw, c'mon, be a friend."

"She'll chew you up and spit you out, that is, *if* she bothers to notice you. If you get her anything she wants, do anything she says, kiss the ground she walks on, she might, and I repeat, she might deign to breathe in your direction."

"Boy, this girl thing is way more complicated than I thought. But she sounds like a challenge."

"If you're a masochist, or suicidal, or have no feelings.

But don't let me stop you if you want to make a complete fool of yourself."

"I'll take that as your blessing for my pursuit of your sister."

"Take it as your epitaph. Now you can answer some questions for me."

Jimmy raised his hand to stop Charlie. Pointing to the sky, he said, "The sun's going down. We should head home."

Charlie got up and walked towards a trail leading away from the circle of stones. Jimmy grabbed his arm.

"Not that way. The Institute's about a half mile down that trail. It's probably the trail you were running on this afternoon. Back the way you came."

Jimmy went behind one of the stones and returned, wheeling a mountain bike.

They walked down the trail and soon came to the river. Turning west, they had to walk carefully along the river trail. Though the sun had not gone down all the way, the trail along the shore was thickly shadowed by the dense growth of trees.

"So, what did you want to know?" asked Jimmy.

"The big house up near The Institute."

"The Mundy estate. Rex Mundy lives there. What about it?"

"Rex Mundy? King of the World?"

"No, Mayor of Coverdale."

"Rex Mundi is Latin for king of the world. It's a weird name."

"He acts like a king sometimes."

"Forget about him. I saw a girl ..."

"Never mind. She's untouchable. Half the guys in town are in love with her, and the other half are intimidated by her."

"Who is she?"

"Gwen Blayney, Mayor Mundy's granddaughter."

"Now *she's* a goddess. What's she like? Has anybody ever asked her out?"

"I don't really know. She keeps quiet in school, only answers questions if the teacher asks her directly. She's so tall. I think maybe a couple of guys might have tried asking her out."

"More, tell me more."

"There's nothing more to tell. She's a mystery. And freakishly tall."

They emerged from the woods and crossed the street. While they walked past the mall parking lot, a police cruiser went zooming by on the river road, siren screaming, lights flashing.

"That place sucks," said Jimmy when they reached the theatre. "It only shows old movies, mostly in black and white. If you want to see anything decent, you have to wait to get permission to go into the city."

"Sounds like my kind of theatre. I love old movies."

"You would."

"Permission to go into the city?"

Jimmy shook his head. "You'll find out soon enough."

They walked on in silence, passing block after block of houses. The ones closest to downtown looked to be about a hundred years old. Crossing a street, Charlie saw an abrupt change in the style of houses. Now, they all seemed to be from the last few years. It was as if all the houses along the street had been built in two stages a hundred or so years apart. They parted when they came to Charnay Street. Charlie's house was to the north, while Jimmy's was south. The two arranged to meet the next day at the park, where Jimmy promised to fill Charlie in on the kids at school.

"One more thing," Jimmy called after Charlie. "Mayor Mundy's best friend is Chief Wycliffe. The Chief is her godfather. He's very protective of whatever is his. Watch out. And don't forget, worst of all, El Baldo wants her."

Charlie smiled and waved thanks to Jimmy.

El Baldo wants the angel. The Chief is her godfather. Both men already hate him. Charlie knew he was doomed.

Chapter Three

The two sections of park in the center of town were jammed with people. Charlie thought that everyone who lived in Coverdale had to be there.

He returned to his family's picnic table with a tray of drinks—non-alcoholic because there were children in attendance. Hundreds of children. Charlie wondered if it was a town rule for every family to have at least five children. His parents were in for a surprise if that was the case.

The welcome-to-town party for the new arrivals, the Bowen and the Standish families, was being hosted by The Institute. Most of the townspeople worked for The Institute, so Charlie was getting to meet just about everybody around. Not that too many folks cared much about Charlie; they seemed far more interested in his father and the work he would be doing. However, whenever the talk drifted towards George Bowen's work, El Baldo would appear, seemingly from nowhere and everywhere, and shut down the conversation. He gave Charlie the stink-eye whenever their paths crossed.

Charlie tuned it all out and scanned the crowd, looking for Gwen Blayney. So far, she was a no-show.

The Standishes, all five of them, did not seem like a happy family. They sat at a table in the center of the eating area, like the Bowens, but they did not mingle much. When people were introduced, the father – Charlie couldn't remember his name

– acted pleased, but his smiles looked forced. The three sons, in their late teens or early twenties, were sullen, and Charlie noticed they were sneaking swigs from beer bottles hidden in their knapsacks. They looked like they might even be a little drunk.

The Standishes definitely were not fitting in.

Charlie's mom was busy talking to a couple of women about gardens, and Ant had run off with a bunch of girls her age. The girls were all dressed to the nines and seemed more concerned about being seen than saying anything intelligent. Ant would fit in perfectly.

Where was Jimmy? He and Charlie had agreed to meet, and Jimmy promised to introduce Charlie to Gwen. Jimmy and Gwen were friends, quite close, according to Jimmy, but Charlie was skeptical.

Someone slapped Charlie on the back, and he sputtered cola into the grass next to the table. The women talking to his mom paused and gave him disapproving looks, then returned to their garden chatter.

"Dude, how's it goin'?"

Charlie looked up into Jimmy's face and calmly grabbed a handful of Jimmy's shirt and used it to wipe cola from his chin.

"Not bad, bud. You're late."

"My big brother's fault. He decided to break the news this morning that he's been accepted to some university in California. My folks were not overjoyed 'cause they want him to go where my dad went, some place in Massachusetts. There was some heated discussing happening, but eventually, my parents went along with the idea of going out west. He scratched his head. Quietly, he said, "Still can't figure out how he got the application out and the acceptance in. Mail's pretty restricted around her."

"Interesting," said Charlie, pretending to stifle a yawn. "Have you seen Gwen?"

"Look, are you sure about this? The Chief already hates you. If you start chasing after his goddaughter, he'll come gunning for you." He looked around the parks. "Where's El? Make sure he doesn't see you talking to her. I've heard things."

"I can handle them. I think. Besides, Gwen can make up her own mind. Where is she?" Charlie hammered the table with his fists. His right leg bounced up and down with a nervous twitch. Soon, the whole table was bouncing, and this brought Charlie more nasty looks from the others sitting there. He grabbed the leg to stop the bouncing. His left leg bounced.

"Take it easy, will ya. She'll be here. She has to be. Her granddad is Mr. Big in town, and he always makes a show at things like this. He brings her along like she's some kind of trophy or something."

There was a sudden surge in the crowd noise at the far end of the park. When Jimmy stood on the picnic table seat to get a better look, he reported that the Mayor and his entourage had arrived.

Charlie stood quickly, forgetting that he was at a picnic table. His thighs slammed painfully into the table, forcing him back onto the bench seat. Rubbing his sore thighs, Charlie carefully got up and tried to see where the Mayor and Gwen were. When he spotted them, Charlie grabbed Jimmy's arm and pulled him towards the Mayor and his dream. Jimmy held back.

"Stay cool, dude. They'll be coming to us. Remember, you're one of the guests of honor." Jimmy paused a moment and studied Charlie's T-shirt. "Okay, you always wear shirts with band names on them, and I've known or at least heard of most of them. But what the heck is a Mott the Hoople?"

Charlie looked stunned, as if Jimmy had said something incredibly stupid. "Egad, I can't believe you've never heard of them. One of the greatest rock bands of the seventies. Pretty much invented punk before they went glam. Oh, the youth of today, so uneducated."

"Cut the crap," said Jimmy. He swiped at Charlie's arm. "Who are they?"

"Ian Hunter. *All the Way from Memphis*." Jimmy's face was a blank. "*All the Young Dudes*." Jimmy's face brightened. "My dad went to a lot of concerts back in the dark ages, like a couple every week. I think that's why he's so deaf, though he won't admit it. Anyway, he used to buy T-shirts as souvenirs, but he never wore them. He gave them to me, so I wear the oldies for special occasions."

"Right, like meeting Gwen. She's going to think you're a freak."

"No way, it's great music. I'll play you some of my dad's old records some time."

"Records? What are those?"

Charlie glared at Jimmy and was about to say something when everyone went silent, and the crowd around the table parted. A tall blond man in a white suit walked towards Charlie. Prominent on one lapel was a pin with a red cross in a circle. The man looked young, quite handsome in a rugged sort of way, not that Charlie thought of the way guys looked much. But this man was striking. When he got close enough, Charlie saw the fine lines radiating from his eyes and the corners of his mouth. There was also a mild earthy smell that seemed to surround the Mayor. It was obvious to Charlie that the Mayor was much older than he looked, maybe even in his sixties.

"Charlie Bowen, so glad to meet you. Rex Mundy." He held out his hand and grasped Charlie's, shaking it vigorously without much pressure. In fact, the handshake was quite limp.

"King of the World," Charlie muttered, a little taken aback. All at once, a force radiated from the Mayor and enveloped Charlie; he could see no one but the Mayor.

"You've studied Latin. Well done."

"Four years, high school," said George Bowen. He stepped in front of Charlie and held his hand out to the Mayor.

The Mayor's face clouded over briefly, and his smile dropped. He looked for an instant as if he was furious that he had been interrupted. But his face cleared just as quickly, and he greeted George Bowen like an old comrade. Charlie was left wondering if the change in the Mayor's face had been his imagination.

Then El Baldo appeared and pulled his father away. As usual, El looked angry.

There was a shimmer as a cloud moved to let the sun shine fully into Charlie's face. He blinked quickly, trying to get the spots out of his eyes. When they cleared, his eyes were filled with a vision: Gwen.

She had been walking behind her grandfather, hidden until the Mayor moved away with El and Charlie's father.

Gwen had to be at least six feet tall, perhaps taller. No wonder half the guys in town were intimidated by her. She was slender, and her calves were well-muscled. Charlie guessed she was either a runner or a swimmer. His mind was a little fuzzy in her presence.

Her blonde hair—there was a slight wave in it—framed her face and was loosely tied back with a red ribbon. Gwen's skin was fair, almost pale, and she wore no makeup. Charlie felt himself drowning in her deep green eyes. They were the same shade as his own.

Jimmy bounced around behind Gwen. He made hand signals that Charlie thought meant he should say something intelligent.

"Allo, Allo, Allo," he said and immediately regretted it. Jimmy's eyes almost popped out of his head. Of all the idiotic things he could have said, he sounded like an English bobby from a crime show. He wanted to turn away and hide for the rest of his miserable life.

But then Gwen smiled. She had dimples and her eyes sparkled.

Charlie was paralyzed and couldn't take his eyes from hers. His chest hurt, and he was short of breath.

"Aren't you the lounge lizard," she said. Her voice was clear and a little husky.

Rex Mundy's voice boomed above the crowd noise, and Gwen moved away from Charlie. She looked back briefly, winked, then disappeared into the crowd behind her grandfather. Jimmy came up to his friend.

Behind Jimmy, Charlie spotted El staring at him like he wanted to kill him. The guy was probably being overly protective of his boss's daughter.

"Allo allo allo? What amazing repartee. You must have had girls following you in droves at your old school. Tell me, have you ever actually kissed a girl? Do you even know what a girl is?"

Charlie's eyes blinked rapidly. He shook his head, said, "I have to throw up," and ran for one of the portable toilets lined up at the edge of the park. The stench inside the cubicle, combined with the heat and his nervous stomach, was enough to cause him to spew his lunch into the holding tank. Coming out of the port-a-potty, Charlie panicked when he couldn't find anywhere to wash his hands and rinse his face.

How primitive is this town? he wondered.

He spotted a drinking fountain over by a bicycle rack and quickly cleaned himself up. There were no paper towels to dry his hands, so he decided he might as well look for Jimmy.

Then Charlie saw something unusual. Several picnic tables had been set aside at the far corner of the park, across the road from the church. Sitting at them were about twenty-five tramps. At least, they looked like tramps to Charlie. However, they were dressed a little more smartly than the ones he was used to seeing in the city.

Charlie walked towards the tables. Jimmy joined him.

"Hey, lover-boy, swept any women off their feet in the last few minutes? Or at least had them doubled over with laughter at your brilliant wit?"

Charlie ignored his friend's jibes. He casually wiped his wet hands on the back of Jimmy's shirt. Pointing at the tramps, he said, "What's the deal there?" They were being served food by a couple of well-dressed women. The women were very respectful to them.

"It's a town tradition," said Jimmy. "Everyone treats the down and outs like human beings. Gets us closer to heaven, I guess. Let's get out of here. Those port-a-potties are pretty ripe." He pulled at Charlie's arm and guided him back to the crowd.

"That's a strange looking church, Jimmy. Know anything about it?"

"How come you're so curious all of a sudden?"

"I'm just interested. Round churches are rare, I think."

"I don't know anything about the church. Kids aren't allowed to go."

"What? That's crazy. Churches love kids. Get 'em early, you know."

Jimmy shook his head. "I don't know. You have to be nineteen to go to that church."

"Well, what about the other churches in town?"

"There aren't any. That's the only one."

"No way! There must be Catholics or some kind of Protestant church. There always are. What about a mosque or a synagogue?"

"Not in Coverdale."

A group of girls walked up to and then between Charlie and Jimmy. They didn't appear to notice the two boys; they were utterly involved in their conversation. Ant walked with them and gave Charlie a momentary hateful glare when he didn't get out of her way fast enough.

Jimmy fell against Charlie and watched the girls walk away.

"She's evil, Jimmy. Give it up."

"That's easy for you to say. You've already had your shot at Gwen."

"Yeah, she likes me."

"Oh, right. Allo allo allo is gonna make her think you're wonderful."

"Not really. She called me a lounge lizard."

"As in 'a lazy reptile' or something?"

"No, twerp. It's a reference to an Ian Hunter tune. She recognized the shirt. She's more perfect than I thought."

"Yeah, yeah. With lines like yours, I'm surprised you even know what girls are. If a girl said yes to going out with you, you'd fall over."

"As if. I've been on lots of dates. Well, several, anyway. And how about you, Romeo? How many girls have you taken out?"

Jimmy hesitated and looked nervous. He said, "Nearly one, but I'm working on it. Your sister's a good place to start."

They both laughed.

"I'm serious," said Jimmy. "Really."

"I think you're trying too hard, my friend. And Ant is about the worst place to start on a quest for a girlfriend."

Jimmy shrugged and stared at the ground. His face was scarlet. "Yeah, who am I kidding anyway?"

"Food. Let's grab some more dogs. Now that my stomach is empty, I'm hungry again."

"Wonderful image, dude. Thanks."

They trotted to the barbecue pit, each taking a couple of hot dogs. While they were at the condiment table, a police cruiser pulled up in front of the town hall. Chief Wycliffe climbed out of the car and walked up the steps. He stopped, turned to face the park, and stood with his arms folded. He watched all the activity at the gathering.

Charlie felt a shiver run down his spine when the Chief's gaze fell upon him. Though the Chief wore sunglasses, Charlie felt the policeman's eyes boring into his soul. That horrible grimace spread across the Chief's face.

"Creep," said Charlie.

"Careful," whispered Jimmy, "you never know who might be listening."

A tramp stumbled by, gave the boys a quick look, and continued on his way.

The Chief never moved.

A flash of white to his left distracted Charlie. He saw Mayor Mundy crossing the street with Gwen not far behind. While Gwen waited at the bottom of the steps, the Mayor joined the Chief at the top. Still surveying the park, the Chief spoke. The Mayor's face became grim, and he nodded a couple of times. The Chief pointed to the south-east, across the park and into the woods on the far side of the river.

Charlie turned to look in the direction the Chief was pointing but could see nothing but the shops across the street. He turned back in time to see the Mayor and the Chief climb into the Chief's cruiser. It pulled away along Sevres Street, turned left at the Loop—Jimmy had informed him that the loop road was indeed called the Loop—in the direction of The Institute, and disappeared behind the trees.

Gwen stood alone at the bottom of the town hall steps. She turned slowly towards the park. Charlie got ready to wave when she saw him. He was sure they made eye contact, but Gwen suddenly looked horrified and turned away. A large, white car pulled up in front of her. A chauffer held the door open while Gwen entered. The chauffeur got in the car and drove off after the Chief's car. Charlie figured Gwen was being taken home. Despite the tinted windows, he waved at the car anyway, hoping that Gwen might be looking back at him.

Charlie grew angry at the Mayor for getting in the way. He would have been able to talk to Gwen properly if it hadn't been for her grandfather.

A moment later, a police cruiser raced past town along the Loop, lights flashing but no siren blaring. It looked to Charlie like two people were in the cruiser's back seat.

It seemed to be going to The Institute as well.

"Don't go getting any ideas, Bowen," said a voice behind him. It was El Baldo, sneaking up on Charlie again.

Charlie turned and looked down at the weasel. He had to stifle the urge to punch in the guy's face. Not being a violent person, the feeling startled him.

Jimmy gasped.

"Shut it, Knox," said El.

El stepped close enough to Charlie for him to smell the little man's rancid breath. Had he been eating in the portable toilets? Charlie took a step back, but El kept close.

"I saw how you looked at her. Don't be fooled. She only spoke to you because she's a nice, polite person. Any other day of the week, you'd be beneath her notice."

Charlie wanted to say something but felt his throat constrict. As much as he didn't want to listen to or believe what El said, there was something in the way he said it that made it hard to dismiss. El put an arm around Charlie's shoulder and squeezed. Being so much shorter than Charlie, El's arm was actually over his shoulder blades. The instant the arm touched him, Charlie felt deep revulsion. He resisted the urge to jerk away. The guy already hated him. No need to make it worse.

"Look, Charlie. May I call you Charlie? Charles is so formal among friends." El smiled. "Look, Gwen is a nice girl, but she's way out of your league. She's destined for much bigger things than a lowly boy in a small town. Trust me on this. I know her."

"But ..." Charlie tried to speak up, but El was persistent.

"No, Charlie. No buts. School starts in a few weeks. You'll meet loads of young girls. You can have your pick of any of them. Any. And I can help there. I know lots of them." El's smile widened to reveal grey teeth spotted with plaque and food.

Charlie began to wonder if any of the adults in Coverdale had the slightest clue about dental hygiene. The stench from El's mouth made Charlie's stomach turn, and he feared he might hurl up his second lunch. This would be a disaster since the barbecues had been shut down, leaving only cold dogs and burgers.

"So, what do you say, Charlie? Are you okay with everything? You understand the situation?" El squeezed Charlie's arm with a little too much pressure as if to emphasize that he wanted the right answer out of the boy.

"Yeah, I guess so," said Charlie. He stared at the ground, unable to look El in the eyes. He felt embarrassed and stupid for even thinking he had a chance with Gwen. There was a lump in his throat, which made him feel worse. He'd been in Coverdale a week. Had seen Gwen twice and only exchanged a few words with her. It wasn't even a proper conversation. What an idiot for getting caught up in a girl so quickly.

El squeezed Charlie's arm one more time, then let go. He patted Charlie's shoulder, saluted, and walked away. He didn't say a word to or even acknowledge Jimmy.

Charlie watched El's back until he disappeared into a crowd. He did observe that, when El approached a woman, she ever so casually moved away from him, closer to her companion or friend. Curious.

"There's a word for him," said Jimmy. "I won't say it because it's unbelievably rude and insulting to that particular body part."

Shaking his head to clear it of El, Charlie said, "Yeah, I know the word and it is an insult to the body part to associate it with that little slimeball."

"Charlie, buddy, don't let what he said get you down. He's full of crap."

"Maybe. But maybe he's also telling the truth. I don't even know her. It's stupid of me to expect her to want to get to know me."

"Let it go. Whether or not Gwen is interested, don't listen

to El. He's very convincing. He even made me feel like a deviate because ..."

Charlie turned to look at Jimmy, who was now staring at his shoes. His face was almost as red as his hair. "Because what, Jimmy?" Charlie went to put a hand on his friend's shoulder, but Jimmy jerked away.

Breathing heavily, Jimmy said, "It's nothing. He found some stuff of mine. Look, Charlie, be careful around him. He knows stuff. He has eyes everywhere, even in your own bedroom."

"Seriously?"

"Trust me. Come on, let's go find something to eat."

"They shut down the barbecues."

"Forget that. I'm talking chocolate. I have a stash."

"You're on."

They walked out of the park on to Sevres Street. Charlie thought no one would miss them.

As much as he wanted to forget what El had said to him, it stuck in his mind. He needed a run to purge the garbage.

Anyway, he might not have a chance with Gwen in the real world, but he still had his imagination. That had got him through a lot of crap at his old school.

Chapter Four

School started on the Monday after the party in the park. It was the middle of July, not September, like a normal school. Charlie had only four weeks off instead of the whole summer, and a good chunk of that had been spent helping with the move. He hadn't read a single book since arriving in Coverdale, although he had finished five before the move, so all was not a total loss. Still, no fair!

To make matters worse, he had to attend prep school. Everywhere else, Charlie would have been starting university. But not in Coverdale. As his father had explained, Coverdale was old-fashioned. Prep school here was considered preparation for university because most teens weren't ready for higher learning. Or being away from home. Besides, it gave Charlie a year to reconsider going to the University of North Massachusetts instead of Oxford, like he had wanted since the beginning of time. Since getting the new job at The Institute, Charlie's father had been adamant about Charlie attending the "company" university.

"Good connections and all that, don't you know," said his father.

Charlie didn't know and didn't care. He'd had to rethink his university plans.

He sighed. "This place truly does suck," he said to some birds that watched him from a fence as he passed.

"Except for Gwen."

Jimmy had waited for Charlie at the corner, and they walked to school together. Along the way, Jimmy told Charlie about the teachers they were likely to get. Most of them sounded fairly normal, perhaps even a little dull. The only person Charlie was warned to look out for was Mrs. Burke, the lady in charge of the cafeteria. If you crossed her in any way, like making a mess of her domain, you could spend any spare periods you had washing dishes and cleaning floors.

Charlie and Jimmy arrived at the prep school. Besides being the cause of doubt about where Charlie's future would lie, the prep school was in the same building as the high school.

Jimmy set him straight. "No, the prep school is part of the high school."

Charlie stopped and stared at the school. "So now I'm just a glorified high schooler. Great," he said. Jimmy shrugged.

An old stone building, Coverdale Temple High was unremarkable except for its huge size. Four storeys high, it dwarfed all the buildings around it. Only the church was larger. The school formed a huge "L" with the bottom leg running east-west. The front door was at the eastern end of the leg. The north-south arm of the school looked slightly newer; its stone was not as weather-worn as the stone of the leg. Its windows were large enough to let in lots of sunlight. But unlike the previous schools Charlie had attended, no grilles were over the bottom floor windows.

Back home—not Coverdale, it wasn't home yet—his high school had been broken into and vandalized at least once a year, despite the heavy grilles.

He guessed that with a police chief like Wycliffe, the criminal element stayed out of Coverdale. He laughed to himself when the image of the Chief eliminating criminals entered his head. This wasn't some crime drama.

He walked up the front steps and spied the cross in a circle again, carved into the arch capstone over the front doors. More interesting were the knights carved into the support pillars on either side of the massive oak doors. They seemed to be watching over the students as they entered the school. Next to the knights were men in what looked like togas. This town was getting weirder by the minute.

The first day went by fairly quickly but started differently from all his previous schools. There was no standing for the national anthem or Lord's Prayer. He was happy about this because he thought it was overkill, having to start each day with the anthem. Plus, he was an atheist but was never allowed to ignore the prayer like some of the students who belonged to different religions.

The students split off into their regular classes after assembling in their homeroom class, where they were assigned lockers and encouraged to sign up for various sports teams. The homerooms were alphabetical, and Charlie's only comprised students with last names beginning with "A" or "B." There were twelve senior homerooms, each with about thirty students.

For a small town, there seemed to be a heck of a lot of students. Charlie wondered how he had missed them at the park. He must have been thinking about Gwen too much.

Charlie was ecstatic when he discovered that Gwen would be in most of his classes, even the basic science course he had to take to round out his course requirements. He couldn't understand why he had to take science when he was only interested in history and English, but at least it would be bearable with Gwen in the class.

He didn't get a chance to speak to her, and when their

paths crossed as they were leaving the geography class, she didn't acknowledge him. Charlie began to believe that Jimmy was right, and his witty repartee had fallen on deaf ears. His cheeks burned whenever he remembered what he had said to Gwen at the park. "Allo, allo, allo." Indeed!

Without warning, El Baldo's words slammed into his head. Charlie instantly felt like a loser for being interested in Gwen. It would be best for him to ignore her and concentrate on his schoolwork. Maybe there were other girls to interest him, not that he had noticed because of his obsession with Gwen.

Obsession. Maybe El was right. Maybe Charlie needed help. He shrugged it off. He was a teenager with a puppy love crush, not a psycho. Stuff it, El Baldo.

Gwen got Charlie into trouble during algebra. She sat two seats ahead of him. The teacher, an old-fashioned crone, insisted they sit in rows in alphabetical order. Whenever Gwen shook her head or brushed her hair out of her face, Charlie noticed the wisps that fell from her temples. It looked so soft, and Charlie wanted to reach out and touch it. During algebra, he had been concentrating on getting a look at the wisps and not on the teacher. When she asked him the answer to a especially easy question, he got flustered and blurted out an answer so wrong the whole class started to laugh.

He shrank into his seat, sure that he was making a wonderful impression on Gwen. Jimmy could barely control his laughter, even after the teacher yelled at him to keep quiet.

Jimmy ribbed Charlie about his math mistake all through lunch. Mrs. Burke scowled at Charlie when he complimented her on the lasagne but smiled when he returned for a second helping. Charlie appreciated good food. Charlie appreciated any food as long as it was on his plate.

The last class of the day was ancient history. He expected to learn about Egyptians, Romans, Greeks, and maybe something of the Orient. He was surprised when the teacher mentioned Celtic and Chinese trade with North America. Most people agreed that Columbus did not discover America and that it was more likely the Vikings. He had read a few books that claimed that the Celts and even the Phoenicians had visited North America. The last thing Charlie expected was to have it taught as part of the regular curriculum.

It promised to be an interesting class.

After school, Charlie went to the gym to sign up for the cross-country team. He was stunned to discover that there was no cross-country team, never had been. A couple of coaches tried to get him to sign up for football, soccer, or basketball, but Charlie declined. He wasn't much interested in team sports. He didn't like the idea of a bunch of brutes trying to crush his skull chasing a funny shaped ball and couldn't sink a basket if his life depended on it. The coaches insisted, and Charlie mollified them by saying he'd take a day or two to decide which team to join.

Jimmy met Charlie outside the gym.

"What'd you go for?"

"Soccer. I'm too short for football and too stout for basketball. How about you?"

Charlie shook his head. "Nothin'. I wanted to run cross country. Those coaches sure are persistent."

"Everyone's expected to be part of a team. It builds character and makes you a better citizen. You must join in."

Charlie looked down at his friend and grimaced. "You're kidding, right?"

Jimmy looked serious. "No. That's what we're told by the coaches, our teachers, our parents, Mayor Mundy."

"It all sounds ominous to me, a bit fascist."

"I don't know what you mean. Just pick a team and join in. A bunch of us are going to the diner for some shakes. You should come along, meet the guys."

Charlie agreed to go. In the two weeks since his family had moved to Coverdale, Jimmy was the only person his own age that Charlie had got to know. He'd been so busy unpacking his books and stuff, organizing his room, reading, running, and trying to avoid having to do Ant's work for her, he hadn't had much free time. It was a good thing he didn't need much sleep.

The lack of internet access frustrated Charlie the most. He'd spent hours trying to figure out what was wrong with his connection. In the end, he'd complained to his father only to discover that internet access was strictly controlled in Coverdale due to the sensitive nature of the work at The Institute. Charlie had to hold in his anger at his father for not telling him sooner. The man didn't seem to realize that "the computers at the school will provide you with all the access you need" was not good enough, especially during the summer when there was no school. He should have guessed there'd be a problem, given the lack of cell phone reception in the town.

Perhaps Jimmy knew some way around the restriction.

And then there was his obsession with Gwen.

He thought about her all the time. Most nights, Charlie was accustomed to reading a whole book in one sitting. Since seeing Gwen, he hadn't read a thing, so it wasn't just the short summer vacation. Now he spent his evenings with his headphones on, listening to his records. He imagined he was in whatever band was playing, and Gwen was in the audience worshipping him. At the end of the show, he would scoop her up in his arms and carry her offstage.

At school, oblivious to his surroundings, Charlie walked into a door and his books and pens went flying. When he bent down to retrieve his things, someone pushed the door open from the other side and smacked him in the head. He went sprawling and banged into the lockers against the wall.

Jimmy doubled over with laughter, fell back against the lockers, and slid down to sit next to him.

Rubbing his sore head, Charlie looked up to see Gwen descending the stairs across the hall. She saw him sitting on the floor, noted the books spread out around him, sighed and passed through the door. She glanced back. There was a slight grin on her face.

Charlie's face went beet red, and he groaned. His chest hurt.

"Don't worry, old chum," said Jimmy happily, "things couldn't possibly get any worse."

Then Chief Wycliffe came out of the Principal's office and saw Charlie and Jimmy. He frowned and walked off in the opposite direction. A few seconds later, El Baldo also came out of the office. When he saw them on the floor, El shook his head in dismay. He looked through the door that had hit Charlie and yelled, "Gwen! Wait a minute. I have to talk to you." Charlie's heart sank.

"My mistake. Things could get worse."

"Yeah," said Charlie, "now the Chief will think a stumbling idiot is after his goddaughter."

"Oh, he already thought that. You've just confirmed it. What about El?"

Charlie looked at Jimmy and frowned. "You saw. He thinks I'm useless and he went off to talk to Gwen."

"You really should pay attention, my friend," said Jimmy.

He pointed through the door. "El called after her and went thataway." He pointed in the other direction. "But the love of your life went thataway. He's messin' with you."

Charlie thought about it. Why would El pull a stunt like that? Maybe Jimmy was right.

"Then again, you could just be a jerk."

"You're such a good and supportive friend, Jimmy. I don't know what I'd do without you."

"That's why you can buy me the first shake."

When they reached the diner, Charlie did a quick detour to check out the theatre next door. He took a deep breath when he looked at the old lobby cards advertising coming attractions. *The Maltese Falcon, Citizen Kane, Lost Horizon,* and *The Killers* were to be featured over the next month.

"Man, those lobby cards must be worth a fortune. Who runs this place?"

"Some old guy named Tyndale. Used to be Chief of Police before Wycliffe. He's supposed to be filthy rich and owns all the movies he shows. He's weird. I wish he'd get some decent movies in."

"Are you kidding? These are great." Charlie was smiling. "I've never seen *The Maltese Falcon* on a big screen. I hope he sells Milk Duds."

"I should have known Mr. I-Love-Seventies-Bands would like old movies. You're not really some old guy whose brain has been transplanted into a young, ugly body, are you?"

"No, I just have good taste."

"Too bad you don't have any co-ordination to go with it."

At the diner, Jimmy opened the front door. It was a fairly large place with ten tables arranged down the middle, each seating four people. Along the right side, four long tables could each seat six or eight people. A counter with stools ran the length of the left side. At the back were several booths, all occupied by young girls, Ant among them. The tables immediately in front of the booths were crowded with adolescent boys. They were hanging on to every word being said by a girl with short black hair in the middle booth.

When Charlie and Jimmy entered the diner, they were met with a chorus of shouts calling them over to one of the long tables. A group of guys Charlie recognized from many of his classes were sitting there talking loudly and making unpleasant comments about the girls at the back. The girls pretended not to notice. Jimmy pulled a couple of chairs from an empty table to the group while Charlie got shakes from the counterman.

Quick introductions were made, and Charlie concentrated hard on remembering everyone's name. He had a bad habit of meeting someone and not immediately catching his or her name. There was always an embarrassing moment later when Charlie had to admit to not remembering.

A heavy-set boy named Dick Wesley made a loud comment about the IQ of the boys at the end tables.

"That wasn't very nice," said Charlie.

"Don't sweat it," answered Dick. He had a straggly beard that was not doing a good job of hiding Dick's acne. "They're just mooning over the stuck-up crowd. They think we're all animals anyway. Nobody cares what we think."

There was a chorus of *yeahs*.

"It can't be all that bad," said Charlie. He stirred his shake. The drink was so thick it was impossible to suck it up through the straw provided. But it was the best shake he had ever had.

"Don't you believe it," said Arnie Goodspeed, whom Charlie recognized from his history and algebra classes. "Hey, you learned to count yet."

They all laughed, including Charlie.

"Charlie's been bitten by the Blayney bug," said Jimmy. He gave Charlie a slap on the back. "He thinks he has a chance with the Ice Queen."

More laughs.

"At least you've got some height going for you," said Dick, "but you've got guts messing with Mayor Mundy and ... never mind."

"He doesn't seem so bad," answered Charlie. "He's a little full of himself. That white suit was too much, but he was okay."

John Roger snorted at the end of the table. "Sure, he's okay, just make sure he doesn't sic that psycho Wycliffe on you."

"Or Justin LaRennes," said Dick. He quickly looked around to see if anyone had heard him. "I wanted to ask Blayney out and somehow he got wind of it. Needless to say, I didn't ask her out."

"I've already had a visit from the Chief and El Baldo, LaRennes. I got too close to The Institute my first day here."

"Dead man," said John and Dick at the same time. "Owe me a coke," they said to each other.

"Just be careful," said Arnie seriously. "Don't mess with Wycliffe."

"Or LaRennes," said Dick, again checking to see if he was overheard.

"What exactly did he do, Dick?" Charlie was curious because Dick had started to sweat.

"Just made it clear that I, and anyone else, should stay away."

While Arnie spoke, the diner's front door opened and

Chief Wycliffe walked in. The place fell silent and everyone concentrated on their food and drinks.

The Chief stepped up to the counter and raised his hand. The counterman moved to the coffee pot with smooth efficiency. It looked like a move he had practiced many times to avoid making the Chief angry and to get him out of the diner as fast as possible. When he had coffee, the Chief scanned the room, grimaced, and left.

He had not made a sound.

People began talking again right away, though they were all a little hushed.

"God, I hate this place," said Paul Whittingham. "I've got to get out of here."

"Good luck," said John.

"What's so difficult?" asked Charlie. "When we graduate at the end of the year, we can do whatever we want. Go to university anywhere we want, get a job in the city. What's the big deal?"

"You don't know Coverdale," said Arnie.

"Those kinds of decisions get made for us," added Dick.

"My brother's going to university in California in January," said Jimmy.

"No way," countered Paul, "your parents would never agree."

"Apparently they have agreed. I was there. I heard it with my own ears. He'll be gone."

"What about North Mass?" asked Dick.

"That's where Dad wants Norm to go," said Jimmy.

"That's where all the dads want their kids to go," said John.

"What's North Mass?" asked Charlie.

"The University of North Massachusetts," said a voice

behind Charlie. The speaker, a stocky blond named Mark Thomson, sat on the bench across from Charlie. "Our school's affiliated with it, and most of the folks from here go there."

Charlie scratched his head. "Right. My father wants me to go there instead of Oxford."

"Who knows?" said Mark. "What teams did everyone sign up for?"

Charlie found he was the only one who hadn't joined one of the school's teams. When pressed, he said he might go for soccer but preferred to skip the whole sports thing altogether.

"Everyone's expected to be part of a team," said Mark. "It builds character and makes you a better citizen. You must join in."

"Wow, that's exactly what Jimmy said to me at the school. What are you guys, part of a cult or something?"

Charlie stared at six blank faces.

Chapter Five

Charlie ran up the steps to the back deck, sweat pouring down his face. After running a circuit of the town, he couldn't wait to hit the shower. The smell of roast beef hit him when he went through the kitchen door. His mother looked up from mixing the batter for the Yorkshire pudding they always had with a roast and smiled at her son. She didn't say anything to him. Neither did he.

After his shower, Charlie thought about the past week at school. None of the guys seemed to think it weird that they all said the same thing about joining teams. Even Jimmy was unaware of it. Under pressure from just about everyone, Charlie had agreed to join the soccer team. It was the best choice since it didn't require him to use his hands and feet at the same time. He kept up with his daily running.

Most classes were okay because Gwen was in them. Charlie passed the time, trying to catch glimpses of her every chance he could. They still hadn't spoken, and his attempt to be partnered with her in science had failed. The science teacher didn't like pairing boys with girls because he thought it would distract them from their work. He was right, Charlie agreed, but it was still a bummer.

The moment he sat at his desk to work on a history assignment, Charlie heard a siren go off. It sounded like an old air raid warning. He went over to his window and looked out.

Over the trees to the north-east, smoke was rising, thick and black.

He raced downstairs, yelling, "There's a fire a couple of blocks over."

No one seemed to be around, and Charlie only heard his mother say, "Dinner's in half an hour."

"I'm going to see what's happening," Charlie said, then left the house at a run.

Several people were already on the street, walking silently towards the smoke. When Charlie asked if anyone knew what was going on, he was ignored. The people were concentrating on where they were going and were oblivious to anyone or anything else. It reminded Charlie of a scene in a movie he had just watched, *The Time Machine*. In the film, cannibals from underground called their victims by using old air raid sirens. The victims were mesmerized, and nothing could stop them from going to their doom.

Charlie saw Jimmy's dad drive by wearing a heavy fireman's coat. Jimmy, in the passenger seat, waved at Charlie as he passed.

Charlie figured there must be a volunteer fire department in Coverdale, and that's why the air raid siren was blaring.

A block from Charlie's house, Charnay Street met Hugues Street. There were woods on the north side of Hugues, and smoke was billowing above them. Running through the woods, Charlie soon emerged onto Blanchefort Street.

Flames spouted from every window and doorway of a furiously burning house. Three fire trucks were already on the scene, and firemen were busy attaching hoses to hydrants. When they were ready, the firemen all stopped and waited. El Baldo emerged from the north side of the house. Charlie guessed he might have been trying to see inside the house because the fire appeared to be concentrated on the south side.

El nodded, and the firemen went to work hosing down the flames.

A large crowd gathered to watch the spectacle. No one spoke. Police cruisers were positioned at each end of the block to hold back traffic. There wasn't any. In fact, Charlie had seen very few cars in Coverdale.

Chief Wycliffe stood by his cruiser with his arms folded. His face was impassive as he watched the action. El joined him. Was that a grin on his face?

Charlie saw Jimmy standing across the street and crossed to him.

"Who lives here?" said Charlie.

"The Standish family. Remember, they moved into town the same time you did?"

"Yeah, they seemed kind of tense at the party."

"I heard my dad say something about Mr. Standish not getting on well at The Institute. I couldn't get any details, though. He was being incredibly quiet, talking to someone on the phone."

"It was probably my dad."

"No way. That's too much like a coincidence. Why would our dads know each other?" Jimmy punched Charlie in the arm to emphasize his point.

"Ow, that hurt. I'm serious." Charlie rubbed his arm. "It was about three days ago. I overheard my dad talking in the study. He didn't sound pleased. In fact, he was pretty angry about whatever it was he was talking about."

With a sudden crash, part of Standish house roof caved in. Sparks flew into the air. Fortunately, there was no wind, so there was no danger that sparks from the conflagration would cause the woods across the street to catch fire. Two firemen ran from the front of the house, chased by flames. The crowd moved back slowly; most people were reluctant to give up their good viewing spots.

An ambulance turned the corner off Hugues Street, made its way past the roadblock, and pulled to a stop beside one of the fire trucks. The EMTs got out but did not appear to be in any kind of hurry.

"They must figure there are no survivors," said Jimmy.

The EMTs were now talking casually to a policeman. One of them laughed, which Charlie thought was inappropriate. Charlie surveyed the scene and noted that the firemen were working hard to extinguish the fire but did not appear concerned about getting inside the building to check for survivors.

"It's almost as if they know there's nothing they can do to save the family," he said.

Jimmy ignored him.

After steady streams of water had been directed onto the house for about half an hour, the fire died out. Two firemen entered the smoking remains of the house. Jimmy grabbed Charlie's arm and pulled him across the road to get a better look. Most of the crowd had moved closer once the danger from the fire had ended.

Before long, the firemen emerged from the house and joined the Chief and El. They conferred for a few seconds. El nodded abruptly, then turned and walked back around the north side of the house. Charlie heard a car start up. A few seconds later, he spotted the Mayor's limo driving away.

The firemen who had been in the house ran to the EMTs, who were prepared to follow them into the house. The firemen waved them off. Instead, the EMTs got some black packages from their ambulance and gave them to the firemen.

"Body bags," said Jimmy quietly.

The firemen with the body bags joined eight of their fellows and re-entered the house.

In a few minutes, they stumbled out of the house with their burdens. The crowd surged forward, trying to get a better look. The grim line of men went to the ambulance, where the EMTs relieved them of those burdens. Five body bags.

The onlookers were hushed, though Charlie heard occasional muttering. A couple of people said something about fitting into the community and how it was all for the best. The most unusual comment came from one of the tramps who had been standing by the woods watching the action. Charlie didn't hear all the tramp said, but he did catch the words "sacrifice" and "cleansing."

The ambulance left the scene and the crowd disbursed.

While his dad stayed behind to make sure the house didn't reignite, Jimmy walked back with Charlie to his place.

Walking down the street, Charlie's thought over what he had just witnessed.

"You know, Jimmy, there was something odd about those body bags."

"Nah, they were full of dead people. If they'd been full of live people, now that would have been odd."

"No, I don't think so." Charlie scratched the back of his head.

"Lice?"

"No. Helps me think."

"Why do you suppose that is? Does scratching loosen the brain cells?"

"Probably. Now, where was I?"

"You thought the body bags were odd."

"Right. They seemed flat, like there was nothing in them.

And the firemen didn't look like they were straining to carry them."

"The bodies would have been burnt to a crisp. There probably wasn't much left."

"No way, they hadn't been burning that long. It's almost as if the firemen were pretending to remove bodies."

"You're nuts. Why would anyone pretend to remove bodies? You're not making any sense."

"It still seems strange to me."

"You've been reading too many conspiracy theory books or watching too many horror movies about small towns where weird stuff happens."

"Could be. I need to get a life."

Without warning, Jimmy stopped, stiffened, and stared straight ahead. "I must warn our leader," he said in a monotone voice, "the stranger is on to us."

Charlie looked at his friend. "Are you mocking me?"

Jimmy said nothing, just continued to stare ahead. Then a smile cracked his face and he laughed.

Charlie walked away. Jimmy followed.

"I could tell Ant you're a real weenie, but she probably already has that one figured out. Or maybe I could make an anonymous call to the Chief and make up a story about you. No, I'll call El."

"Hey, come on. Buddy. Don't even joke about El. I was only kidding. You're right. There is a conspiracy. The bodies were taken away for weird scientific experiments at The Institute. But please, don't tell Antoinette? Anastasia? I'm a weenie."

"What about the Chief?"

Jimmy shrugged. "There's not much I can do there. He already thinks the worst about me."

"That's too bad. What's been said?"

"Never mind."

"Okay."

"I'm forgiven?"

"You're forgiven if you say you're sorry."

"I'm sorry."

"You'll never mock me again."

"I'll never mock you again."

"Kiss my foot."

"I'll kiss your ... No way!"

Charlie was laughing now.

They reached Charlie's house and parted company, laughing at each other. Charlie watched Jimmy walk down the street for a few seconds, and then entered his house.

His father stood at the kitchen door. He did not look happy.

"And where have you been? Dinner's been on the table for half an hour. We're all finished."

"Uh, sorry, Dad. There was a fire over at the Standish place. It looks like all five of them were killed."

The last sentence shocked his father. His face went white and he looked around the room nervously.

"That's a tragedy, Charlie, but we all have to try harder to fit in."

"I don't know about fitting in, Dad, but this town sure is weird."

"There's nothing weird about Coverdale. It's a good little town where people can live safely."

"Oh, sure. And we have a maniac Chief of Police, and the guards around The Institute have machine guns. El ... Mr. LaRennes is incredibly uptight and nasty."

"We do sensitive work up at The Institute. There are spies

all over the place."

"Oh, come on, Dad. Spies. In Coverdale. That's silly."

His father remained momentarily silent, so Charlie took the opportunity to sit and tuck into his dinner. His mother had taken his plate from the oven where it had been kept hot.

Charlie's father sat across the table from him.

"Charlie, I want you to try harder to fit in around here. I don't want another visit from the Chief. And especially not from Mr. LaRennes."

"Dad, I'm doing the best I can. The Chief's a thug anyway. He just likes to throw his weight around. That badge and uniform give him a thrill. Same with El ... LaRennes"

"Don't talk about Chief Wycliffe and Mr. LaRennes that way!" His father stood and stared down at Charlie. "I'll not have my son showing such disrespect for the authorities in this town."

Charlie shoved a forkful of roast beef into his mouth to avoid saying more. When his father got this angry, keeping quiet and taking any yelling with the proper contrition was best. His father's anger usually dispersed quickly once he had done a bit of yelling.

Charlie's mom stayed busy doing the supper dishes and said nothing. These days, she rarely said anything except to comment about the garden. Charlie looked at his mother for a moment.

When did she become so domestic? Where did the free spirit that Charlie so admired go?

Ant waltzed into the kitchen and placed an empty glass near the sink. She did not offer to help her mother with the dishes. She never did.

Charlie noticed something on her wrist.

A tattoo.

Charlie spoke up, sensing a chance to divert some of his father's anger. "Hey, Ant, what's with the tattoo?"

Ant stopped and sneered at Charlie, "It's for the Sisterhood of the Temple, zitface."

Charlie's hand automatically went to the tender spot between his eyes.

"Leave your sister alone, Charlie. We're talking about you."

"But Dad, she has a tattoo. And what's the Sisterhood of the Temple?"

"It's a girl's youth group from the church," said Charlie's mother from the sink.

Charlie looked over at his mother and noticed the wristband she always wore. It covered the exact spot where a Sisterhood tattoo would be if she had one.

Charlie knew he had to calm down and stop seeing conspiracies everywhere.

George Bowen leaned down closer to Charlie.

"Everyone's expected to be part of a team, Charlie. It builds character and makes you a better citizen."

Charlie's eyes widened in horror at what his father was saying.

"You must try harder to join in."

Interlude One
1686 CE

Jacques Lajeunesse drew deeply on the pipe and coughed until his eyes watered. He hated this tobacco stuff, brought up to Quebec by those cursed English, but if he wanted to fit in, he had to smoke. All the soldiers from the garrison smoked, and if there was one thing Jacques wanted to be, it was a soldier. As a cook's assistant, he was ignored for the most part by the soldiers, except when the food was particularly awful; then he was the brunt of their curses and kicks, the cook having conveniently disappeared. Perhaps now he would have a chance to get to know some of the men.

The unit of French troops had stopped in a clearing an hour ago to rest for the night. There had been no sign of the Iroquois all day, and Captain LeDuc was getting anxious. The Iroquois had been warring with the French for the past few months, and the merchants in Quebec and Montreal wanted the fighting stopped—their profits from the fur trade were down, and that was something they would not tolerate. Now, Captain LeDuc sat with two of his Huron scouts and perused a map of the area. Jacques wished he was there with them, planning strategy, earning promotions, saving France's North American colonies, and defeating both the Iroquois and the English. For now, though, Jacques would have to be content trying to get one of the men to treat him like a person rather than a slave.

Jacques looked around the bivouac. Most of the men had bedded down for the night, trying to get some sleep on the rough ground. A few were still talking and smoking, and a couple played cards. These were the men Jacques was sitting near; perhaps they would ask him to join their game. He could see a couple of the pickets patrolling just beyond the trees and shadows moving through the trees around them. His imagination was playing tricks on him, Jacques thought. This tobacco was powerful and made his head spin. He'd listened to too many rumors about silent killers that were supposed to lurk in these woods.

Drifting off to sleep, sure the men around him would never notice him, he thought he saw a ghost gliding through the trees. A dream, nothing more.

He was awakened abruptly by a booted foot kicking him in the backside.

"Get up, you lazy piece of trash." It was the cook with his usual morning greeting.

Jacques grunted and shook the sleep from his head. The sun was already up and the men were moving about, some gathering their equipment, others relieving themselves by the trees.

"Go find some water," the cook said and threw a cooking pot at Jacques.

Jacques caught the pot, mumbled, "Yes sir," and stumbled into the woods in the direction he thought the river lay. It was the same every morning. Never a kind word, only abuse heaped on abuse. Jacques was indentured to the cook, and there was no way he could get away without hurting his mother back in Montreal.

The sun filtered through the trees, and a cool breeze was

on his face. Jacques tasted the tobacco from last night, coughed and spat, and wished he wouldn't try so hard to fit in. He pulled a piece of moose pemmican from a pocket and bit off a chunk. He chewed in hopes of getting the foul taste out of his mouth.

The woods were quiet.

Jacques stopped walking and turned around. He couldn't see the camp anymore or hear the men moving about.

The canopy made strange shadows move between the trees.

Silence.

Even the birds were quiet this morning.

A chorus of whoops.

A volley of musket fire.

Screams. Shouts.

More musket fire.

Jacques dropped the cooking pot and fell to the ground behind a fallen tree. He peered between two branches in the direction of the sounds but could see nothing but some smoke rising through the trees.

More screams.

Someone running.

Four men, French soldiers, burst through the bushes and ran past Jacques' hiding place. He got up to follow the men, but something huge lumbered into Jacques from behind, knocking him to the ground. Jacques squirmed around and looked up into the terrified face of the cook. The fat man was panting and crying, and there was a bad smell coming from him, far worse than usual.

Fear.

The cook glared at Jacques. "Iroquois. Hundreds of them. Must have killed the guards. No hope. Run for your ..."

An arrow exploded from the cook's throat, showering Jacques with crimson, and his tormentor crashed to the ground.

Jacques didn't wait to see where the arrow had come from; he sprang to his feet and ran for his life. He could hear the Iroquois coming after him, but he kept running, never looking back. He felt warm wetness soak his trousers.

He knew any chance he had of becoming a soldier was gone.

Musket fire.

A scream. A cry for mercy cut off abruptly.

The war whoops of the Iroquois.

Ahead of him, Jacques saw a break in the trees.

The river!

Jacques ran harder. The Iroquois were still behind him. Maybe they were also at his sides because he was sure he could see men running there.

He ran so hard, his thoughts only of escape, that he didn't notice he had left the woods, stumbled down a riverbank, and run headlong into a river. The force of the water tripped him up, and he fell face-first and sank to the bottom. Jacques let the blackness and silence envelope him, welcoming the cool comfort of the water. Then the need to breathe took hold and he struggled to the surface.

Jacques was halfway across the river, facing the far bank. He turned when he heard screams from behind him, and his eyes beheld unimaginable horrors.

The Iroquois were on the riverbank. They had caught the first four soldiers Jacques had seen running. Two of the soldiers, obviously dead from the way blood pumped from their wounded throats, were being scalped. Four Iroquois held down another while several more hacked at him with their axes. The last man attempted to run along the river but was hamstrung as he ran past a warrior. Four or five more fell upon him, and Jacques saw a geyser of blood cover them.

Letting out a scream, Jacques swam for the far shore. Dragging himself out of the water, he heard shouts and the echo of musket fire. Puffs of dirt erupted all around him.

They were shooting at him. Lucky for Jacques, they were as bad at shooting as he was.

He scrambled up the riverbank and into the trees at its top. Pausing briefly behind an old willow, Jacques looked back to see if the Iroquois were crossing the river.

He saw something strange.

One of the braves began to run into the water but was pulled back by a pair of his fellows. All the Iroquois stood at the water's edge and stared across the river, right at him, Jacques was sure. One of them gestured, speaking to the warrior who had tried to cross. Every one of the Iroquois looked nervous. Abruptly, they turned and disappeared into the woods.

All was silent again.

Jacques was mystified. Why had the heathens turned away? They could easily have captured and killed him. Hacked him to pieces or scalped him like those men on the shore.

After resting for a few minutes, and when his legs had stopped shaking, Jacques moved away from the willow. A few minutes later, he was shocked for the second time that morning.

He was standing at the edge of a grove of oak trees, in the center of which there was a stone well.

Jacques had heard of no white settlers in this area, and the *courier de bois* were unlikely to erect anything so permanent.

Curious, Jacques walked over to the well and looked in. The sun was overhead now, and he could see to the bottom. Dry as a bone. In fact, it looked like the well opened up down there.

Strange.

Quiet.

The grove was silent as a grave. Jacques looked up into the trees to see if there were any birds. None.

He sat on the lip of the well to think. The only thing left for him to do was try to return to the fort and tell the Commandant what had happened to the soldiers.

Jacques looked around, unsure of the way back.

A whoosh.

Stinging pain in his left arm.

Jacques looked down in time to see his right arm fall into the well. Blood pumped from the stump. In shock, he fell back and down the well.

There was an echoing crack when Jacques hit the bottom and his neck broke. It didn't kill him immediately.

As he lay on his back at the bottom of the well dying, Jacques tried to see who had attacked him. He could only move his head slightly. The sun was directly over the well. Shapes moved across the opening, momentarily blocking the light, but Jacques could see no details.

Darkness began to overtake Jacques, and he tried to remember his mother and home. He looked to his right, and all thoughts of home fled from his mind.

"*Diable*," he said and darkness reigned.

Chapter Six

The school hallways were abuzz with talk about the fire and the deaths of the Standish family. Yet no one seemed to mourn the passing of the Standish boys because they hadn't attended the school, and only a few of the senior boys even knew them. The flag flapping in front of the school had not even been lowered to half-mast out of respect for the dead. During the morning announcements, nothing was said.

Charlie thought this showed precisely how much the townspeople stuck together.

Ancient history class got terminally strange for Charlie. He was used to reading about the Romans and how ruthless and determined they were in their quest to create an empire and that no enemy was allowed to survive unpunished. In fact, plenty of times, the Romans returned the land to the natives and set them up as overseers of a new Roman territory. The Romans knew how to turn enemies into, if not friends, at least allies. Charlie had always thought the Romans, in the early days, were no worse than any of the other civilizations that had grown up around the Mediterranean Sea or in the Middle East.

Charlie's history teacher, Mr. Taverner, thought the Romans were the evilest people who had ever existed. He went on at length about how they had stolen lands from the rightful rulers and how the Roman Empire had done more to set back civilization than any other empire that had ever existed. When Charlie tried to say something good about Rome—architecture, literature, art, organization—the teacher scowled at Charlie as if he were crazy.

"There is nothing about that so-called civilization that can be considered good, Mr. Bowen. Now, please keep your ludicrous ideas to yourself. You are disturbing the rest of the class."

Charlie remained silent for the rest of the period.

After class, Charlie tried to talk to Mr. Taverner about his views. The teacher told Charlie that he didn't have time for ridiculous notions. He snorted and strode off to the teachers' room without another word.

A few other students from the history class had watched Charlie speak to the teacher. When Charlie looked at them, they snickered and went to their next classes.

With his cheeks and ears burning, Charlie went to his science class. He was unable to concentrate on his work, disturbed by Mr. Taverner's comments and his own embarrassment. It also didn't help that Gwen was looking particularly beautiful today. Twice Charlie got caught daydreaming by the science teacher and was warned about not paying attention.

During lunch Charlie kept quiet. The other guys at his table in the cafeteria were talking about the various sports teams they were on and ignored Charlie. Even Jimmy got caught up in the sports talk. Charlie didn't mind because he didn't think Jimmy would have understood how unusual Mr. Taverner's views were.

The only bright spot was Mrs. Burke, the cafeteria lady. She seemed to sense that Charlie was feeling low, so when she served him the day's special chili, she gave him an extra-large helping. When Charlie thanked her, she grunted and told him to move along; he was holding up the line.

As soon as the final bell rang, Charlie raced to his locker to retrieve his knapsack. He was so intent on his task that he didn't notice Jimmy arrive.

"Coming to practice?" Jimmy stood with his arms crossed while he waited for Charlie's answer.

Charlie closed his locker and noticed that Jimmy was carrying his soccer gear.

"I can't today."

"You've already missed two practices. If you miss many more, the coach will toss you off the team, and that's never happened to anyone that I know of. Everyone's ..."

"I know, I know, I'm not a very good citizen. Look, Jimmy, just explain to the coach for me, okay? I had too much chili for lunch and it's affecting me."

Jimmy backed away. "No problem, bud. We wouldn't want you making the pitch any muddier than it already is."

They walked towards the front door.

"Are you okay, Charlie? You've been quiet all day. Was the drubbing you took from Taverner that bad?"

"Yeah, I guess I was just surprised by it. I always thought teachers were supposed to encourage their students to think for themselves."

"What planet are you from? This is Coverdale. The teachers do all our thinking for us."

They reached the front doors of the school and parted company.

"Oh, Charlie, was that you in science class?" shouted Jimmy from down the hall.

Charlie looked back at his friend and saw several kids from his science class. They were all looking his way. He guessed Jimmy had already told them his story about the chili.

"No, it wasn't me. Someone at the back was fooling with the gas taps."

"Right," said Jimmy and ran off.

Charlie ignored the jeers coming from down the hall and left the school building. He headed across the street to the town library.

The library was another old stone building. Charlie realized it looked like the school, town hall, and even the theatre. It was as if they had all been built at the same time. Only the round church seemed to be different, older. Much older.

Inside the library, everything was silent, as it should be. A couple of tramps sat in a lounge area reading newspapers. The librarian at the main desk didn't appear to mind their presence.

Charlie went to the desk to ask for directions. The librarian, a grey-haired lady, looked at Charlie with suspicion when he asked where the card catalog was located.

"Everything's on computer now," she whispered, pointing to a small room next to the reading lounge.

Charlie went to the room and sat at one of the three terminals. The computers seemed incongruous in a room with wood floors and dark oak paneling. They were top of the line, appeared new, and barely used. Light flooded in from a large window.

Charlie thought about trying the internet again but decided not to bother. It had never worked the few times he'd tried and had only earned him trouble at home when he was reported. He entered his request on the computer but didn't get the response he was seeking. There appeared to be no local history section in the library. Frustrated, he returned to the main desk to make inquiries.

"We don't have a local history section, young man." The librarian hissed rather than spoke.

"You're kidding, aren't you? Every library has something about the town it's in."

"I never kid," said the librarian dryly. She returned to the books she was scanning.

"Can you direct me to the local newspaper files, then, please?" Charlie asked, trying to be as polite as possible. He did not want to offend this lady anymore, though he couldn't figure out what he had already done.

"You have to make a special request to see the files."

"Then I'd like to make a request."

"All the old papers are on microfilm. The last months' worth is off being filmed."

"I don't want to see the recent files. I want to look at the oldest files you have."

The librarian was silent for a moment. She stared at Charlie through squinty eyes and let out an exasperated sigh.

"The microfilm reader is out being repaired. You can't see the files."

Charlie made fists and punched his thighs, trying to hold in his frustration. He took a deep breath and said, "You couldn't have told me that to begin with? Thanks for your help, anyway. Have a nice day."

He turned away and stalked to the entrance, biting his tongue to hold in his anger.

"Rassa frassa, old bat." He hoped no one had heard him.

Behind him, the librarian hissed. He turned back, and the look the librarian gave him could have frozen lava.

Charlie didn't think that she had heard him. He decided she simply liked to hiss and was generally in a bad mood.

He hurried out the door and down the front steps.

Later that night, after the supper dishes had been cleared away, without Ant's help, Charlie sat in his room reading. The textbook's author for his ancient history class held the same views as Mr. Taverner. Charlie checked the publisher, the University of North Massachusetts Press. That was the same school where many of the kids went after graduation. He would have to rely on his own meager collection of history books.

Before Charlie could gather his thoughts further, the front doorbell rang. He left his room and went to the top of the stairs. Below, his father opened the front door and Chief Wycliffe strode silently in, followed by El Baldo. They went straight into the kitchen, but not before the Chief glanced up the stairs, right at Charlie.

Charlie's heart sank. He crept down the stairs and stood by the kitchen door, hoping to hear the conversation.

"Whatcha doin', zitface?"

Startled, Charlie turned to look into the sneering face of his sister. He rubbed the sensitive spot between his eyes and said, "I was going to get a drink, but Dad's in there with the Chief and El ... Mr. LaRennes."

Ant gave him a look like she didn't believe a word he had said and then skipped out of the room.

Charlie heard chairs scrape the kitchen floor and raced up the stairs. The Chief and his father came out of the kitchen. Just before the Chief walked out the front door, he looked up at Charlie again. His face was impassive.

El wasn't with him.

"Charlie!" George Bowen shouted. "Get down here immediately."

Charlie shuffled to the top of the stairs.

"Did you call me?" he asked innocently.

His father, barely containing his anger, looked up at him. "Down here, now."

Charlie came down the stairs slowly. He was sure his father was angry about something the Chief had said, but he couldn't think of anything he had done wrong. Charlie had made sure he stayed well away from The Institute while he was out running, and he didn't so much as jaywalk while downtown.

And where the heck was El?

"Sit down." His father pointed at the couch.

Charlie sat and looked up at his father as he paced the living room.

"The Chief says you've been causing trouble again, Charlie. What have you been up to?"

Charlie shook his head. "I don't know."

"Don't give me that. You must have been doing something. Why else would the Chief come here and warn me about you?"

"The man's nuts, Dad. I haven't done anything. He's got it in for me."

"Think, Charlie. What were you doing today? Who did you offend?"

"Why are you taking his side? Don't you believe me?"

"You've done nothing but cause trouble since we moved to Coverdale. I won't have any more of this." His father's face got redder by the minute. He paced faster and swung his hands through the air, barely missing the lamps on the end tables. "What did you do?" He said this so loudly Charlie was sure Jimmy could have heard it from down the street.

Charlie was stunned by his father's anger. This wasn't like his dad. Sure, he got mad occasionally, but recently, he seemed to blow up and get uncontrollably angry all the time.

John Buja

It must be pressure at work, Charlie thought, trying to find a reasonable explanation.

He tried to remember everything that had happened during the day. It couldn't be Mr. Taverner; he had dismissed Charlie as if he were some kind of nut. It must have been the librarian. But what was so bad about wanting to look into the town's history? Charlie didn't think his father would be happy to hear that Charlie was checking up on the strange goings on in Coverdale. Then again, how else could he explain what he had been doing at the library?

Charlie decided that part of the truth might smooth things over and calm down his dad.

"I was trying to read up on town history." He explained about the librarian and the microfilm reader. "You know how I am, always wanting all the facts. I figured I could fit in better if I knew more about Coverdale, its history, and its traditions."

His father stopped pacing and thought for a minute. Charlie could almost see the wheels turning in his father's head as he tried to digest the information.

"Good," his father said, "that's good. You're learning. Trying to fit in is a good thing. Perhaps you were just being too pushy with the librarian. Not being polite enough."

"Yeah, she did seem a bit touchy. Probably hates long hair or something."

Charlie's father appeared to have calmed down considerably. Relieved that the situation had relaxed, Charlie stood and walked to the kitchen door.

"Do you want a beer? I'm going to have a soda."

His father nodded *no* and picked up a newspaper from one of the end tables. He sat down heavily in his recliner.

In the kitchen, Charlie paused to catch his breath. He leaned against the counter and tried to calm his nerves. His hands shook a little.

Charlie didn't like lying to his father, though he hadn't truly lied. He simply hadn't told the whole truth.

The Chief's visit and his father's reaction made Charlie even more determined to find out what was going on. He'd use all his capabilities to find out what mystery lay behind the quiet facade of Coverdale.

No one was going to stop him.

No one.

"Come out here, Charlie, now."

"Oh, crap." He looked through the kitchen window to see the source of the command. Now he knew where El had gone. But why hadn't his father mentioned it?

Charlie grabbed a soda from the fridge, not bothering to get one for El, and went outside. The sun was still too high for the trees at the back of the property to provide shade. El sat beneath the table umbrella, and though there was another chair there, Charlie elected to sit in the heat of the sun.

"Yes?" Try as he might, Charlie found it impossible to say anything more to El. He disliked him so much he feared what he might say or do if he lost control. That shiny, bald head needed to be introduced to a brick. Charlie shuddered at the thought. He'd never been violent or even had violent thoughts, especially not about another human being. *Then again, El wasn't exactly human, was he?* He thought and chuckled.

"Something amusing you, Charlie?" El's voice was calm and quiet.

Charlie shook his head. "Remembered an old joke about a lady and a snake."

"Tell me," said El. He wasn't smiling.

Now what? Charlie didn't know any jokes about ladies and snakes. Time for a distraction. "So, what brings you out on this fine evening?"

El smiled. "I think you know, Charlie. You might as well tell me all about it. I can help you. I'm really good at helping people. Ask Jimmy. I've helped him a lot with his problem."

Before saying anything, Charlie had a sip of soda. El sounded so friendly, almost genuine. He was suspicious about the man's intent but felt an overwhelming urge to unload all the angst and uncertainty he'd been holding in for the last few weeks. And he'd helped Jimmy? What was Jimmy's problem besides liking the wrong girl?

"Okay, Mr. LaRennes."

"Call me Justin. We're all friends here." The smile on El's face looked sincere, but Charlie couldn't be sure how far below the surface it reached.

"I keep doing the wrong things. I ran somewhere I wasn't supposed to. I asked questions I'm not allowed to ask. I like a girl who doesn't like me. I'm just not fitting in here."

El nodded. "How were you to know the areas that are off limits in town? You were new. Maybe you should have asked first, but you're so young and impulsive. Wrong questions? There are no wrong questions, Charlie, only wrong subjects. All you need to do is think first, then ask your question. Do you understand? It's all because you don't think before you leap."

Charlie wanted to throw up. What El was telling him was such garbage and insulting. Very calmly, he said, "I guess you're right. I need to think things out more."

"That's right, Charlie. And as far as liking the wrong girl, well, lots of the boys in this town have made the same mistake. They quickly learn how foolish it is to even think those things. When you're just a young boy, you get crushes on all the wrong people. I'm sure you had a crush on your own mother at some point. No, no, it's perfectly normal and she is quite pretty. What about your sister? Again, perfectly normal."

What El was suggesting was not perfectly normal. Charlie felt disgusted by what El implied about his own family members.

"I can see you know I'm right," said El. He got up, walked over to Charlie, and put a hand on his shoulder. Charlie suppressed a gag when he caught a whiff of El's breath. "Just remember your station, your position in life. Don't try to rise too high or you'll get slapped down in the worst way. The lady in question isn't interested in you. Stay away." He patted Charlie's shoulder and then walked into the house.

Charlie heard his father say something, but it was muffled. No doubt, his father was apologizing or sucking up to his master.

When he went back inside, his father looked up at him. "All sorted? You really should be grateful to Mr. LaRennes. If it wasn't for him, your foolish and juvenile antics could have caused me considerable trouble at work. We don't want that, now, do we?"

Unable to think of anything to say to that, Charlie shook his head.

"Good," said his father. "Now, why don't you head up to your room and think about all the people you have inconvenienced and all the trouble you keep stirring up. Try to think of others before yourself for a change. Right? Good. Good night, Charlie."

Walking upstairs to his room, all Charlie could think was, *who is that guy downstairs, and what happened to my dad?* He seriously needed to sort himself out before he screwed up everything.

Chapter Seven

"Remember, you guys are to meet us at the restaurant at five. We eat dinner, then go to the movie."

"Okay, no problem, Mom," said Jimmy.

He and Charlie watched Jimmy's parents walk off towards the pedestrian mall. The two boys turned and headed the other way.

When Jimmy told Charlie that he and his parents were going into the city on Saturday to shop and see a movie, Charlie grew excited for the first time in a week. He didn't want to ask his parents to take him to the city. His mother wouldn't have been interested anyway, and his father might have been suspicious. Charlie was able to invite himself along with no trouble. But Jimmy's parents insisted on calling Charlie's father to double-check that he had permission to go. Lucky for Charlie, his father was in a good mood today. Jimmy had been glad of the excuse not to spend the afternoon shopping with his parents. As much as he wanted the new game, his parents could be hard to take when shopping. His dad loved a bargain and would spend hours comparing prices, he explained to Charlie. His mom only liked clothes shops, which Jimmy hated.

Charlie needed to get away from Coverdale for a while. Though he knew El was full of it, the man's words had eaten away at Charlie for the last week. He had withdrawn into himself and stayed in his room for the rest of the weekend.

Eating was a chore. None of his books held the slightest bit of interest for him. When he put on an album, he lasted maybe one minute into a tune before he lost the urge to listen.

Even running didn't snap him out of his funk. Getting up at five in the morning was always perfect because he could get out for a run and be home in time to beat Ant to the shower, grab breakfast, and head off to school. Last Sunday, he had readied himself and reached the end of his block before he stopped. Staring into the trees across the road, Charlie had wondered why the hell he was bothering to run. Nobody cared. It didn't help with anything. All he got out of it was sweaty clothes, aching muscles, and blisters.

He had coasted through school the last week. Feeling isolated and unworthy, Charlie had avoided Jimmy as much as he could, feigning a sore stomach or some other lame excuse when he couldn't get away in time. He'd not answered a single question or volunteered anything during any of his classes. What was the point? The teachers thought he was an idiot, his fellow students laughed at him, and he was stymied when it came to one of his passions: history. Research in Coverdale was not only fruitless, it was dangerous.

If there was a bright spot during the week, it was seeing Gwen at school. However, that was brief because he knew thinking about getting anywhere with her was futile. Charlie knew he should be thinking about one of the other girls in school. Nice as they might be, none of them sparked any interest in him. Hell, he couldn't even get interested enough to take care of his usual nightly need. Now that was serious since he hadn't missed a day in four years.

One thing Charlie didn't want was to end up in a dead-end life like his father, married to a woman who had lost all her lust for life. Cruel as it was to think that way, Charlie absolutely did not want to be anything like his parents.

Seeing the school counselor might have helped, but Charlie didn't want anyone to know what was going on. He worried that word would get out that he was having problems. Talks with the counselor were supposed to be confidential. In a town like Coverdale, with guys like El Baldo and the Chief running around checking on everyone, Charlie was certain he'd be getting another visit to sort him out. No, he'd sort things out himself. He always had. He always would.

"Hey! You alive in there?"

Charlie blinked several times when something waved in front of his face. It was Jimmy's hands. "What the ...?"

"You went away for a while there, my friend."

The concern on Jimmy's face made Charlie feel guilty for cutting his only friend out of his life for the last week. He knew it was unfair to use Jimmy to get into the city and then keep him in the dark. There was a hot dog stand across the street, so he pulled Jimmy there.

When they both had a couple of dogs and were sitting at a picnic table, Charlie said, "Look, Jimmy, I'm sorry about the last week. I've been a crappy friend shutting you out."

"Yeah, I was wondering what had happened. You seemed so miserable. Even my witty quips couldn't snap you out of it. That is, when you didn't avoid me or run away. Tell me."

Charlie told his friend everything: the hassle at the library, the visit from the Chief, how his father had reacted and not supported him in any way.

After hearing about the exchange with El Baldo, Jimmy got angry. "Who the hell does that guy think he is? The asshole is always interfering in other people's business and giving them crap advice. Someone needs to shut him up."

"He told me he helped you with your own problem,

Jimmy."

Jimmy's jaw dropped and his face turned red. He stared at Charlie and a tear slipped from his left eye. "What did he tell you?"

"Nothing more than that he helped. Why? What's so terrible?"

Jimmy shook his head. "I was much younger and stupid. I had some dumb ideas that I stupidly let slip out. El Baldo heard about it somehow and talked to me about it. Instead of helping, he made me feel worse. He promised not to say a word to anyone. I've been living in fear ever since."

"What could be that bad?"

"Nothing. But it's Coverdale and El Baldo. He'll make anything seem like the end of the world. I've outgrown it, so case closed."

Charlie let it drop. Jimmy would tell him if he felt Charlie needed to know.

"Back to the matter at hand. That old bat at the library is a royal pain," Jimmy said. "She used to scare the crap out of me when I was a kid. She guards that library like it's her own private domain."

They finished their hot dogs and then crossed back over the road.

"The library's around the corner," said Charlie. "It shouldn't take too long to find what I need."

"That's cool with me," said Jimmy, "so long as we have enough time to get to the computer store so I can pick up that new game."

When Charlie told Jimmy why he wanted to go to the city library, Jimmy had no hesitation in joining him.

"I'd love to find some deep, dark secret about the town. Maybe find out why Wycliffe is such an uptight jerk."

"I don't know about finding out about the Chief," said Charlie, "but there should be something about when the town was founded."

The city library was a large stone building, somewhat like the Coverdale library. A cornerstone at the front had the date 1874 carved into it. Charlie guessed that since the architecture in Coverdale resembled the city library, the town must have been founded sometime around the mid-1800s.

"You want me to look for anything?" asked Jimmy when they reached the computer catalog.

"Yeah," said Charlie. "There's a series of old atlases done sometime in the last century. See if you can find them and get the one for the county Coverdale is in. Dundee, isn't it?"

Jimmy shrugged. "If you say so. Geography's not my thing." He walked towards a sign that said 'Reference Room' and disappeared from sight.

Charlie sat at a terminal and typed in "Coverdale town." He kept his head low, not wanting to attract attention. Not that anyone would notice one more person checking out the catalog. He felt slightly paranoid, expecting the Chief to come around the corner and sneer at him. Or worse, El to pop out and start asking awkward questions.

The search returned references to a town in New Brunswick, a place in England, and the musician.

"Nuts," said Charlie. The person at the next terminal gave him a look that told him to keep his comments to himself.

He typed in "Dundee County" and was rewarded with two listings. Both books were available. One was from 1897, the other from 1953. Charlie wrote down the reference numbers on the notepad he had brought along.

Charlie then called up the city newspaper index. He tried Coverdale again and was met with the same no references message.

"Doesn't anything happen in this town?" This time, he was quiet.

There were a lot of references to Dundee County, which he dutifully copied.

By the time Charlie finished with the catalog, Jimmy had returned from the reference room.

"I found the atlas you want, but it's not allowed out of the reference room."

"That's okay. I'll get the books I want and bring them there."

"How long do you think it'll take you to look up what you need?"

"Getting antsy about that game?"

"Yeah. I don't know when my parents will be coming back to town."

"Why don't you take off to the store? Meet me in the reference room when you're done. Once I get to researching, I lose all track of time. I won't even notice you're gone except for the lack of smell."

"Yeah, right, Mr. Chili Butt. Don't go blind reading."

Charlie and Jimmy separated at the stairs.

The two books on Dundee County were easy to find, and in no time, he was sitting down at a carrel in a corner of the history section. It was quiet there, and no one from the main aisle could see Charlie while he worked.

Neither book was indexed, much to Charlie's frustration. That meant he would have to go through both page by page looking for references to Coverdale. He decided to do the 1897 volume first since it was only a hundred and twenty pages long.

The book was full of old photographs of buildings and

people from the county. The book had been written for the one-hundredth anniversary of the founding of the county by the president of the local historical society.

There were no photographs of anyone or anything from Coverdale. The town was never mentioned.

Charlie assumed this meant Coverdale had been founded after 1897. That was strange considering the style of architecture in the town.

He picked up the 1953 volume, a massive tome with lots of photographs and maps. Charlie paused for a moment. He stared at the book and its five hundred pages. Charlie sighed at the thought of the number of hours it would take to plow through the book. Was it that necessary?

Then he remembered the Chief and El and how his dad seemed to believe every bad thing about Charlie.

"Screw you," he said into his sleeve.

He started to flip pages.

Nothing.

Absolutely nothing.

It was as if Coverdale didn't exist. None of the maps showed anything where Coverdale should have been.

There was something about a haunted forest. According to the natives of the area, there was a forest in a valley where no members of the tribe would venture. Even the fierce Iroquois kept their distance. The Jesuit missionaries who had first visited the area had been unable to get the natives to elaborate. It was as if they were scared to even talk about the place.

The Scottish settlers who had founded the county made no mention of the forest or the legend.

Baffled by the mystery of where Coverdale was, Charlie left the carrel and went to the microfilm room. He found the film reels for the city newspaper. He was about to begin scanning for Dundee County articles when he spotted an old card catalog. Curious, he investigated.

The catalog was an old index of the city paper, done in the early eighties. This must have been the source for the computer catalog, except the cards had much more information on them. After each entry, there was a brief notation about the article.

Charlie pulled out the "D" drawer and sat at a carrel. He found Dundee County and began to thumb through the cards. There were many county council meetings, social reports, stories about the county's regiments during the wars, and even a few weather reports.

But no Coverdale.

The latest entry in the card catalog was for mid-1983. There was no way Coverdale had been founded after that late date.

"By the light of the silvery moon, where are you?"

He checked his watch and found two hours had passed since Jimmy left for the computer store. Charlie didn't think Jimmy would know where to look for him in the library, so he rushed to the reference room where they had agreed to meet.

The reference room had three large tables arranged down the middle, with the stacks going off to each side. Charlie walked down the left aisle looking for the atlases when he spied a large black book on the last table. It looked like one of the atlases he was seeking.

Sure enough, it was the historical atlas for Dundee County, compiled in 1880. Charlie didn't expect to find anything if Coverdale hadn't been founded before the turn of the century. He figured he should be able to see what was on the land occupied by the town before that time, though.

Charlie checked the master map of the county. He found the river that ran through the town and followed its course through the county. There were a few small villages along the course of the river in 1880, but none were named Coverdale.

That was another strange thing: the river was called the Dundee, like the county, not the Pannon. Following the course of the river carefully, he couldn't find the bends at Coverdale or the bay near where he'd seen the circle of standing stones. The bend should have been easy to recognize.

Turning to the township map that should have had more details and a listing for all villages and post offices, Charlie found only forest and swamp in the area now occupied by Coverdale.

It was as if the town and the valley it sat in didn't exist.

Then Charlie had an idea. He quickly returned to the computers, found an unoccupied one, and googled "Pannon." Maybe he could at least find the source of the name. That might provide a clue. What came back didn't help. There was a Pannon wine region in Hungary. During Roman times, the area was the province of Pannonia on the Danube.

Charlie logged off and returned to the reference room and the atlas. That was a total waste of time.

A hiss to his left made Charlie look up.

Jimmy crouched in the stacks, looking panic-stricken. He beckoned Charlie to come to him.

"What's up?" he asked.

"Keep your voice down." Jimmy put a hand over Charlie's mouth. "She might hear you."

Charlie pulled the hand away. "Wash your hands. You smell like hot dogs. Who?"

"The woman with the tattoo."

Charlie felt his stomach drop.

"Who? Where?"

Jimmy pulled Charlie to the back of the stacks and hid behind a pillar. He looked about cautiously, then spoke.

"I spotted her out there," he pointed towards the hall outside the reference room, "when I came back in. I've been looking all over for you."

"I was upstairs in the microfilm room."

"She has the same tattoo as the women in Coverdale. That Sisterhood thing."

"Did she see you?"

"I don't think so. I was crouched down behind a cart. I'd dropped my jacket and was picking it up. I saw her hands reach out from the other side of the cart and grab a couple of books. That's when I spotted the tattoo. We've got to get out of here."

Jimmy made a move to go, but Charlie held him back.

"Wait. I've got to put the books back. If she spots them, she'll know someone was snooping."

"I'll get the atlas. You get whatever else you were using. Meet me at the front door."

Jimmy slid around the pillar, and Charlie moved to the reference room door.

He peered out and nearly had a heart attack when Jimmy appeared at his side.

"You almost scared the crap out of me," whispered Charlie.

"I heard. She's wearing a white dress with red trim. She's about forty. I thought that might be useful."

"Thanks," said Charlie as he checked the hallway. It was empty.

Charlie returned to the history section and found the books he was using where he had left them. Careful to get the numbers correct, He replaced the books on the shelf, double checking the library numbers to be sure they were shelved correctly.

He remembered the card catalog drawer. Had he put it away? Maybe.

Rather than take a chance, Charlie returned to the microfilm room. When he entered, he thought he saw something white disappear around a far corner. He quickly checked the card catalog, saw everything was in order, and headed for the library entrance.

Outside, there was no sign of Jimmy. Charlie's heart thundered in his ears, and his palms were sweating. If Jimmy had been spotted, he was in deep trouble.

As he moved past a pillar, someone grabbed his shoulders and pulled him into the shadows.

"We've got to stop meeting like this."

"You've got to stop scaring me like this. You're giving me palpitations."

Jimmy smiled at Charlie and gave him a thumbs-up sign.

"I don't think she spotted me. Shall we join my parents for dinner?"

"I could use something to eat," said Charlie. "I think I lost twenty pounds in the last few minutes worrying about getting caught."

Charlie glanced back and thought he saw someone in a white dress watching from a third-floor window. But when he tried to concentrate there was no one there.

He decided he was being paranoid.

Chapter Eight

Charlie spent a nervous week waiting for the Chief to visit the house and speak to his father. The thought that El might show up made him physically ill. After Monday's upset from some of Mrs. Burke's chili that genuinely had kept him in the bathroom at school for an hour, Charlie stuck to bland foods for the rest of the week. By Friday morning, there had been no visits, so Charlie decided that neither he nor Jimmy had been spotted at the city library.

Since he couldn't find out anything about the history of Coverdale, Charlie thought about concentrating on Gwen. Even though El had told him she wasn't interested and had made some disgusting suggestions, Charlie felt he should give Gwen a chance to shoot him down. It was only fair. Much as El got him to feel two inches tall and useless, he knew he had to overcome it and at least try to speak to her. They'd been in school for a month now and still hadn't spoken, though they had spent a large chunk of the school day in the same classes or passing in the halls. On his way to school that morning, he tried to talk himself into having the nerve to walk right up to Gwen and say something. A simple "Hello" would suffice.

He would have to concentrate hard not to say something stupid like, "Allo, allo, allo." His ears burned at the memory of his triumphant introduction to Gwen.

The moment Charlie saw Gwen in their homeroom, his brain turned to mush. When he passed her on his way to his seat, she looked up at him and smiled. He promptly tripped over his feet, knocked over a couple of desks, and landed tangled around his knapsack. He straightened up the mess and safely sat in his seat without further damage. Refusing to look up from the textbook he pretended to read, he tried to tune out the laughter. Nervous sweat dripped down his forehead.

His day only got worse when he reached science class. Charlie had a lot of problems trying to perform a simple experiment involving wires, transistors, a battery, and a light bulb. As much as he tried, he could not concentrate enough to wire the circuit correctly so the light would go on. While lights flashed all over the classroom, Charlie became increasingly frustrated. Anger got the better of him, and he tried to destroy one of the colorful transistors but only succeeded in stabbing himself in the palm of his hand with a wire. Wincing in pain and annoyed at himself for being an idiot, he swept the wires into his lab station sink.

"Cool it, fool," said John, his lab partner. "If Caxton sees you playing the idiot, he'll keep us both after school until we get this thing to work."

"Don't worry, Mr. Roger, I know you can do the experiment." A voice boomed from behind them.

Charlie and John turned to face their science teacher, the short and rotund Mr. Caxton. He played with his little black mustache as he frowned up at Charlie.

Stifling a giggle, Charlie did his best not to think of that fat Belgian detective from the TV, Hercule whatsit.

"If you think science is so amusing, Mr. Bowen, you won't mind appearing in this lab at the end of the day to complete your experiment."

Charlie's eyes widened, and his jaw dropped. He had definitely planned to talk to Gwen after school. This day just kept getting worse.

"B-b-but ..."

Mr. Caxton held his palm up in Charlie's face. "No buts, Mr. Bowen. I don't care if it's the weekend. Your Friday fun will have to wait."

The teacher walked away, gesticulating with his hands. "Science waits for no man," he boomed to the class. "Good work always comes first." He clapped his hands twice and sat down at his desk.

The bell ending the period drowned out Charlie's muttered curses while he retrieved the wires from the sink and stuffed them in the drawer under the lab station.

At the end of the day, Charlie waited with a heavy heart to see if Gwen would pass his locker on her way out of the school. The final bell rang, and he waited ten minutes, cutting it short to get to the science lab. Being late for detention would only irritate Mr. Caxton more, and then he would really lay into the sarcasm. The teacher had a way of making you feel small while seeming to compliment you on something you had done. Charlie enjoyed it when Caxton was on a roll, but being the brunt of the teacher's wit was another thing entirely. He knew it was all in fun, the complete opposite of El.

There was no sign of Gwen.

It was all Charlie could do not to trip and hurt himself when he saw Gwen in the science lab. She sat at her lab station, trying to complete the same experiment Charlie had to perform. She was concentrating so hard she didn't notice him enter.

Mr. Caxton, reading at his desk, motioned for Charlie to start working, and then he returned to his science journal.

Fifteen minutes later, there still hadn't been a flash of light from anywhere in the lab.

"Perhaps, Mr. Bowen, you and Miss Blayney should put your heads together and see if you can get out of here before midnight."

Charlie looked up at the teacher, startled, scared, elated, stunned. He was speechless.

"All, all, allo," said a husky voice from across the room.

"Quite," replied the teacher. He grinned without looking up.

Charlie wondered if everyone in town knew about his gaff when meeting Gwen.

He moved carefully over to Gwen's lab station. He didn't bring anything lest he drop it, set fire to the room, or stab himself in the thigh with a pencil.

Gwen smiled, Charlie's heart flipped, and she said, "Have you had a good look at yourself lately?"

Confused, Charlie checked his reflection in the lab window. His hair looked neat, and he had no food stuck in his teeth.

The zit! His hand went to the tender spot.

"No, you twit," Gwen said, tapping Charlie's chest. At the touch of her hand, he got an immediate erection and sat quickly to hide it.

Realization hit Charlie. "The T-shirt. You're making a Uriah Heep reference." His heart beating so fast he thought it would push itself out of his chest. He tried to think of something intelligent to say but was saved by Mr. Caxton.

"If you two lovebirds don't mind, I have a dinner engagement at seven. I'd like to be there."

Both Gwen and Charlie had red faces when they set to work on the experiment.

Charlie watched Gwen try to get the light to flash, and then Gwen watched as Charlie tried. They sat for a few minutes, staring at the mass of wires and transistors, when Charlie had a brainstorm.

He picked up a wire and attached it to the battery.

"What if we do this," he spliced two wires together, "then this," he hooked up a transistor.

"Then take this," Gwen picked up the light bulb, "and put it here."

The light flashed.

"Hallclujah!" cried Mr. Caxton. "I'm starved." He rose from his desk, shoved the journal into his briefcase, and headed to the lab door. "Come on, get out. You did it. I'll put the materials away on Monday." He winked.

Surprised at the teacher's generosity, Gwen and Charlie practically ran out of the lab, down the hall, and out the front door.

On the sidewalk, they stopped and took deep breaths.

"It was really easy, after all," said Gwen.

"It just took some concentration and a fantastic lab partner," Charlie said, blushing.

"What makes you think you're so fantastic?"

"I-I-I didn't mean me."

"I'm kidding. Are you always this jittery?"

"Only when I'm awake." Trying to think of something witty, he blurted out, "I'm so hungry for something spicy."

"Are you thinking of getting a burger with hot sauce and shake at the diner to celebrate our success?"

Startled, Charlie could only stare in wonder at Gwen.

"Just as I thought."

Gwen wrapped her arm around Charlie's and steered him towards the diner. Charlie remained silent, stunned that he was walking with the girl of his dreams.

And all he had to do was make a fool of himself in class.

He felt immense relief that a particular part of his anatomy remained calm and didn't make a show of things.

When they got to the diner's entrance, Charlie saw there weren't many people inside. He reached for the door, but Gwen pulled him away.

"Do you mind if I check with Mr. Tyndale at the theatre first? I want to find out what time he wants me there tomorrow."

Gwen led Charlie down the alley between the theatre and the library. At a back door, she rang the bell. Charlie heard the sound of the bell inside the old building and footsteps approaching the door.

An old man who looked about a hundred, stooped and leaning on a cane, pulled open the door. He wore a purple velvet smoking jacket and a cravat. A smile spread across his face when he spied Gwen.

"Come in, my dear. It's so good to see you."

When they were inside, Gwen said, "This is my friend ..."

"Charles Bowen," said Mr. Tyndale. He shook Charlie's hand. "May I call you Charlie? Such a pleasure to finally meet you. Gwendolyn's spoken so much about you. A great student of history and classic rock. Also witty with a penchant for slapstick."

Charlie looked over at Gwen, who stood there with a huge smile. She shrugged.

"I approve, Gwendolyn," said Mr. Tyndale. "Don't let Justin mess this one up." She gave him a quizzical look. "Now, Charlie, Gwendolyn, and I must confer. Why don't you explore a little? We shan't be long."

While Gwen and Mr. Tyndale talked, Charlie wandered into the theatre's lobby. There were old movie posters everywhere, some dating back to the silent era. In a showcase near the candy counter were dozens of lobby cards, all signed by the actors starring in the films. Charlie stared in wonder at the signatures—Cary Grant, Errol Flynn, Marlene Dietrich, Peter O'Toole, and more.

"You like the old ones?"

Charlie was startled out of his reverie by the appearance of Mr. Tyndale at his side.

"Yes sir. Especially Humphrey Bogart, Burt Lancaster, and Jimmy Stewart."

"I have them all, you know," said the old man. His eyes were gleaming, and he didn't try to hide his glee. "I've met them all, too. Lovely people, mostly. Magic."

"I'll never get to meet any of them," said Charlie. "I'm too young, and most of the best actors have already died."

"They'll never die so long as we can watch their work," said Mr. Tyndale. "Why are you such a fan? I thought a young one like you would be more interested in the flashy special effects things out now. All those explosions and sex and blood."

"Back in the city, there's a cable channel that only shows movies from before 1975. It's on all night. I don't sleep much, so I'd watch if I wasn't reading. Too bad we can't get the station here."

Tyndale clapped his hands and did a little dance around his cane. "I supply that station with all its films. That's why it has such good copies."

Charlie giggled and said, "That is so cool."

Then Charlie remembered that Gwen was there. He couldn't believe he'd forgotten her, even for a moment. She was at the candy counter, dusting the popcorn machine. It used only real butter. And there were lots of packets of Milk Duds among the candy.

"Gwen," it felt odd speaking her name but comfortable, too. "Why are you here anyway?"

Gwen stopped dusting and joined Charlie and the old man. "Mr. Tyndale lets me work the ticket booth before the show. Then I get to see the movie from the projection room."

Mr Tyndale tugged at Charlie's sleeve. "I'm sure if you show up on Saturday, Gwendolyn will let you in for free. Not that I charge much anyway. I'm a very wealthy man, you know. That's why I can indulge myself in my hobby. My colleagues think I'm a little mad, but I've done my bit for The Institute. It's time I had some fun."

"We'd better get going if we want to eat," said Gwen.

When they reached the back door to leave the theatre, Mr. Tyndale called out to Charlie. "Here," he said and tossed a packet of Milk Duds. "Dessert."

When they got there, the only people inside the diner were a couple of Coverdale policemen at the counter having pie and coffee. Gwen and Charlie took a booth at the back, ordered, and sat silently for a few minutes.

Charlie wanted to ask Gwen all kinds of questions, but he was too nervous to speak. He was relieved that he hadn't destroyed anything or killed anyone since they had been together, but he decided not to put ketchup on his fries just to be safe. Gwen was dressed all in white.

"So, tell me about the t-shirts," Gwen said, breaking the deadly silence.

Charlie explained about his father, and Gwen added that her father, too, had liked many of the same bands. When she suggested that Charlie come over sometime and see her record and CD collection, he was sure she was only being polite.

More silence.

The food came. Charlie couldn't resist the ketchup and

patiently waited for it to drop out of the bottle. Smacking the bottom to speed it up was a sure-fire recipe for disaster.

"Who's your favorite actor," asked Gwen. "Wait, don't tell me. Bogart or Stewart. Maybe Lancaster. I listened when you were speaking to Mr. Tyndale."

"Right. And Myrna Loy. Who's yours?"

"Daniel Craig, who else?" Gwen laughed at the look of surprise on Charlie's face. "I like modern movies, too, you know."

"Me, too," Charlie added quickly.

They were quiet while they ate. Charlie knew he'd spew food all over Gwen if he tried to speak.

"Dessert?" Charlie held out the packet of Milk Duds.

Gwen wrinkled her nose and said, "Raspberry pie with vanilla ice cream is dessert. Those are an appetizer."

They ordered. They had been so intent on each other and their limited conversation that they only now noticed that the diner had filled up. Mr. Caxton sat at the next booth with a woman in a white dress. Charlie couldn't see her face, but something about her felt familiar.

When they had finished their pie and ice cream, Charlie pulled out the Milk Duds. He shook the packet and attempted to pull it open. The cardboard resisted, so he pulled harder. Milk Duds flew all over the booth. Both Gwen and Charlie scrambled to catch them before they hit the floor.

"Suave," said Gwen and popped a Dud in her mouth.

"And sophisticated," said Charlie. He didn't feel the least bit embarrassed by the candy disaster.

"We're a regular Nick and Nora," said Gwen.

They got up to leave, and Charlie tried to get a look at the woman with Mr. Caxton. He failed. At the counter, Charlie insisted on paying.

"But I asked you out, sort of," said Gwen.

"But I'm the guy. It's a guy thing. I must pay."

"Can we at least go Dutch?"

"Why Dutch? Why not Norwegian? Or Spanish?"

"It is one of the great questions of the day."

The bill, paid by Charlie alone, they left the diner. They hesitated outside. Charlie casually kicked at the wall of the restaurant.

"Can I walk you home, Madame?"

"You'd better, sir. It's about two miles, and it's getting dark."

Charlie perked up at this comment and then slapped his forehead.

"Oh no, I'm a dead man. I forgot to call home and let them know I'd be late."

Gwen remained silent.

"Never mind. Walking you home is worth any hassle I get from my folks." Gwen smiled. "Anyway, my mom won't even notice I'm not there."

Gwen took Charlie's arm again and they walked in silence. It was a warm night, though a slight, cool breeze rustled the leaves in the trees lining the park. They walked along Sevres Street to the Loop and turned north. Soon it left the built-up section of Coverdale and passed through a tunnel of trees. It was dark under the trees, and the woods were silent. He was certain he saw movement in the shadows, but there were no sounds, not even animals or night birds. Gwen snuggled closer to Charlie. Charlie's heart did flips.

He told himself to enjoy the moment and not to rush things. Keep it nice and clean. And if there was movement, the darkness would hide anything obvious.

Thinking there wouldn't be anyone around to hear their

conversation, Charlie said, "What Mr. Tyndale said about Justin not spoiling things. What did he mean? Tell me if I'm being nosy."

Gwen stopped and sighed. She stepped away from him. He thought he'd ruined everything.

"I'd hoped this wouldn't come up, Charlie," she said. "I know you've met Justin LaRennes, that baldy-headed piece of shit."

"Ah, yes. We call him El Baldo, or just El."

"Nice. You and Jimmy?" He nodded. "El thinks he owns me, but he's a disgusting worm, and I want to scream every time he gets near me. His breath is horrific. He scares all the boys in school. None of them have even tried to ask me out."

"I nearly hurled the first time we met." Hadn't even one of the guys tried to ask her out?

"He's told me things about you, Charlie. Not very nice things about, well, who you really like."

"That son of a bitch. He made gross hints when he tried to warn me off you. He told me I was beneath you, that you were destined for greater things than a simple boy like me."

"Oh, I am, Charlie." She smacked his arm when he looked serious. "Goof." Gwen took his hand and they walked along the road. Charlie felt an instant reaction when she touched him. She leaned closer and quietly said, "Don't be embarrassed. It's normal and I'm flattered. Now let me spoil it by talking more about El."

Charlie gently squeezed Gwen's hand and felt a pain in his chest. Excitement, happiness, anticipation. He hoped he wouldn't hurl. Was he being presumptuous?

"El will try to gaslight you, Charlie. He's done it to me enough times. But I can get past it now with a little effort."

"Yeah. He got me the other week."

"Was that when you were sulking around school, looking like you'd lost your best friend? I could tell something was wrong because you were so quiet and couldn't look at me."

"Yes. What he said hurt. I knew it was a load of crap, but it kept gnawing away at me. And my dad didn't help. He's so concerned about his position at The Institute that he believes anything bad anyone says about me."

"Look, Charlie, never believe a word that El says. If he tells you water is wet, double check. He's a troublemaker, a manipulator, a pathological liar. All he cares about is himself and controlling people. He wants to be in charge but have everyone think he's a nice guy who's trying to be helpful. He loves to play people off against each other. The way he did with us."

"Thanks, Gwen. I needed to hear that. He's so convincing."

"Any time he tries it with you again, talk to me, and I'll get you out of it."

"I'll do the same for you."

"I know."

They emerged from the trees at an intersection where a road branched off the Loop to The Institute. Gwen's home was across the way.

When they reached the gates of the Mundy estate, Gwen went to a box on one of the gate posts. She opened a small door and punched a code onto a keypad inside. The heavy iron gate swung open, and they entered the grounds.

Charlie saw the Chief's cruiser parked on the laneway near the house. His heart sank.

"I'm a dead man," said Charlie. "If the Chief sees me with you, he'll throw me in jail."

"Uncle Willy? He's a pussycat."

Charlie's eyes widened and he burst out laughing. He laughed so hard he began to choke when he tried to say, "Uncle Willy."

They stopped a few feet from the front door, and without thinking too much about it, Charlie said, "Gwen, would you like to go out with me sometime? I'll understand if you say no."

She seemed a little shocked by the request, but before she could answer, the large oak front door of the Mundy mansion swung open. Chief Wycliffe stepped out, followed by the Mayor. A few feet further in, Charlie spied El, standing with his arms crossed. He looked furious, and Charlie felt El's eyes boring into him. He shivered.

The Chief smiled at his goddaughter. When he condescended to notice Charlie, he had such a look of contempt that Charlie shrank back behind Gwen. This seemed to make the Chief's look even more intense.

Then Charlie remembered "Uncle Willy" and started to giggle.

The Chief got in his cruiser and sped away.

The Mayor waited at the door. He cleared his throat and raised his eyebrows.

"Gaslight him," Gwen said so quietly Charlie could barely hear it. "Zipper." Then, louder, "Good night, Charlie. Thank you for walking me home."

"You're welcome, Miss Blayney."

She ran into the mansion.

The Mayor retreated and closed the door without saying a word. Before the door closed, Charlie saw El reach out for Gwen as she tried to get past him.

Charlie realized Gwen hadn't answered and was tempted to knock on the door. But the look the Mayor had given him dissuaded him. And there was EL. He didn't want to get Gwen into more trouble than he had already caused her. He turned to jog down the laneway. When he got to the gate, he saw that it had closed after the Chief had left.

Charlie didn't know the code and didn't want to bother the Mayor.

What had been the best day of his life had suddenly turned sour. He tossed his knapsack over the wall and heard something break when it landed. While scaling the stone wall next to the gate, he caught the backside of his jeans on a shard of shale on top and tore them.

Now, he would have to face his father's wrath when he got home late from school without having called to leave a message. And he'd have to explain how he ripped his pants open.

But Gwen seemed to like him, which couldn't be bad. Not bad at all.

Maybe the day wasn't such a disaster after all.

Chapter Nine

Charlie looked down at the composted manure pooled around his feet. His runners and socks were buried in the black mess. He tossed aside the plastic bag that he had just cut open and stepped out of the pile. Charlie leaned against the fence and pulled off each runner to empty the black clods. While he spread the manure across the flower bed, he pondered the great injustice of parents.

Grounded for a week.

He couldn't believe it.

When he returned home last night, still dancing on cloud nine after spending time with Gwen—having touched her and held her arm and hand—his father was waiting. Charlie's mother was in the kitchen reading a gardening magazine, and Ant had been perched at the top of the stairs, a nasty grin on her face.

"Where the hell have you been, boy?" his father had shouted.

"Out," was all Charlie could say. He could feel the warmth spreading across his face. He couldn't look his father in the eye.

Plus, he didn't want to mention Gwen at home. It was none of their business, and he feared that if his family knew about her, they'd find some way to spoil it.

"What? We're not good enough to get a call informing us of your plans? Speak up, I'm waiting."

"Forgot."

"Well, you can forget going out for the next week. You're grounded."

Charlie had been startled. Grounded?

"No way. I was just a bit late."

"Five hours isn't a bit late, sonny."

"But grounded, that's so unfair. I'm eighteen. You can't ground me."

"As long as you live in this house, rent-free, I can do whatever I want."

"Oh, for gosh sake, this is ridic ..." Charlie had seen the sweat running down his father's face. The man was about to lose it. "Uh oh."

"'Uh oh' doesn't even begin to describe the trouble you're in, sonny-Jim." There had been silence for a few moments. "Do you have anything else to say?"

Charlie had thought for a moment about telling his father who he had been with but decided that would only get him into more trouble, not less. He expected another visit from the Chief and El anyway, and there was no need to throw more fuel onto the fire.

"No, sir. I apologize for being late and not calling. It won't happen again, sir."

His father had appeared somewhat mollified by Charlie's change in attitude. The man had relaxed and sat down in his recliner.

"Alright. Go apologize to your mother for ruining her dinner. And volunteer to help her with the garden tomorrow."

Tomorrow had come quickly, and now Charlie was covered with dirt, manure, and peat dust. His mother had mapped out where she wanted flower and vegetable beds in the spring. Charlie had been granted the task of removing the sod from the beds in the backyard. Once that was done, and it had only taken him two hours of steady digging, he had to move several dozen wheelbarrows full of topsoil from the driveway to the new beds.

Then came the fun part. Charlie's mother had purchased a couple of bags of peat moss and about a dozen bags of manure. They were supposed to make the ground more fertile, but they only gave Charlie a headache. The wind caught the peat as soon as he sliced the first bag open. It had billowed around him, choking and blinding him.

Once he had the peat moss under control, Charlie had found the manure almost as co-operative. At least the stuff didn't smell. It wasn't gross or anything because it had been well-rotted. It was the thought that counted, though.

Charlie hoped his hard work all day might make his father more reasonable. He was anxious to get to the theatre and see if Gwen would let him in free. Maybe she would even invite him to join her in the projection booth.

He could still dream.

By lunchtime, Charlie had finished the work his mother had assigned him. Though he was dirty, he was pleased with what he had accomplished. He felt like a farmer – like he should go out and milk a few cows.

When George Bowen joined his wife and son on the back deck for a lunch of sandwiches and potato chips, he seemed to be in a good mood.

"The work's going well," said Charlie, hoping his father would agree. "We should be finished in no time."

"Charlie's worked very hard today," added his mother.

His father simply said, "Discipline is good for you."

Charlie concluded his father was still honked off at him. He could forget about seeing Gwen at the theatre tonight.

"What do you want me to do next, Mom? Maybe ask Ant to give us a hand?"

"No," his mother said through a snicker. "Your sister isn't much given to garden work."

"She's not much given to any kind of work if you ask me."

"We didn't."

"Sorry, sir."

"Maybe you could clear out that nasty patch of weeds in the corner there."

Charlie's mother pointed at the northwest corner of the yard where a great patch of briars and assorted weeds grew. Though sod must have been laid there when the house was built, the grass hadn't taken for some reason. Now the patch was overgrown and ugly.

"It would be a good spot for a compost pile," said Charlie's mother. "We'll get some chicken wire and wood from the hardware store next week and build a small enclosure for the pile."

Charlie forced a smile at the thought of more garden work next week.

With lunch over, Charlie grabbed a rake and some shears and walked over to the briar patch. He leaned the rake against a nearby tree and began to cut down the weeds. It was awkward work because he didn't want to kneel down. The briars would tear apart the skin of his knees. Charlie soon realized that shorts were not the best clothing to wear when gardening. He had to crouch and cut, and several times he got weeds up in his shorts or fell back and got briars in the backside.

Charlie stood, stretched, and yawned. Sweat flowed freely down his face and arms. He thought about taking off his shirt, but the neighbors were out on their deck, and Charlie didn't feel like a show-off.

There was a noise from the woods a few feet away. Charlie stopped and looked in the direction of the noise. The Bowen house had no back fence, and the yard opened directly onto the woods. About a hundred yards through the trees ran the Loop.

The noise again. A slight rustling, like a small animal.

"Don't say anything."

It *was* a small animal. Charlie recognized Jimmy's voice.

Charlie kept his head down and continued to cut weeds.

"I'm grounded. Do you want to get me into more trouble?" Charlie glanced at his mother, who was sorting out some tulip bulbs. His father was nowhere to be seen.

"What do you want, Jimmy?"

"It's important. I had to speak to you." The voice seemed to come from behind an oak tree, but it was hard to tell. "I need details, man. Details."

"What are you talking about?"

"Last night. You and Blayney. What happened? Are you engaged yet?"

"Nothing happened," said Charlie, a little irritated at his friend's nosiness. "We had something to eat, I walked her home."

"You're kidding, right?" The voice had now moved to the left a few feet. "Something must have happened. Did you kiss her?"

"No. The Mayor and the Chief came out the front door before I got the chance."

"Are you going to see her again?" This time, the voice came from far to the right.

"Can't you stay in one place?"

"No. I have to pee. It always happens when I'm trying to

hide."

Though he was reluctant to talk about last night in case he jinxed any further chance of seeing Gwen, he said, "I asked her out, but she didn't give me an answer."

"That's a first. But it's over already. If she wanted to see you again, she would have given you an answer right away. Or El would have said something. You might as well give up."

"I thought you were my friend. You're supposed to give me encouragement."

Charlie's mother left the back deck with a handful of bulbs and went through the garage to the front yard.

"She calls the Chief Uncle Willy."

"Oh, crap."

"Yeah, I thought it was funny, too."

"No, I just stepped in some."

Charlie guffawed and kept working. There was silence from the woods for a while, followed by the sound of trickling water.

"Are you peeing in my backyard?"

"I'm marking my territory."

Charlie threw a lump of dirt in the direction of Jimmy's voice.

"You jerk," came a quick reply. "You made me pee on my shoe."

Charlie bent forward to grasp a large clump of briars. He needed to use both hands to pull it free, and when it came away from the earth, he fell back with a jarring thud. Charlie tossed the clump into the woods, in the general direction of Jimmy, and rubbed his behind.

Something glinted in the sunlight.

"Hey, Charlie."

"Hold on, Jimmy. I've found something."

Charlie knelt next to the hole made by the clump of briars he had just pulled. There was some shiny thing at the bottom. He reached in and pulled out a coin. Charlie brushed off the dirt that had adhered to the coin and examined it closely.

On it was a man's head, with a wreath and an inscription. Charlie could make out some of the letters: AVGVST S CAESA.

"Augustus Caesar," Charlie said quietly. A Roman coin.

"What is it?" asked Jimmy.

Without hesitation, Charlie answered, "A dime. I'm rich."

"Now you can afford to buy Gwen a piece of bubble gum. If she'll have you."

Charlie ignored Jimmy and placed the coin in his pocket. He bent down and dug some more dirt out of the hole. More coins.

"Jimmy, I have to go inside for a while. Nature calls and I don't feel like marking my territory. I'll see you at school on Monday."

Charlie didn't know why he kept quiet about the coins. An image of El popped into his head and he knew he absolutely had to keep his mouth shut. He quickly surveyed the surrounding area for spies or cameras. Looking up, he saw no drones in the sky. This town was making him paranoid.

"No problem, bud. And don't worry, I'm sure Gwen will want to go out with you."

In the bathroom a few minutes later, Charlie washed off the coins. There were three more with the Augustus Caesar inscription, two with TIBERIVS, and one with an owl and what looked like Greek letters.

What are Roman and Greek coins doing in my backyard, he wondered.

Charlie stuffed the coins into his pocket and returned to

the garden. He stopped by the garage to get a spade and went to the briar patch. Most of the weeds had been cut down, and Charlie decided to dig the ground over. That way, he would have an excuse to look for more coins.

Standing over the hole where he found the first coins, Charlie began to dig. It didn't take him long to hit something metallic. Checking first to see if anyone was watching—there wasn't, as far as he could tell—Charlie knelt down and brushed away the dirt with his hand.

There was a box buried there. Most of the wood had rotted away, but some metal fittings, heavily rusted and brittle, had survived.

Inside the box was a trove of coins. There must have been hundreds. At a glance, Charlie could see more Roman coins, some with Greek inscriptions and a few with writing he didn't recognize.

Then he heard his father approaching. Charlie quickly threw dirt back into the hole and covered his find.

"How's it going?" asked George Bowen.

"Not bad, sir. I'm digging over the roots here so the weeds won't grow back."

His father checked over the work Charlie had done and shook his head.

"Good, good. There's nothing like a little hard work to get rid of rebelliousness. Very good, Charlie."

A little mystified by his father's words, Charlie thought about asking if his grounding could be lifted.

"Um ..."

"Before you say anything," his father interrupted, "I want to tell you that I'm going to shorten your grounding."

Charlie was relieved at his father's words. He'd get to see Gwen tonight, after all.

"Yes, you've worked very hard, and I think you deserve some consideration. Though you must remember, I am your father, and while you live under my roof, you do what I say."

Charlie nodded despite the urge to tell his father to stuff it. What Charlie heard sounded a bit too much like a sermon for his liking. He wasn't a kid anymore.

But he was anxious to see Gwen.

"Right then, you're only grounded until Thursday instead of next weekend."

Charlie was too stunned to speak.

George Bowen walked back into the house with a satisfied look.

Charlie stared down at the dirt that hid the box of coins.

"I hope you're worth something." He wanted to run away from Coverdale and make a life for himself.

"What's worth something, Charlie?" El stood a few feet away. He must have come through the garage after his father had left.

Not showing any signs of surprise or shock, Charlie calmly said, "Hm? Oh, just talking to myself about me. I don't seem to be able to do anything right. Now I'm grounded for being home late last night."

El came right up to the edge of the dug-up area. "About that," he said. "I told you she wasn't for you, but you went ahead anyway. Now, that was downright stupid and juvenile of you."

"I don't understand, Mr. LaRennes. All I did was walk Miss Blayney home when it got dark." He felt confident that Gwen would not have told El anything about what happened. "We both had detentions. Later, I went to the diner for a burger, and she was there. She allowed me to sit with her, and we talked about what a pain science is."

"I don't believe you," said El.

"It's true. She's so much smarter at it than me. When she explained what I was doing wrong, it was so helpful. I guess I kept asking her questions because I want to do well in science class. My dad's a scientist, you know. Maybe, if I'm lucky and study hard, I can get a good job like him."

"I don't think you will ever be as smart as your father, Charlie. He truly is brilliant. You should settle for something that you're capable of comprehending. Carpentry, perhaps. Or landscaping."

"Thank you, sir."

"And you shouldn't bother Miss Blayney with your idiotic questions. It's your fault she was out so late last night. And she is much, much smarter than you."

"I know, and I'm sorry. By the time we finished eating, it had gotten dark, so I walked her home. I mean, you wouldn't expect a young girl to walk home in the dark alone, would you? Especially one who's as special and important as Miss Blayney. That would be rude and very ungentlemanly."

"Perhaps."

"There's no perhaps about it. Back in the city, you read a lot about young women being assaulted when they walk home alone at night. I know Coverdale isn't the big city, but I still have big city concerns. Can't shake 'em."

"That's very noble, Charlie. Still, I did warn you about her."

"No worries, Mr. LaRennes." Charlie laughed. "I know my place and I was completely polite with Miss Blayney. We barely spoke the whole way to her house." He hoped he wasn't laying it on too thick.

"Really? What did she say to you before she came in the house?"

Charlie remembered what Gwen had said a moment before she thanked him for walking her home. She must have known something like this would happen. He deliberately thought about something embarrassing and humiliating to make his cheeks go red. He wanted El to believe his story. "It's really embarrassing." He looked down at his feet. "She told me my fly was down. I used the bathroom at the diner and must have forgotten to pull it up. Happens to me all the time." When El smiled, Charlie continued. "I bet everyone in the diner saw it. It's just lucky there wasn't anyone out on the Loop to see."

"You need to be more careful, Charlie. That was a stupid thing to do."

"Tell me about it. Er, if you see Miss Blayney, could you thank her for me, please. I was so shocked last night; I was rude and said nothing. I wouldn't want her to think any less of me than she already does."

"Of course, Charlie, I'd be happy to pass along your thanks to Miss Blayney." He stared at Charlie for a few seconds. Charlie stared back but looked away as if he couldn't stand the scrutiny. The truth was, he couldn't stand to look at the weasel-faced little shit.

El nodded. "I'm glad we had this talk, Charlie. I simply wanted to be clear you understand how things are."

"Oh, I do, sir. Totally."

"Good. I have important work to do. I can't be wasting my time putting foolish children on the right track."

With that, El turned and walked away. Charlie sighed and watched El walk up the deck steps, cross it, and go in the back door. He didn't bother to knock. Through the kitchen window, he saw El and his father speaking. Well, he saw El speaking as his father stood there and listened.

When El left, Charlie's father stood at the back door with a beer. When Charlie waved, he got no reaction. His father shook his head in disgust and walked back into the house.

"Well, that was fun. I hope you're okay, Gwen."

He returned to digging but in a spot well away from the coin stash.

Chapter Ten

Did teachers conspire to have tests on the same day? Charlie had to wonder. He had tests in six of his seven classes today. Perhaps being grounded for the weekend hadn't been such a bad thing after all. He'd had plenty of time to study, not that he needed to review much, except in science.

He wanted to get through the tests so he could get to the library and look up the coins. In one of his history books, he found that Augustus Caesar had ruled Rome from 30 BCE to 14 CE, and Tiberius had been Emperor from 14 to 37 CE. He was interested in the Greek coins, but the coins he couldn't identify piqued his interest a lot more. Charlie figured he must have discovered some old collector's hidden treasure, or perhaps it was some colonial guy's stash. Wherever the coins came from, Charlie was sure they didn't belong in Coverdale.

Charlie wasn't able to speak to Gwen during most of the morning. She had rushed into homeroom as the final bell rang and rushed out again as soon as the dismissal bell sounded. He tried to get her attention a couple of times in the halls, but Gwen hadn't seen him.

"I hear you got the experiment worked out," said John when he Charlie outside the science lab.

"Um, yeah. How did you know?" Charlie looked at his lab partner closely but could read nothing in John's expression.

"Mr. Caxton had dinner with my aunt and mentioned you

and Blayney worked things out. That's good to hear."

"What do you mean?"

Before Charlie could get an answer, John slipped into the lab.

"Hi, Charlie."

Charlie spun and faced Gwen, who had approached him silently from the stairs.

"Hi, Gwen. Sorry about Saturday night. Not showing up and all."

Gwen looked puzzled.

"The movie. What Mr. Tyndale said." Charlie was flustered by Gwen's response. Didn't she remember they were going to meet?

Gwen looked behind Charlie, then shrugged. His heart sank. The bell rang.

Mr. Caxton came to the lab door. "Are you going to join us, Miss Blayney and Mr. Bowen? Your fate awaits you."

Without another word, Gwen walked into the lab. Before entering, Charlie looked in the direction Gwen had stared and saw El turn the corner down the hall. Had he been spying?

"Mr. Bowen? Today, if you don't mind."

He followed the teacher into the lab, aware that all eyes were watching him.

The test was a breeze, much to Charlie's relief.

Charlie was held up after the class by Mr. Caxton, who wanted to remind him to review the experiment because it would be on the final exam for the semester. Charlie barely paid attention to the teacher, trying to stay aware of where Gwen was going. He saw her leave the lab and was about to throttle Mr. Caxton when the teacher dismissed him.

Charlie raced to the door, narrowly avoided knocking some beakers off a shelf, and left the lab. He looked around the hall eagerly.

Gwen poked her head out from an alcove by the lockers across the hall. She smiled at him. Charlie's heart resurfaced and he went to her.

"Not much time. El's lurking, watching me," she said when Charlie drew near. "Saturday's fine. We'll talk sometime before. Gotta go. Next class."

She left Charlie standing dumbstruck.

Gwen Blayney, the most beautiful girl in the world, had just said she would go out with him this weekend.

Life was good.

He turned to go to his next class and crashed face-first into an open classroom door.

Charlie didn't get the chance to speak with Gwen for the rest of the day. He did spot El several times, always coming around a corner or out of a classroom door. Didn't he have anything better to do than spy on kids?

During lunch, Jimmy bugged him for more details about Charlie's date with Gwen on Friday night. Despite Charlie's denials, Jimmy insisted it counted as a date because food had been shared. Milk Duds counted as food.

According to Jimmy, it wasn't much of a date because no kissing had occurred, but Charlie could make up for that on Saturday.

"Can I come along?" Jimmy asked.

Charlie looked horrified. "Why on earth would I want you to come along?"

"You might need on the spot advice, encouragement. Someone to distract the Chief when he decides you're assaulting his goddaughter. Or El when he sees you're invading his territory."

"I'm not going to be assaulting anyone, goofball. Besides,

I can take care of 'Uncle Willy.'"

"Just thought I'd try." Jimmy seemed genuinely disappointed.

"Listen, Jimmy, please don't bring Gwen up again. Okay. I'll explain later, but it's important."

"Sure." He seemed a little confused, but when Charlie indicated that El was in the stairwell nearby, Jimmy touched the side of his nose. He got it.

When the last bell of the day rang, Charlie dashed to the town library to check on coin books. He had little time because his father told him to be home right after school. Charlie calculated that if he ran from the library, he would be home at the same time as if he'd walked.

At least his grounding gave him another excuse to miss soccer practice. A further upside was that he'd probably get kicked off the team.

When Charlie entered the library, the old bat librarian was at her post at the main desk. He went out of his way to smile politely at her and walked to the computer catalog. He soon found the book he was looking for, grabbed several other books to conceal his main interest, checked it out, and ran home.

He got home early. Gwen's acceptance must have given him added energy.

The house was empty. His father must still be at work. He'd no doubt be late home again. It's okay for some, Charlie thought. Ant was probably at a Sisterhood meeting. She'd been attending a lot of them since the welcome party. His mother had left a note saying she would be home by five. She was shopping.

Charlie had a good forty-five minutes of solitude.

He quickly changed into some grubby clothes and went to

the garage. Armed with a trowel and a cardboard box with some plastic bags, Charlie returned to the briar patch. He also brought along the wheelbarrow and several bags of mulch to place around the hole. It should provide a little barrier to prevent spying eyes from seeing what he was doing.

He carefully used the trowel to remove dirt from above the box. Once he had all the dirt from the top of the box, he slowly scraped away earth from the sides. The box was about one by two feet and about a foot deep. The wood was so fragile and rotted that small pieces fell off every time the trowel touched it. When he reached the bottom of the box, Charlie found there was no way he could remove it without the thing falling to pieces.

He paused for a moment. He'd watched enough archaeology shows to feel bad about the damage he was doing to this artifact. Though Charlie had no idea how old it was, it still should be preserved. Unfortunately, with so little time and the fear that El might suddenly show up and discover what he was doing, there was no way to save the box in one piece. He checked his watch. It would take him far too long, and he only had about twenty minutes of freedom.

He took hold of one of the iron clasps that held the lid and pulled. It came away easily, with a little bit of wood still attached. He placed it in one of the plastic bags. Pieces of wood, these felt more like sponge than wood, he put in another bag. He began to panic when he filled five bags with coins and still had more to come. In the end, he had scooped coins and dirt into ten more bags.

The bags went into the cardboard box, but it was too flimsy to hold the weight when he tried to lift it. As quickly as he could, Charlie placed the bags in the wheelbarrow, careful not to burst any. He took one of the mulch bags and set it on top of the stash. Seeing that it didn't do much to cover anything, he slashed it open with the trowel and spread the contents out. When he was finished, it looked like he had a barrow full of mulch. He put the two remaining bags on top.

Charlie hesitated momentarily, wanting to dig around the briar patch to see if anything else was buried there, but there wasn't enough time.

Satisfied that he had retrieved everything he could, Charlie refilled it with dirt. He had to scrape some soil from around the hole to smooth the area out because the box had taken up a lot of space. It still looked depressed, as if something had been removed. Charlie ran over to the fence and grabbed a pile of branches and large weeds that he had cleared from the area on the weekend. He tossed the stuff on the cleared patch and kicked it around a little. Anyone looking would think there was just a mess here. He could fix it later when he had more time.

When he hefted the wheelbarrow, it was so heavy he immediately dropped it. The combined coins, dirt, and mulch must have weighed over a hundred pounds. Ready now, he raised the barrow slowly. It was difficult to negotiate the path back to the garage with so much weight on the barrow wheel, but he made it without tipping it over.

He heard a car pull into the driveway. His mother was back from shopping.

Maneuvering the barrow close to the side of the garage, he set a spade, rack, and some more mulch on top. No one should bother to check it out. He was the only one doing any of the heavy garden work anyway. Ant would never lower herself to manual labor or anything involving dirt.

He had just walked into the laundry room from the garage when his mother came in the front door. As fast as he could, he tore off his soiled pants and shirt, then rolled them into a ball. This he set on the washing machine. He threw his sweaty socks on the pile. Standing there in his underwear, he panicked. There was a pink towel on the counter. He quickly wrapped it around his waist and went into the kitchen.

"Hi, Mom."

"Charlie!" She sounded excited. "Come and see what I found. You won't believe it." She dumped out some shopping bags on the kitchen table.

Feeling grotty with sweat and dirt and uncomfortable being half naked in front of his mother, Charlie was torn between making up a fib about a stomach ache so he could get to the bathroom and a shower or keeping in his mother's good books.

He spent the next half hour listening to his mother explain about the various packets of flower and vegetable seeds she had bought on sale.

By the time all the seed packets had been discussed, including possible recipes for the vegetables, Charlie's father arrived home. Ant followed a few minutes later.

"Wow! You've got a fat belly," said Ant when she saw him. He chose not to reply but looked down to ensure his belly wasn't sticking out too far. It wasn't.

"Charlie, you stink. Go get cleaned up for dinner. Don't keep your mother waiting." His father got a beer from the fridge and went to his recliner to read the paper while he waited for dinner.

Ant ran upstairs. Charlie heard the bathroom door close. Bitch.

Waiting in his bedroom for Ant to finish in the bathroom, Charlie shucked his underwear and tossed it in his laundry hamper. He'd do a load of laundry after dinner. He could clean up his mess, and it might also give him the opportunity to get a bag of coins to take to his room.

Ant eventually left the bathroom, but she left a fearsome stink behind. Gagging, Charlie got in the shower just as his mother yelled, "Supper's ready."

After showering and dressing in record time, Charlie made it down for dinner before the rest of the family had eaten too much. His father gave him a filthy look.

"Sorry I'm late, sir. I was working on the garden for Mom." His father shrugged and kept eating.

Charlie wolfed down his spaghetti, much to his mother's surprise; Charlie wasn't usually a big fan of pasta. He waited patiently while his sister, seemingly aware of his desire to get somewhere else in a hurry, took her time finishing her dessert. Ant sat for a few moments when she was done deciding if she wanted more pie. Charlie stewed silently, wondering if there was some kind of psychic link with his sister that allowed her to bug him so much.

With the dishes finally done, Charlie ran to his room to get his laundry.

"Doing a load, Mom," he said. No one answered.

When the washing machine was going, he looked into the living room. His father sat reading while his mother sat with a pencil and pad. She'd been drawing a layout of the garden. He knew she would spend hours deciding what to plant where. There'd be a ton of work for him there later in the week. Ant was probably in her room doing something he couldn't care less about.

As quietly as possible, Charlie went to the wheelbarrow and dug a bag of coins from under the mulch. He'd managed to snag one of the first ones he'd filled, so it didn't have much dirt mixed in with the coins.

He was ignored when he made his way up to his room. Once there, Charlie didn't expect to be interrupted because his family was used to him sequestering himself in his room while he studied. But he'd have to keep an ear alert for the washing machine.

He opened the bag of coins and took a moment to decide whether or not to sneak them into the bathroom for a cleaning. There were some clods of dirt amongst the coins, after all, and Charlie didn't relish the idea of getting dirt all over his desk.

Things were decided for him when he heard Ant go into the bathroom, lock the door, and turn on the radio. She was about to take one of her hour-long baths.

Using a printer paper box top as a tray, he sat at his desk and began to go through the coins one by one. He carefully separated the coins from the clods of dirt and used a pair of handkerchiefs to rub off any caked-on dirt.

He sorted the coins according to their inscriptions as he went.

It took several hours, and a rough count told Charlie there were over three hundred coins in the thirty piles in front of him. This was only one bag of fifteen. What had he found in his backyard? Blackbeard's treasure?

He needed something to store them in that would keep them separate.

Charlie went downstairs. Ant was long gone—his parents didn't seem to care about her being out late even though she was only seventeen; it was so unfair. His father still sat in the recliner, now reading a science journal. His mother was in her studio working on a book cover. She hadn't done that for a while. Charlie was glad she was regaining some of her artistic drive.

In the kitchen, he found the box of freezer bags his mother

had purchased that afternoon and stuffed it under his sweatshirt.

With a can of soda in hand, Charlie returned to his room.

Again, neither parent paid him any attention. That made him mildly angry. There was no point in being secretive if no one knew about it.

In his room, Charlie put each pile of coins in its own bag. He then placed the bags in a cardboard box, which he hid in his closet.

Charlie had kept one coin from each pile to use with the coin book from the library.

Most of the Roman coins were from the reign of Augustus Caesar. All had the emperor's head on one side with the reverse side showing a bull, the god Apollo with a lyre, two men facing each other, or an oak wreath. There were some coins from the time of Julius Caesar and a couple from Tiberius's reign. The Greek coin with an owl was from Athens. Charlie also had an Antioch stater, a Pontius Pilate hepton, and a bronze Herod the Great. One Greek coin bore the head of Alexander the Great. Ptolemy I of Egypt was on two coins. There were several coins that Charlie could not find listed in the book. He assumed these were either examples of coins that had not yet been discovered elsewhere or fakes the collector had picked up.

Charlie sat back, his mind a jumble of thoughts. He couldn't even begin to estimate the value of the hoard he had found. Just the thirty coins he had kept out to use as reference were worth a hundred thousand dollars.

Fifteen bags with roughly three hundred coins in each. *Did he really have over four thousand coins?*

How much would they be worth?

He was rich! Rich beyond his wildest dreams!

But what were all these ancient coins doing in his backyard? They represented almost every ancient civilization that had existed up to the Romans.

Charlie stared out his bedroom window at where he had been digging.

Had some ancient pirate buried his treasure in this valley? A Roman Blackbeard?

What other mysteries lay buried beneath Coverdale?

Interlude Two
975 CE

They had to be close behind him. On silent feet, they had ambushed the foraging party. While men screamed and roared, the killers made no sounds as they slaughtered everyone except for Eric, the youngest among them, who had held back to relieve himself behind a tree.

When Eric had first heard the commotion of battle, he had panicked and tried to rise too quickly. His baggy wool trousers and underpants caught at his knees, and he fell on his backside into the mess he had just made. Standing quickly, he pulled up his soiled underpants and tied the string around the waist. By the time he had his trousers up and secured, the sounds of battle had ceased.

He had moved swiftly and as silently as possible towards the last place he had seen the party. They could only be a short distance away. When he had broken through the trees into a small clearing, he'd found his fellows sprawled about, bleeding and dead. One who had still lived, Wulf, attempted to stand. He was cut down with a single stroke by a ghost in white wielding a gigantic sword.

Eric had been unable to stop his cry. The ghost had turned to face him. He'd signaled to the other ghosts around the clearing, and they had all moved silently toward Eric.

That was all Eric had needed to see. To his everlasting

shame, he had turned tail and run. At some point while he ran, he'd felt a sharp sting on his right arm. The sword he had been carrying fell to the ground and blood spurted. There had been no one near who could have wounded him.

It must have been the ghosts.

Now, he was almost finished. His legs ached, his arm throbbed, and he was lost in the silent forest.

His pursuers *had* to make some kind of noise as they chased him through the woods. No one could remain quiet on all these dead leaves and underbrush. The cold air bit at Eric's throat while he tried to keep up his pace, lungs ready to burst. His eyes watered from the cold wind and the pain of the wound in his right arm. Blood flecked the tree trunks and bushes when he raced past. Crashing through a large bush, Eric's feet met air and he plunged down a small hill. Twigs and dead leaves that blanketed the ground scraped his face raw. Hesitating only momentarily, Eric tried to hear the white ghosts tracking him. The only sound was his own pounding heart.

Total silence. Not even the animals made a noise in this haunted place. Could he have died and gone to the realm of Hel, goddess of the lower world? But that would mean he had not died a brave death in battle. How could he? He was a coward who had run at the first sign of danger.

A twig snapped.

Jumping to his feet, Eric ran in the direction he thought the river lay. He had to get back to the longship and warn the others. There was no hope for the rest of his party; the phantoms had wiped them all out, even Hrolf the Berserker. Eric used his wounded arm to pull his sword from its scabbard. It was gone, he remembered, lost in his haste to escape, never once having tasted the blood of his enemies. His shame at his cowardice burned within him.

Distracted for an instant by a wave of pain from his wound, Eric didn't see the low-hanging branch that snared his long, blond hair. Yanked back by the clutching limb, Eric smashed against a tree trunk. Winded, he forced himself to breathe again, knowing that he would die a dishonorable death if he didn't move. What hair hadn't been torn out by the branch was securely entangled, and no amount of pulling would release him. Eric tore his dagger from his belt with his left hand and hacked at the tangled mass. A few times the blade bit into his skull. The angle was awkward, made worse by his growing panic. Finally, he was free.

Still no sound from behind.

The sun was going down, and it was becoming dark under the canopy of the trees. Clouds had rolled in from the west, but even if the sky had been clear, it would not have helped Eric find his way. He knew nothing of navigating by the stars. If only he had paid more attention to where the party was going instead of listening to the stories being told by Uncle Einar.

Blood ran into his eyes from his self-inflicted head wounds and momentarily blinded him. His right arm snagged on a tree trunk, and the sword cut was ripped open even more. The red natives were not supposed to have swords, just bows and clubs. The lightning wave of pain that reached his brain nearly made him pass out. He couldn't help but let out a loud scream.

They'd be able to easily locate him now.

Holding his throbbing right arm with his left hand, Eric tried to see anything that looked familiar. Uncle Einar had been too interesting for Eric's own good. Too often, Eric's father had chided him for listening to the old man's tales of war and the gods. Lucky Einar, now he would be meeting his gods in Valhalla.

Then he saw it. Through the trees there was a glow. The campfire.

Heartened by the sight, he gathered his strength and ran towards the light. Hope filled his heart, and even the pain of his arm seemed less now.

It must be a big fire, he thought, the nearer he got to the camp, to glow so brightly above the trees. He broke through the trees, saw the river, and slid down an embankment to the narrow beach. Eric saw that he was around a bend in the river from where they had dropped anchor that morning. Running along the beach, stumbling as the sand gripped his feet and tried to make him fall, he tried to calm himself and prepare what he had to say to his father, Harald. Before he rounded the bend, a rock tripped him, and he sprawled in the sand.

He coughed sand out from his mouth and tried to claw it from his eyes. Eric was aware of sand grinding into his wounded arm, but he bit down hard so he wouldn't cry out. A Viking did not show pain to his fellows when his wounds were so slight.

He raised himself to his feet. Men shouted in a language he did not recognize. Eric hunkered down behind a fallen tree at the bend of the river and looked towards the camp.

The longship was on fire!

The great sail with its wolf's head had already been consumed by flames, and the mast toppled and crashed into the river while Eric looked on, shocked to the core.

There was no sign of his father or any other men who had remained at the camp. A few swords stuck out of the sand and over by the remains of the campfire; yes, it was his father's helmet. The sand was churned up as if a battle had taken place.

Dark patches on the sand had to be blood.

Odd shadows caught Eric's attention. A short distance down the beach from the deserted camp, Eric thought he saw movement.

The ghosts.

He was sure he saw a pair of them walk into the cliff in front of the burning longship. They seemed to be carrying something.

Eric paused to consider what he should do. Everyone from the longship except himself had to be dead. His father would never have deserted the ship without a fight. Any hopes of founding a new colony in this land had been dashed by the appearance of the ghost warriors.

Revenge was all that mattered. Revenge and dying well in battle.

Eric tore a strip of cloth from his tunic and wound it around the gash in his arm. Blood still flowed freely from the wound, and his head was a little cloudy from blood loss. Pulling together all his inner strength, Eric rose from his hiding place and strode boldly across the beach towards the burning longship. He paused to pick up his father's helmet and set it on his head. It was a bit large; Eric's father was a huge man, and Eric had only seen fourteen summers. Eric winced as the cold iron scraped across the knife cuts. Eric picked up one of the abandoned swords. He saw no point in picking up a shield. With his wounded right arm, he'd have to carry the sword with his left hand.

Walking shakily towards where he had seen the shadows, Eric noticed a small pouch in the sand. He stooped to retrieve it, stood, and opened it. Inside were several acorns his father hoped to plant in the new colony. Harald had taken the acorns during a raid on Britain many years before. Now, he would never see the trees growing, return to his wife in Vineland, or see the fjords of home again. Angrily, Eric tossed the pouch at the cliff and strode across the beach. He felt the heat of the burning ship, a welcome warmth in the autumn chill.

When he reached the cliff, Eric saw a cave a few feet above the sand. A huge willow had obscured the entrance from the river. There were strange footprints in the sand leading to the cave. Eric followed.

The cave was dark and dank, the silence oppressive. Eric clutched his sword tightly in his left hand and advanced into the darkness. The constant throbbing from his wound kept him alert. With his right hand outstretched to touch one of the cave's walls, Eric moved cautiously, ready for any attack. About twenty paces in, there was no wall to his left. Eric decided to check this branch of the cave.

The branch was pitch black and smelled like the slaughterhouse back at the Vinland colony. He ran his hand along the wall and realized he was in a cavern.

Eric tripped and fell against a pile of something soft yet firm. He rolled to the ground and yelped in pain when something sharp pierced his left leg near his groin.

There was a scrape and a flare, and light filled the cavern. Blinded by the sudden light, Eric tensed and held his sword out, ready to strike.

Silence.

When his eyes became used to the light, Eric found that a broken sword had impaled his leg. The pile he had fallen against was his comrades, bloody, cut to ribbons, and thrown in the cavern as if they were offal. There was Hrolf the Berserker, but how ...?

Eric turned away in disgust and looked into the face of his father. Harald's severed head lay a few feet from Eric's outstretched sword hand.

Screaming in rage and agony, Eric leaped to his feet. The sword that had pierced his leg slid out, severing the femoral artery as it went. Blood poured down Eric's leg, but that didn't stop him. Calling out to Odin and Thor, he charged towards the source of the light. Blinded by berserker rage and pain, he didn't realize that he had passed out of the cavern and into the main vault of the cave. He met no resistance. Still running, he didn't notice that the light was following him. Finally, he stopped running as the blood pumping from his leg slowed to a trickle. Light-headed, he dropped his sword and fell to his knees. Harald's helmet slipped from Eric's head, and released from the helmet's weight, Eric looked up, ready to die.

What he saw made him happy.

"Freija," said Eric Haraldson, then he died.

Chapter Eleven

Before going to bed Tuesday night, Charlie slipped into the kitchen, took a brick of cheddar cheese out of the fridge, and sliced off half. He was sometimes lactose intolerant. Whether or not eating dairy would set him off was a crap shoot, but he hoped it would work. Cheese was one of the things that usually gave him a bad attack. In his room, Charlie ate the cheese. Usually, he didn't pay attention to what he ate, so he didn't know how much cheese would set him off. Most times, he had about four or five hours before the cramps started.

At five o'clock, pain ripped across Charlie's abdomen. He barely made it to the bathroom before his bowels exploded. Before sitting, he'd managed to pull the bathroom trash can next to the throne. Good thing. While waiting for the second wave, he felt that familiar sensation in his throat as if he was wearing a shirt with a collar that was too tight. He emptied his stomach into the trash can.

Midway through his second vomit, his bowels again released. This was the part Charlie hated most about these attacks: fire at both ends.

Taking in huge gulps of air, he waited for the sensation in his throat to go away. As soon as it did, he knew he wouldn't be vomiting anymore. It was also a signal that, after an hour of agony, his bowels were going to stop assaulting him.

He quickly cleaned himself up and returned to bed. A shower would have been better—he felt disgusting and not totally cleansed—but he needed to look sick when the rest of the family got up.

An hour later, he heard his parents downstairs having breakfast. The thought of food put a lump in Charlie's throat, but he swallowed it. Walking slowly, he went down to the kitchen.

"Mom, I'm going back to bed in a minute. I've been up half the night in the bathroom. Something I ate must have disagreed with me."

His mother looked sympathetic. "Did you want something to soothe your stomach? Some juice? A big glass of milk?"

She was sweet and meant well, but Nell Bowen was a little clueless. George Bowen, on the other hand, had no sympathy.

"You need to be more careful, Charlie. Lately, you've been acting like a child and not watching out for yourself. One of these days, you'll get into serious trouble that I won't be able to sort out. I'm not risking my job at The Institute just so you can be thoughtless and selfish."

Charlie was stunned by what his father said. It was becoming more apparent to him that his place in his father's life was to be nothing more than a showcase son who would make his father look good. He thought it best not to answer. Instead, as his father brought a spoonful of cereal to his mouth, Charlie made gurgling sounds and pretended he was about to hurl. He ran out of the kitchen, hearing the sound of a spoon clattering onto the table and his father cursing.

Ant was in the bathroom, so Charlie went to his room and crawled into bed.

Nell Bowen had been pressed into service, helping the Sisterhood serve meals to the tramps. She was required to put in one day a week at the town hall, where the meals were prepared and distributed. Today was her day. Before leaving, she checked in with Charlie, but he acted as if he was sound asleep, so she left.

Ant had already left for school, and his father would have been gone for an hour.

The plan had worked perfectly.

Charlie had the house to himself for at least five, maybe six hours.

He quickly got out of bed and took a shower. He contemplated the day ahead while dressing in old sweats and a t-shirt.

Charlie microwaved a couple of scrambled eggs, made a Western sandwich, and ate it as fast as possible.

He was ready.

The space between the garage and the side of the house was not visible from the street. No one would see Charlie at work unless someone was spying on the house from the woods at the back of the yard. He could get the coins into the house and hide them.

There was some hesitation about where to clean them. The laundry room had a huge plastic tub perfect for washing something extremely dirty. However, if someone came home, he wouldn't be able to hide the coins. The bathtub upstairs would give him a better chance of hiding them before he was discovered, but there was a risk of scratching the enamel with the metal coins and dirt.

Feeling extremely nervous and worried it might set off his stomach, Charlie brought the first bag into the laundry room. He carried it in a bucket to ensure there wouldn't be any dirt dropped on the floor.

It took him fifteen minutes to clean the coins from the first bag. Damn! It would take him more than three hours to finish at this rate. Checking the clock, he saw that it was only nine. There was plenty of time if he worked steadily.

At noon, he was in the middle of cleaning the final bag. A few of the bags he'd filled in a rush at the end had fewer coins and loads more dirt. Even so, in his bedroom closet, thousands of coins waited in a couple of plastic storage boxes to be dried and sorted.

The front doorbell rang. Charlie froze and cursed. Who would be calling at this hour? His family would simply walk in. He hadn't heard of any salesmen going door to door in Coverdale. It was probably against some town by-law anyway.

Drying his hands, he thought about ignoring his visitor. But what if it was someone who expected him to be there? Someone sent by his concerned mother?

Peeking through the peephole, Charlie felt his stomach drop.

El stood there with that shit-eating grin of his. He waved to Charlie.

Thinking the worst, Charlie opened the door. With his weakest voice and shivering a bit, he said, "Yes?"

Fortunately, he was sweating from hauling the coins, which added to the impression that he was still sick.

"Charlie! May I come in?" El looked concerned, but Charlie knew the concern was not genuine.

"I'm feeling pretty sick, Mr. LaRennes. Bad stomach. I've spent most of the morning on the toilet."

"That's a shame, Charlie. Still, surely I can come in to see that you're all right."

"Maybe not," said Charlie. "It might be a bug."

"Not to worry, Charlie. I'm strong as an ox. I rarely ever catch anything." El stepped forward, pushed past Charlie, and walked into the living room.

Appalled at the nerve of the guy, Charlie closed the door. He shuffled after El. Sitting on the couch, he waited for El to sit. He needed to keep him in here and out of the kitchen. The door to the laundry room was open. El might see what Charlie was doing.

El walked straight to the door between the kitchen and living room. He quickly looked into the kitchen, then walked around the living room, examining everything on the shelves. Nervous sweat ran down Charlie's neck. What did El want?

"No offer of a drink, Charlie? That's hardly being a good host." El smiled at him.

"Like I said, I'm sick. I don't want to spread my germs. I want to go back to bed."

"If you're sick, you should be in bed. How sick are you, Charlie?" El sat in George Bowen's recliner, leaned back, and raised the footrest. He was making himself at home. Charlie wanted to strangle the man for his gall.

"I am sick, Mr. LaRennes. Why would I fake it?"

"Why, indeed? Perhaps to avoid school? Perhaps to avoid a certain young lady that you've been harassing?"

Charlie felt his anger rising. The things this scumbag was suggesting were ridiculous. Then again, he was avoiding school to take care of the coins. Still, to bring Gwen into it was too much.

"Mr. LaRennes, you and Miss Blayney have made it clear that I have no business with Gwen. I don't think I've been harassing her, as you say. We are in several of the same classes. Yesterday, I kept my distance."

"You did, Charlie. I appreciate that." How did he know that? "I simply want to be sure you're heading in the right direction in that regard."

Charlie pushed down the urge to tell El to get stuffed. Instead, he said, "I know what I have to do, Mr. LaRennes. I know I need to keep my nose clean, or my father might get in trouble at work."

"Yes, Charlie, it was your father who informed me that you were ill. I felt it the friendly thing to check up on you."

"Thank you, Mr. LaRennes. I appreciate your concern, but I can take care of myself."

"Of course you can, Charlie." He got out of the recliner and stood in the center of the room, looking down at Charlie. "Was there anything else you wanted to tell me?"

Charlie shook his head. "No, sir. I just want to go back to bed before I have to throw up again."

"All right, Charlie. I'm still skeptical, but I'll let that pass." He walked to the front door. "No, don't get up. I can let myself out." He opened the front door. Before stepping out, El said, "I only have your interests at heart, Charlie. I want to see you succeed. If you need anything or feel like you want to tell me something, my door is always open. Goodbye, Charlie."

El let the front door slam closed behind him. Charlie didn't move. He waited for his nerves to calm down. When he held up a hand, it shook. El had scared the life out of him. How did the guy find things out? Did he know about the coin stash? No way, Charlie had been especially careful.

Charlie got up and crept to the front door. Looking through the peephole, he was shocked to see El standing on the sidewalk next to a limousine. He looked right and left, then took out a small notebook. Whatever he wrote in it, Charlie was sure it was about him and something bad. El put the notebook back in his pocket, climbed into the car, and it sped away.

Not giving himself another moment to delay, Charlie raced back to the laundry room to finish cleaning the last coins. He deposited them in one of the boxes in his closet, then scrubbed down the laundry tub to remove all evidence of dirt and mud. For good measure, he threw his sheets in the wash.

Returning to his bedroom, Charlie sat at his desk to think. It had been exactly a month since the family moved to Coverdale. In that short time, Charlie had found a new best friend (Jimmy), the love of his life (Gwen), a deadly enemy (El Baldo), and someone who would happily kill him (the Chief). His own father had turned on him while his mother slipped further into oblivion. His sister? Forget about that waste of space.

What the hell was going on in Coverdale? The secrecy, the isolation, the strict rules, the weird history, the almost robotic expectation that everyone would know their proper place in society. The Institute. Throw in the standing stones and the stash of coins, and you have all the makings of a Gothic mystery.

Charlie needed to do something and talk to someone. Gwen was the one he wanted to see the most, but at the moment, that was out of the question. Jimmy. He could trust Jimmy, couldn't he? But when and how? Thanks to El, Charlie was completely paranoid about being watched. He also thought the phones might be tapped. It was getting extreme and ridiculous. What to do? Charlie decided to go for a run. It always helped him think and clear his head. Except, he couldn't go now. He was supposed to be sick.

He checked the time and knew his mother would be home soon, followed by Ant. His father would be home sometime, but Charlie didn't care anymore.

His sheets were clean, so he made his bed then took

another shower to clean off the sweat and nervousness of the morning.

In the kitchen, he made a green salad, prepared some garlic bread for the oven, and took out a frozen pizza. Dinner would be ready soon after his mother and Ant got home.

Two hours later, with Ant not thanking him for making dinner and his mother sitting in her studio staring at a blank canvas, Charlie was about to set out on a run.

His father arrived home.

"Where do you think you're going, Charlie?" George Bowen blocked the front door so Charlie couldn't leave.

"Out for a run, sir."

"No, you're not. You're grounded. Remember?"

Charlie wanted to scream. He knew from the look on his father's face that it was pointless to argue. Besides, he wanted as little interaction with him as possible.

Without another word, Charlie returned to the house and went to his room. He decided to spend his sentence sorting the coins and checking their values.

The first ten coins he checked were worth over twenty thousand dollars.

An hour later, the front doorbell rang. Charlie went to his bedroom door to listen. Was it El again?

"Charlie can't see you right now, Jimmy," said his father. "He's grounded. You'll have to see him at school."

What was Jimmy doing here? And did his father have to rub it in about being grounded? He was eighteen, not a kid.

"All right, I'll see that he gets it." The door shut. "Charlie!"

Charlie went downstairs, where his father waited.

"Your friend, Jimmy, brought this." He handed Charlie a small canvas bag. Inside were two fat books. "He said there was an assignment due tomorrow and wanted to make sure you didn't miss it. Why can't you be a responsible person like your friend, Charlie?"

"Thank you, sir," said Charlie.

Back in his room, he took the books out of the bag. There was a note that read:

Chapter four. Important. Write a report for tomorrow.

He opened one of the books and found an envelope tucked in chapter four. Opening it, he found another note.

Dear Charlie,

I pressed the gnome into helping me and threatened to remove body parts if he didn't get it right. He's okay, by the way.

I told El Baldo that you annoyed me with a load of stupid questions at the diner on Friday, and that was why I was late. I told him you were a pest and that I didn't want you around me. I also said you spent most of the time with your fly open. He seemed to believe me.

Just so you know, everything I told him is a lie.

See you at school. I can't wait for Saturday night. Come to the ticket booth at five, and we can talk. Bring food.

Love, Gwen.

Charlie read the note a dozen times. He read the last line two dozen times.

If Jimmy was playing a joke on him, he'd kill him. If it wasn't a joke ... he couldn't go there. He might jinx it. She was probably just being polite.

The rest of the week was going to be a nightmare of waiting.

Chapter Twelve

The rest of the week dragged on painfully. All Charlie thought about was his coming date with Gwen. At school, Charlie was careful to avoid her and the temptation to say something to her. The last thing they needed was for word to get back to El. Charlie knew he would be in for another uplifting visit if he set one foot wrong before Saturday.

Charlie was still officially grounded until Thursday night and was eager to get out for a run. Since he slept so little, he could have gone early in the morning, before his parents got up, and no one would have been the wiser. However, he knew something would go wrong: El or the Chief would spot him, his father would get up early and notice him missing, and Ant would squeal. Why take any chances?

Jimmy kept giving Charlie knowing looks and saying, "Waaw, eh!" every time he saw Gwen pass in the halls. It got to be a bit annoying because Charlie didn't want to draw any attention to himself. Jimmy explained that someone had to make fun of him for being dumb enough to fall for the untouchable Gwen Blayney. Jimmy knew something was up between them. He'd carried the note to Charlie from Gwen, after all. Charlie felt it would be better to keep his friend in the dark about the details in case EL got pushy. There weren't many details anyway.

Charlie did admit to Jimmy that Gwen was extremely good looking. No, she was beautiful. That hair, those eyes he could drown in, those legs that went on for days. He had to remain seated a few times in class when his mind drifted, and he thought of her in a bathing suit.

Only once did he walk into a locker door because he was watching her.

After supper Friday night, Charlie jogged through town, then took the river trail to the circle of standing stones. Jimmy waited there with a knapsack full of soda and munchies. Charlie sat next to him on one of the fallen stones.

"Took you long enough," said Jimmy. He passed Charlie a can. "I've been waiting for hours."

Charlie looked pointedly at the mountain bike leaning against a stone pillar and grunted.

"You should try running or at least walking more. That belly of yours is starting to block the sun."

Jimmy looked appalled. "This is not a belly, it's love handles ..."

"But you've got no one to love except your left hand."

"Hey, buddy, I'll have you know I have lots of friends. I'm ambidextrous. Anyway, soccer practice gives me plenty of exercise."

"Is the coach still mad at me?"

"He's beyond mad. Now he just thinks you're a bum."

"Speaking of which, for a small town, Coverdale sure has more than its share of tramps. What's the deal? It's not like there's a railroad running through here or the weather's really nice."

Jimmy stuffed a handful of potato chips in his mouth and said, "Glumph fra da know about that. People around here treat them well, though; give them food and clothes."

"It's almost like the Middle Ages when people revered crazy folks. They thought they were closer to God or something."

"Who knows? Are you going to eat that other lemon tart?"

Charlie crammed the tart in his mouth before Jimmy could take it. Tears rolled down his cheeks when he bit down on the foil cup which held the tart.

"Tell me you're not really that much of a klutz." He seemed concerned. "Please. People *are* starting to talk."

Charlie carefully removed the foil cup. His friend looked so serious, yet Charlie knew behind those eyes lived a joyful heart.

It was time to take Jimmy into his confidence with more than simply passing notes. Charlie reached into his pocket and pulled out one of the Roman coins he had found.

"What do you make of this?" He handed the coin to Jimmy.

Jimmy's eyes widened. "An Augustus bull! When the heck did you get this? It's worth a fortune."

"I found it, along with some others. How do you know what it is?"

"My dad collects coins big time. He has a chest of drawers full of old coins and some bills. Sometimes he lets me touch the protective plastic sleeves the coins are in."

Charlie wrestled with whether or not to tell Jimmy about how many coins he had found. No. Best to wait until he had sorted out the situation. The last thing he wanted was to get Jimmy in trouble.

"Don't tell a soul, okay. I want to check out a few more things first."

"My lips are sealed."

"I know. You don't have a girlfriend."

Jimmy scowled at Charlie.

"Not bad. Almost as good as Uncle Willy."

Jimmy jumped up and began goose-stepping around the stones. "Ve haf vays of makingk you talk, Englander svine."

Charlie cowered back. "I know nothing. Nothing."

Jimmy kept marching, then stopped and rubbed his shins. "Man—oh—man, how did those guys do that for so long?"

"Iron discipline and blind obedience," said Charlie. "Speaking of which, I'd better head home. The last thing I need is for my father to ground me again."

"Waaw, eh, waaw."

"You're a pig," said Charlie. He gathered up the empty soda cans and munchie wrappers and stuffed them into Jimmy's knapsack, leaving a half-eaten Boston cream doughnut exposed at the bottom where Jimmy's fingers would jab into it later.

They sat quietly for a short while. Charlie stared at the stars through the trees. Jimmy seemed to be arguing with himself, but Charlie decided not to interrupt. Jimmy said he came to the stone circle to think out his problems and relax. Charlie knew Jimmy would tell him what the problem was when he was good and ready.

Finally, Jimmy broke the silence. "Charlie, there's something I need to tell you."

Charlie sat up straight and looked at his friend. Jimmy seemed nervous and kept shifting his gaze around the circle.

"I don't want to go out with your sister anymore. I never really did."

Relief flooded through Charlie. "Hey, bud, no problem. Ant's a ball buster, anyway. There are plenty of good women out there without her attitude. There may even be one with bad enough taste that she'd go out with you."

Jimmy grinned and said, "Yeah, right." It sounded to Charlie as if Jimmy had something caught in his throat. "I, um

...” Sweat broke out on Jimmy’s forehead and he looked away from Charlie.

“What?”

“Never mind.” Jimmy hesitated, then added, “Maybe we should get going.”

“Sure, whatever you say.”

Charlie ran down the trail to the river while Jimmy followed on his mountain bike. He had no trouble staying ahead of the bike on the trail, but once they reached the road, Jimmy sped past.

He disappeared into the dusk with a hearty, “Waaw, eh, waaw.”

Back home, Charlie walked up the stairs in time to see his mother exit his bedroom. He immediately panicked, thinking she might have found the coins. She had never been one to pry and had always respected Charlie’s privacy. But maybe with her change in demeanor and his father’s change in attitude, things were different now.

“What’s up, Mom?” Her hands were empty.

“Oh, Charlie, I didn’t hear you come in. I just put your clean laundry on your bed. I would have put it away, but you do have your system.”

“Thanks, mom.” He gave her a hug, but she did not return it. It felt like he was hugging a mannequin.

Charlie went into his room and locked the door. His father often said that locked doors were unnecessary in their house because everyone respected everyone else. Things had changed, though. For all Charlie knew, his father might be searching his room for ... what? Contraband that went against Coverdale rules? Hidden plans to overthrow the oppressive regime that ruled the town? An incredibly valuable stash of ancient coins that would most likely set Charlie up for life?

Then there was Ant. She spent almost all of her time with her Sisterhood of the Temple cronies. They went around school as if they owned the place. It was almost like they were cheerleaders except out of shape, inflexible, and not interested in anything but themselves. They did have that cheerleader contempt for anyone not on the football team down pat.

Would Ant spy on him?

Damned El Baldo. He was making Charlie extremely paranoid.

Nothing looked like it had been moved in his room. His desk was the way he left it a few hours ago. The pencils were still crossed next to the notepad. A sweater hung in front of the desk drawers exactly as he had placed it.

In the closet, the two plastic storage boxes of coins remained hidden under a pile of magazine boxes holding his old toys. Charlie never threw anything away.

Rooting around in the closet, Charlie slipped and banged against the wall. It moved. This was an older house, built sometime in the late 1800s, like most of the town, but it seemed pretty solid. Tapping the wall lightly, it sounded hollow.

Charlie moved the toy boxes out and set them by the bed. He shoved the coin boxes to the far side of the closet and tossed a couple of jackets on them. On his knees, Charlie felt around the edge of the closet wall. There definitely was a gap between the wall and the corner molding. He had seen the molding before and thought nothing of it. Looking at it now, he wondered why anyone would put molding inside a closet.

He gently pushed against the loose wall. There was a click, and the wall slowly swung away, revealing a dark space. Charlie recoiled in case it was full of spiders, but nothing came rushing at him. He got a flashlight and shined it in the hole.

Next to his closet was a small alcove about six feet deep and two feet across. The ceiling was about the same height as the shelf above the hidden door inside the closet.

Something reflected the light from the far end of the alcove. Carefully crawling through the door, Charlie got closer. Leaning against the back corner was a sword about thirty inches long. It looked like something out of the Middle Ages. Next to it was a wooden-handled mace topped with a spiked ball. Both weapons were covered with thick dust. Attached to the wall above them was a small mirror. This was what had reflected the light.

Charlie crawled into the alcove to get a better look at the weapons. He couldn't stand up but could get to his knees. The mace was heavy and revealed rust stains all over the ball when he blew off the dust. He guessed this might be dried blood. The sword was also heavy. Checking the blade, Charlie found it to be dull and chipped.

Turning to return to his closet, he spotted something behind the open door. This was a Brown Bess, a musket used by the British army in the eighteenth and early nineteenth centuries. It, too, was covered with dust.

Before exiting the alcove, Charlie checked to see if any other walls opened into a closet, possibly Ant's next door. To his relief, none did.

Back in his closet, he examined the hidden door and found a small hook that could be used to pull it closed. He carefully and quietly heaved the coin boxes into the alcove then pulled the door shut. The toy boxes piled in front of the hidden door kept it out of sight and unlikely to be opened accidentally.

Curious now about what he had found, Charlie went into the hallway. The space on the wall between his and Ant's rooms had a cold air return vent near the floor. He hadn't seen that on the other side of the wall, so the alcove didn't extend all the way to the hall. A table stood against the wall with a vase of artificial flowers. On the wall itself hung a couple of his mother's paintings.

He stepped over to Ant's bedroom door and knocked quietly. She didn't answer, so he took the chance she wasn't in and opened the door. When no screams met his entrance, he went in. Quickly surveying the room, he noted that Ant's closet was not on the same wall as the alcove but opposite against the bathroom wall. Her bed stood against the alcove wall.

Unless someone noticed and took the time to measure, the extra space between the rooms would not be obvious. Even more curious, Charlie went downstairs through the kitchen and onto the back deck. His room was directly above the kitchen, while Ant's was over his father's mostly unused office. From down here, nothing looked out of the ordinary.

Now Charlie had another mystery to solve. What was the story of the alcove? Who had owned this house before the Bowens, and did they know about it? Perhaps the library might have information on who built the house. He thought that was a stretch since the place didn't have anything he was looking for when it came to the town.

There was one more mystery. What the heck were those weapons doing in there, and whose were they?

Chapter Thirteen

Saturday morning, Charlie worked like a fiend to get the garden ready for his mother. Even though it was already August, she wanted to plant some late vegetables and flowers to get a head start. The whole time he dug dirt, hauled manure, and spread mulch, Charlie's mind was on Gwen and their first official date later today. It was still a huge secret, and he wondered what they would do afterward. Would Gwen want to maintain the secrecy to avoid any hassles from El? Maybe her grandfather, the mayor, wouldn't approve either. Their togetherness would be doubly damned.

At one, his mother let him get away. He spent extra time in the shower scrubbing off the dirt and ensuring every inch of his body was sparkling clean. Half an hour was spent on getting all the crap out from under his fingernails. Ant complained about him taking so long in the bathroom, but Ant would have complained no matter how much time he took. It didn't bother Charlie in the slightest. He had a date with Gwen.

She had said to meet her at the theatre ticket booth at five and to bring food. Charlie checked his secret money stash – what was left of the cash he had earned at his part-time job back in the city. He still had several hundred dollars, more than enough to finance some dates with the most beautiful girl in Coverdale. With the town being so cut off from the outside world and trips to the city limited, Charlie hadn't had many opportunities to spend his money. He was relieved that he didn't have to ask his father for an allowance or an advance. That was never going to happen again.

Dressed in his best black jeans, Deep Purple t-shirt, and Aerosmith touring jacket, Charlie arrived at the diner at a quarter to five. The place was hopping, and he hoped there wouldn't be too much of a wait for his takeout order. Fortunately, the cooks were used to being busy and were super-efficient, so Charlie left the diner with three whole minutes to travel the hundred or so yards to the theatre. He was relieved that none of the patrons noticed or wanted to talk to him. He did not want to explain what he was doing.

His breath was fresh. He had eaten half a roll of mints and promised himself he wouldn't have onions on his burger. However, he remembered that Gwen liked onions on her burger, so he took the chance with them. They'd both have onion breath.

With a nervous stomach, Charlie approached the ticket booth. To his horror, it was empty.

"Psst! Over here." He looked around the booth to see Gwen leaning out of a front door. "Come on, Charlie."

He hurried to the door and entered the theatre.

Charlie gasped when he saw Gwen. Her bangs had been gathered and tied back with a red ribbon. This held the rest of her flowing blonde hair behind her ears so the wisps from her temples framed her face. No barrettes or hair pins. Gwen wore a red T-shirt and white jeans.

She took his hand and said, "This way. Mr. Tyndale said we could eat in the storeroom next to the projection room. It also has a large window so we can watch the movie in private." Gwen led him up the stairs, past the balcony entrance, to the third floor. They had to take a few steps down to the storeroom. Charlie guessed they were now directly behind the last row on the balcony.

"I set things up, Charlie. I hope you like it."

Gwen opened the door and let him through. The center of the small room had been cleared, and a small table was set up. It was laid out with plates and cutlery for two. In the middle of the table was a small vase with some lavender roses.

"The roses are from Mr. Tyndale. They're supposed to be symbolic of mystery and enchantment and something else." She blushed. So did Charlie because he knew what something else was, and it had happened to him the first time he saw Gwen.

"He's cool with us being together? He's not going to report me to El or the Chief?"

Gwen smiled. "Mr. Tyndale is not a fan of theirs. He refers to El as 'that back-stabbing, slimy, little scumbag.' He tolerates Uncle Willy because of me."

"I don't know what to say, Gwen." He liked saying her name.

"How about, 'Here's the food.' I'm starving." She sat at the table and patted the chair next to her for him to sit. Charlie liked that he wasn't across from her but next to her.

He set the bag down on the table, then took out the food.

"Two burgers each, onions, tomato, ketchup, pickle on the side. Two extra-large orders of fries smothered in malt vinegar. Be careful. If you eat too many fries with malt vinegar, your sweat gets very yellow. Trust me." He unwrapped the burgers and put them on their plates, followed by the fries. "Please excuse my fingers." Last, he took out "Two vanilla milkshakes. You have exquisite taste, and I have lactose pills."

Charlie sat and stared at Gwen. They were silent for what

felt like several minutes, but was only a few seconds. Gwen seemed to be examining his eyes carefully. Charlie's heart thumped.

"Eat," said Gwen.

They tucked in.

"When I passed the river, the mist looked like smoke on the water." She pointed to Charlie's sweatshirt. "Have you been to a lot of concerts?"

"My father used to take me all the time since I was ten, though in the last year, he's been too busy with work. I was going with friends from school a lot. He used to go almost every week when he was a teenager, hence the shirts."

"He sounds like a nice guy, your father."

Charlie thought for a moment, then grunted. He couldn't bring himself to agree with Gwen, and that made him feel sad. "Back then, no matter how bad things got, there was always enough money for concert souvenirs."

Gwen hesitated for a second, then laughed. "I wish I had known my parents," she said. She stared down at her plate.

Tentatively, Charlie put a hand on her shoulder. "I'm sorry, I should have thought about what I was saying."

Gwen looked into his eyes and smiled. Charlie's heart melted.

"Don't worry about it, Charlie. They died when I was six months old. I don't even remember them. Granddad's been good to me, and Uncle Willy does what he can."

Charlie winced at the mention of the Chief. "I think he hates me."

"Once he knows we're together, he'll have to like you. He's a big pussycat."

He liked the sound of that. "Yeah, you said so before. Speaking of being hated by someone, how'd it go with El last

Friday?"

Gwen laughed. "The second I walked through the door, he grabbed my arm and demanded to know what was going on between the two of us. That's when I told all that bull about you being annoying and stupid and walking around with your fly open."

"You laid it on a little thick, didn't you? I mean, don't tell him anything, but don't make me out to be a total loser."

Gwen patted Charlie's hand and he felt a thrill run up his arm. "With El, you have to be as nasty as possible or he won't believe you. The guy really is a piece of shit. Pardon my language."

"When it comes to that prick, anything goes." Charlie finished off his first burger. Gwen finished hers a moment later. He liked how she ate with gusto.

"Damn, I forgot," said Gwen. She got up and went to a bag on a shelf by the door. When she returned, she held a bottle of wine and two glasses. "Do you indulge?"

Charlie hesitated. Should he tell her the truth? Always. "Back in the city, a lot. Some friends got me a mickey of whisky for my eighteenth birthday. I drank the whole thing over a couple of hours, puked it up, then put away some beers. I haven't got very good taste in booze because I don't have much experience. I do like wine."

"Wow," said Gwen. "I sneak a drink from grandfather's cabinet whenever I have the house to myself." She held up the bottle. "It's good stuff from grandfather's cellar. Worth a bit, too." She opened the bottle and poured them each a glass. "To us." They clinked glasses.

"Always," said Charlie.

When they had finished eating and cleaned up the mess, they sat in two comfortable looking chairs in front of the window. The view of the screen was perfect—no heads would be in the way. Gwen had brought the wine bottle. She refilled their glasses then put the bottle on the floor next to her chair. Charlie was feeling quite happy, and she seemed relaxed.

The movie that night was *Lost Horizon*. It was about survivors of a plane crash in the Himalayas who stumbled upon a secret valley where people live forever. It was one of Charlie's favorites.

There was a quiet knock at the door. Gwen said, "Come in."

Mr. Tyndale entered and walked up to them. "Good to see you again, Charlie. I hope you're comfortable."

"These seats are perfect. Thank you."

The old man chuckled. "There's plenty of room out there. We rarely ever sell out. In fact, I don't think we've ever had more than half the theatre full. People in this town don't appreciate the good old stuff like us."

"Their loss," said Charlie.

"Did you like the roses?" They both nodded and blushed again. Mr. Tyndale smiled.

Emile the florist knows everything about flowers and what they mean. He knows a lot of things that are useful to know."

"Anyway, I thought you two would like a bit of privacy. I brought you these." He handed them each a large box of Milk Duds. "There are more if you run out. Enjoy the show."

He walked to the door. "And no hanky-panky. Unless Gwen says it's okay. This door does lock." He turned off the light and left them alone.

Charlie was shocked. "Gwen, I would never ..."

"Ever?" The theatre went dark, and the screen curtain opened. "Give it a week."

It was hard for Charlie to pay attention to the movie at first. He was so incredibly excited being there with Gwen. She seemed so ... perfect. During a romantic part, Gwen took Charlie's hand in hers. They held hands for the rest of the movie.

It was about nine-thirty when the film ended. They were both feeling no pain, having polished off the whole bottle of wine. When they stood, Gwen stumbled and Charlie caught her.

"My hero." She gave him a peck on the cheek.

They both stood staring at each other.

"We need some air," said Charlie. "I need to regain control of my senses."

"Me, too," said Gwen. "Right now, I'd be willing to do something that I'd rather enjoy sober and less rushed. Would you care for a walk in the park, Charles?"

"That would be fabulous, Gwendolyn."

They linked arms and left the theatre.

The night was cool and clear. There was no sign of mist. Then Charlie realized Gwen had been making a joke earlier and mentally kicked himself for not getting it straight away. Charlie was overwhelmed by the number of stars he could see in the night sky. In the city, the bright lights had obscured all but the brightest stars and the moon. Arm in arm, they walked around the perimeter of the park until they came to a bench across from the church.

They sat. Gwen moved closer to Charlie, and he put his arm around her shoulder. He felt completely relaxed with Gwen. The butterflies had gone as soon as they had started talking in the storeroom. When they were silent, it didn't seem awkward but natural, as if they were just enjoying each other's presence.

"What do you want to do after you graduate?" asked Charlie quietly. He already hoped Gwen's plans included him, though he knew that was ridiculous so soon after they had met.

"Paint."

"Houses?"

"Yes, and landscapes, people, anything that suits me."

"Oh, you want to be an artist. I thought you meant you wanted to be a house painter."

Charlie winced when Gwen jabbed him in the ribs with her elbow.

"What about you, twit?"

"I'm not entirely sure. I'd like to dig up ancient ruins, discover lost civilizations, and solve the mystery of the Sphinx. Or maybe spend all my time going through old books and documents, researching and writing great scholarly works of history. Or be the lead guitar player in a rock band."

"Can you play guitar?"

"Air." He strummed a few riffs.

"I can see us now. You half buried in the mud trying to excavate an Egyptian pyramid while I'm painting a landscape with the Nile in it."

"We could have a special gallery show my discoveries and your paintings."

"We'd have to be rich, though. That way we could spend all our time doing what we like."

"You never know," he said. Should he tell her about the coins? No. Keep that as a surprise for later.

Charlie shook his head and realized what they were saying. Gwen was thinking about a future with him.

Her beautiful face was so close Charlie could feel her breath.

"Are we being presumptuous, thinking this way?" She

turned her head to look at Charlie. "What do you think, Charlie?"

Charlie looked deep into Gwen's eyes and the butterflies returned. He was tempted to say something foolish, like, "I love you," but resisted the impulse. Instead, he smiled and squeezed Gwen's shoulder.

A breeze started up and Gwen shivered. Charlie checked his watch and saw that it was well past ten o'clock.

"I'd better get you home. We wouldn't want Uncle Willy out looking for us." He took off his jacket and wrapped it around Gwen's shoulders.

They walked in silence along the Loop, arms around each other's waists. When they got to the gate of the Mundy estate, Gwen punched in the security code, and they walked up the laneway.

They stepped up to the oak front door. Gwen put her arms around Charlie's shoulders and drew him closer.

"Since we shared our dreams, I guess that means we're going steady."

"Do people still say that?" He couldn't believe his ears. Charlie's heart hammered as he looked into Gwen's eyes. "Wow, it's so great that you're tall. My neck isn't being strained."

"Shut up and kiss me goodnight, twit." She pulled his face to hers.

Charlie's mind roller-coastered. He pulled back his waist slightly. Gwen pulled him back.

Gwen kissed him again, moved away a step, stroked Charlie's face and opened the door.

"Think of me," she whispered. She went in and closed the door.

Charlie could barely catch his breath while he walked

down the laneway. The girl of his dreams truly existed, and she was now his girlfriend.

Now what? He didn't know what to do next.

A smile spread across his face, and no matter how hard he tried, he couldn't get it to go away. He was smiling so hard, it hurt. Terminal grins, he called it.

Just as he reached the gate, expecting to climb the wall again, the gate swung open to release him from the estate.

Charlie looked back towards the house, knowing Gwen was thinking of him.

He walked into the gate, hitting it hard with his right knee.

Charlie limped home, feeling as if he ruled the world.

Chapter Fourteen

Gwen wasn't at school on Monday or Tuesday, and that worried Charlie. Had someone found out about them, and was she being held against her will as punishment? No one had come to the house on Sunday to give Charlie royal hell for daring to take the daughter of Mayor Mundy on a date, let alone get a little tipsy with her, exchange suggestive innuendos that weren't at all subtle, and kiss her.

Claiming a heavy homework load, Charlie had stayed in his room most of Sunday. In truth, he had spent his time using the coin books to value his stash. By day's end, he was well over ten million dollars richer, though he couldn't think how he would ever be able to benefit from his haul. What if someone found out and claimed it as theirs or as town property since it was found in the town.

Charlie had taken a break from the kind of thinking that spoiled his fun and had gone for a run where he could imagine what he and Gwen would do when they were able to be together.

At school, he didn't dare inquire after her in case someone got the right idea about them. Jimmy made some silly comments that were meant to elicit some kind of news about Gwen, but they fell on deaf ears. Even the rumor mill was empty. That was good. No need to rile El.

Wednesday after school, Charlie decided to try Mr. Tyndale. The old guy seemed nice enough, and given how he thought of El—a backstabbing, slimy scumbag—he thought there might be some help in that direction. The theatre was closed, and when Charlie tried knocking at the front and back doors, no one answered.

Frustrated, Charlie went to the library to look up books on architecture. At the very least, he could try to figure out when his house was built. Given how secretive the town was about its past, he didn't think there was any hope of finding the previous owner. All that his search turned up was his house was likely built sometime after 1850 but before 1910. That definitely narrowed it down. Something that did stand out, though, was that the houses around Charlie's were definitely not built at the same time. Their styles were from after the 1920s. His home must have been on an old farmstead or estate, and the town had gradually expanded to absorb it.

When he left the library, he saw a group of men in the park having a heated discussion. Among them were El and Mr. Tyndale. Tempted to try and listen in, Charlie thought better of it and headed home. He'd gone about a hundred yards when he heard his name called.

Turning, he was surprised to see Mr. Tyndale walking towards him. He walked back to meet him.

"Charlie, my boy, so good to see you."

"Thank you, sir. It's good to see you, too. I tried the theatre earlier. I was hoping to ask you a few questions."

"Really? Fire away."

Charlie checked to see if El was still around, but he and the other men were walking towards the town hall. "Okay, first, when was my house built?"

"1862."

"Who built it?"

"My grandfather."

That shocked Charlie. "So, it was your house?"

Mr. Tyndale smiled. "I never owned it, but I lived there until I went away to college. While I was gone, my father died, and my mother sold the house to one of the church elders. I always resented that because I wanted a chance to buy it. By the time I found out, this was several years later, my mother had moved out and the new owners were in."

"Why didn't your mother let you know about the sale? Oh, sorry, that was rude of me."

"Not at all, my boy. My mother was a greedy bitch who couldn't say no to a packet of money for a house she always hated. She later married into one of the prominent families in town."

"Dare I ask which one?"

"The Blayneys."

"What? Does that mean you're related to Gwen?"

Mr. Tyndale chuckled. "I am, but not the way you might think. When I returned from college, I became Chief of Police. I married my stepsister. It wasn't thought of as a scandal back then, especially in this town. There tend to be a lot of close family ties here, only a few of which should never have happened. If you get my drift."

Charlie shook his head. "Not really."

"Gwendolyn is my great-granddaughter. However, she doesn't know it. My son, the current Rex Mundy, kept the Blayney name because, at the time, it was much more important in our circles than Tyndale. Gwendolyn's mother was my granddaughter."

"Why do you keep your relationship secret? Am I being nosy again?"

"No, no. You have a stake in this, though you don't know it yet. However, it's safer for Gwendolyn if she's not associated with the Tyndale name. I'm considered a bit of a gadfly by the town bigwigs."

"Like that backstabbing, slimy scumbag?"

Mr. Tyndale laughed until he coughed. Charlie patted the old man's back until he regained his composure. "Gwendolyn's been talking. She trusts you. I like that."

"Me, too. A lot."

"Any more questions?"

Charlie hesitated to ask about the alcove.

"You found it, didn't you? Is it empty?"

"No. There are three items in it."

"Good. The new owners didn't find them. They're yours, Charlie. Use them as you see fit."

That was an odd thing to say. Why would Charlie have any use for medieval weapons and an old musket?

"Before you go, Charlie, Gwendolyn asked me to give you a message. She'll meet you at your house at ten tomorrow morning. She wants to go to the fair with you. I think it's going to be a statement to the powers that be."

Charlie slept less than usual that night. The anticipation of meeting Gwen and going public with their relationship was exhilarating and scary. How would people react? Would the Chief shoot him? Would El try to gaslight him to death? Would his father's head explode at the scandal of it all?

In the end, Charlie didn't care what any of them thought. Gwen was all that mattered.

At four in the morning, Charlie got up and took a long run to clear his head. It was still dark, so Charlie ran down to the Loop, followed it around town, and then up towards the Mundy estate. By the time he got home, the sun was up, and Charlie was looking forward to the day. His shower was so long and thorough that he used all the hot water. There'd be hell to pay when Ant found out, but too bad.

Charlie ate a hearty breakfast and was going to his room when the rest of the family was heading down to eat. No one said anything. Before entering his room, Charlie heard Ant scream from the bathroom. The hot water tank was extremely slow.

Remembering how he was when Gwen was around, especially when she held his hand, Charlie took care of business twice. That should help blunt any untoward thoughts or desires, at least until the afternoon.

At nine-thirty, Charlie got a deck chair and went to sit on the front porch to wait for Gwen's arrival. He was stunned fifteen minutes later when the Mayor's limo pulled up in front of his house. The Mayor got out and held the door open for Gwen. He kissed his granddaughter on the cheek and got back in the car. Gwen watched it pull away towards downtown.

The Mayor had ignored Charlie. Or maybe he didn't see him. No, Charlie decided the Mayor had deliberately snubbed him. He must be furious about Gwen's choice of boyfriend.

Charlie stood and waited for Gwen to come up to the porch. He figured he should at least introduce her to the family, even if the family didn't deserve to know her. He always wanted to keep his romantic life private and had never brought home a girlfriend or mentioned any interest. Gwen, however, was not someone he could avoid bringing home.

Gwen walked up the driveway to the garden path and then to the porch. Charlie had to take a few deep breaths when he saw her. Today, her hair was tied back with the customary red ribbon. Her white sundress had little yellow flowers on it, and with the sun shining from behind her, it was thin enough to show off the outline of her incredibly long legs. They appeared even longer since the sandals she wore had two-inch heels. She had painted her toenails.

"Hello, Charlie," she said when she stepped up to the porch. She leaned forward and kissed him lightly on the lips. When she pulled away, and he followed, she said, "Save it for later, tiger."

"You look fantastic, Gwen. I don't think I've ever seen anything as beautiful and radiant."

"Flattery will get you everywhere, my love. Are you going to introduce me to the family?"

"Do I have to? I'd rather not."

"Yes, Charlie. It's the polite thing to do. Besides, I want to see your sister's face when she finds out we're together. She doesn't say much nice about you with the Sisterhood."

Charlie was a little hurt by that. He had always hoped that his sister's antagonism was something that only happened for show when he was around. Ant must seriously dislike him for some reason.

"We'd better go in, but only for a quick intro. The last thing I want is to hang around the family when you're here."

Charlie opened the front door and let Gwen in.

His parents and Ant were still in the kitchen talking about what they expected from the fair. He knew his father wanted to schmooze with as many bigwigs as possible, and Ant planned to show herself off to all the boys. His mother ... he didn't know what she wanted.

"Everyone, this is Gwen," said Charlie. "We're walking to the fair together."

Silence.

Ant looked horror-stricken. George Bowen gasped. Nell Bowen smiled.

"Charlie's being bashful," said Gwen. "That's why I love him. Really, we're going steady. Girlfriend – boyfriend. You know."

Charlie wanted to crawl under a rock. But did Gwen say she loved him?

"So nice to meet you, Gwen," said his mother. She came over and gave Gwen a hug. "You lucky girl."

"Lucky girl?" Ant huffed. "You've got terrible taste in boys, Blayney." Ant walked out of the room. Gwen grinned.

His father rose and walked up to Gwen with his hand out to shake hers. "Miss Blayney, I'm so happy to meet you. I'm George Bowen. I met your grandfather, the Mayor, at the welcome party a few weeks ago. I'm sure he remembers me."

She took his hand and shook lightly. "He meets a lot of people, Mr. Bowen. Charlie's a great guy, very underappreciated. I'd been wanting to meet him since the first time I saw him running by my house. It was such a good thing we both had detentions a couple of weeks ago. We got to know each other over a science problem. Charlie's brilliant. I hope I didn't get him in any trouble because I kept him out so late. We were having so much fun I wouldn't let him go. I didn't even spare him enough time to call home. Silly me."

Gwen smiled sweetly at George Bowen and then batted her eyelashes. Charlie enjoyed seeing his father trying to decide what to say while his head swiveled between his son and the Mayor's granddaughter.

"Come on, Charlie. There's a fair to attend and lots of games and food and fun to be had." She pulled Charlie to the front door and shouted, "Bye, everyone," without looking back.

When they were on the street, Charlie started to laugh.

"Did I do all right?" Gwen squeezed Charlie's hand. "I wanted to shock them."

"You were amazing. I could kiss you."

"I'm waiting."

He put his arms around Gwen and pressed his lips against hers. She broke away and said, "Good, they're watching."

The rest of the morning passed by in a flash.

It was the Coverdale Triennial Fair, and the park was crammed full of people. Tents and pavilions had been erected, and from their cool shade, people sold baked goods and crafts, old clothing and candy, books—nothing that interested Charlie—and whatever else had been cluttering up their garages and attics for the last three years. There were pony rides for the children, hayrides for the adults, games of chance and skill, a pie-eating contest, and awards for the best preserves and chili. There was even a small circus in a tent across from the school.

The whole town had turned out.

Charlie walked hand in hand with Gwen, feeling ten feet tall because he was with the most beautiful girl in the town. Jimmy, who met them at his house on the way this morning, tagged along and cheered Charlie on as he won stuffed animals for Gwen at several of the games. All three had loaded up on cotton candy, cake, soda, and ice cream.

The sun was shining, and a slight breeze lightly ruffled the flags and pennants that hung from every available pole or window.

Mayor Mundy made the rounds, judging pies, complimenting cooks, kissing babies, and shaking hands. He had been amiable towards Charlie and had gone so far as to invite him for Friday's holiday dinner. Charlie was stunned. Gwen said it would be boring. Jimmy wondered why he wasn't included in the invitation.

Chief Wycliffe roamed the perimeter of the park, eyes hidden behind dark glasses. Although it was hard for Charlie to take 'Uncle Willy' seriously anymore, he avoided the Chief anyway. He thought it best to keep out of trouble now that he and Gwen were together. Another grounding would be disastrous. Although, after what Gwen had said to his father this morning, groundings might be a thing of the past.

When the notices for the fair first appeared on bulletin boards at the school and on lamp posts around town, Charlie was mystified. He learned from Jimmy that the Coverdale Triennial Fair was a tradition carried on from the old country. It was celebrated every three years and was *the* big event in the town.

The old country. Charlie thought that wherever the old country was, that must be where the cross in the circle originated. The symbol was evident everywhere, not just on pennants and flags. It appeared on pins, plates, and even as ornamentation on the horses' traces. One manifestation of the symbol, in particular, intrigued Charlie. When they passed a couple of policemen conversing by a cold drinks stand, Charlie noticed both men had tattoos on their forearms. However, the cross and circle pattern was changed to resemble a cross on a shield.

Curious.

Tables were set out for the evening meal, served up by The Institute Social Club. Charlie felt a mild satisfaction while he watched his aproned father carry food trays around and place them on the tables. The downside was that he and Gwen were forced apart for the meal. She had to join Mayor Mundy at the head table; families were expected to eat together. At least Jimmy had gotten his parents, brothers, and sisters to join with Charlie's at the same table. Charlie would have someone to insult besides Ant.

The meal, barbecued chicken and ribs, was excellent.

Charlie ate plenty despite having sampled too much of Mrs. Burke's prize-winning chili around lunchtime. By the time the plates and trash were cleared away, the sun had gone down.

The church bell began to ring.

All the adults gathered on Sevres Street, which connected to the ring road enclosing the church. Several dozen teenage girls, including Ant, corralled all the children.

Charlie was astounded. Ant was helping out, almost babysitting. That wasn't like her. Gwen was helping, too. He missed her.

The adults formed a procession and slowly moved up the road in the direction of the church. Strangely, the local tramps, about twenty of them who had been sitting at their own tables, led the way.

Charlie went to join the procession but was held back by Jimmy.

"It's adults only, bud."

"What, aren't we considered adults? We're eighteen."

"Around here, you're nothing until you're nineteen," said Paul. He, Mark, and Arnie had come up behind Jimmy and Charlie while they were observing the proceedings with the adults.

"We're crap," added Mark.

"What're you guys gonna do now?" asked Arnie.

"What the flip?" said Charlie. A look of confusion masked his face when he saw the children being herded along the street to the Town Hall. "Where are they going?"

"The Sisterhood chicks," Paul said and spat. "They'll be taking them off to amuse them while the adults do their thing at the church. Bunch of stuck-up bitches."

Charlie bristled at Paul's comment. "Watch it, clown. Gwen's over there. Careful what you say about her."

"Cool it, Charlie." Jimmy placed his hand on Charlie's chest to hold him back from Paul. "The guy's got a point. Most of those girls wouldn't give us the time of day."

Charlie looked down at his friend. "Can you blame them, short stuff? Anyway, Gwen's not part of that crowd."

"She's got the tattoo," said Mark. "Maybe you'd notice if you took your eyes off Gwen's chest for a minute."

Jimmy stepped forward. "Bag it, Mark. Watch what you say about Gwen, or you'll have to deal with me. And no one gets to insult Charlie while I'm around. Except me." Turning to face Charlie, he asked, "Well, do you look anywhere else?"

Charlie said nothing, but his face turned red.

"Thought so. Is that a booger hanging out your nose?"

Charlie quickly checked his nose, flicked his fingers at Jimmy, and smiled.

"Getting along with LaRennes, Charlie?" Mark stood with his arms crossed, waiting for an answer.

Charlie decided it was best to tone things down. "I've encountered him, Mark. He seems all right. Mostly."

Mark huffed and turned away.

"Let's throw stones at the old bridge pilings," said Arnie.

"That sounds exciting," said Charlie without enthusiasm. "Why don't we follow the girls and see what they do?"

"No point," said Mark. "The Sisterhood has some kind of ceremony it performs whenever the adults are in church. We're definitely not welcome."

"Come on, Charlie, let's go to the old bridge. It's a tradition," said Jimmy, pulling at Charlie's sleeve.

"Yeah, in a minute. I have to whiz. I'll catch up."

He trotted off towards the portable toilets. When he reached them, he looked back to make sure the guys were heading for the bridge. Seeing that they were, Charlie detoured around the toilets and behind the pony rides. The last of the adults were going through the church's front doors. Just like at the school, the doors faced east. He ran across the road after the doors closed and around the back of the Town Hall.

From inside came the sound of female voices chanting. The Hall's basement windows were dark and the first-floor windows were too high for him to see into.

He decided to try his luck at the church and ran across the road.

Under the trees that bordered the church grounds, something struck Charlie as odd. He paused for a moment beneath a massive oak and stared at the grass spread out before him.

"This is where the cemetery should be," he said quietly. "But there's nothing here except that small stone building."

Set to the northeast of the main church building was a low structure. To Charlie, it looked Greek, with columns and a sloped roof. He dashed across the open area to the small building. There were no windows. At the side facing the church was a heavy wooden door covered with carvings, most notable of which was at its center—the cross in a circle. Charlie guessed it was some sort of tomb. A pea stone path led to a door at the side of the church.

Moving as silently as possible, Charlie crept to the church. He could hear the congregation singing a hymn, though he didn't recognize the tune.

The walls of the church were covered with ivy. He gave it a tug and figured it would hold his weight. Charlie climbed carefully to one of the high stained-glass windows. When he looked down to see how far he had climbed, Charlie was almost overtaken by vertigo. He was about fifty feet up the side of the church, and the roof looked about another hundred feet higher. The church had appeared massive from the ground, but now Charlie felt like an insignificant insect on the side of the building.

Charlie found a small pane in the corner of the window that had clear rather than colored glass. Peering into the church, he tried to see what was going on. The picture was distorted because the pane was of thick, hand-made glass, and the surface was uneven.

The congregation stopped singing and sat down. It looked to Charlie as if the local tramps were leading the service. The clothes of the men at the front of the church seemed ragged, though it was hard to tell through the distortion.

There was a small choir box to the right of the altar, and there seemed to be two people kneeling before it.

Charlie thought they appeared tied up, but it was hard to tell through the thick glass.

He tried to see his parents. The church was jam-packed with people. If all the town's adults were here, there must have been several thousand people there, maybe more. He finally found his parents near the middle, with Jimmy's folks.

The congregation rose again and started to sing. Charlie saw movement near the altar. The two people who looked tied up were led to the altar. They didn't appear willing.

There was something familiar about the pair.

A tingling at the back of his neck made Charlie look to the choir box.

There, looking straight at Charlie, was Chief Wycliffe.

Charlie shrank back. There was no way the Chief could have heard him climbing the wall. And it was darker outside now, so Charlie wouldn't cast a shadow on the window. It must have been his imagination.

When he took another look inside the church, the Chief's

seat in the choir box was empty.

Trying to remain calm, Charlie quickly climbed down the ivy. As soon as he hit the ground, he ran for the tomb; it was the closest place to offer him cover. Peeking around the side of the tomb, Charlie saw that the coast was clear. He dashed across the grass to the oak trees, then to the sidewalk on the other side of the street.

He heard a door slam somewhere over by the church. Staying crouched behind a tree, Charlie tried to breathe quietly. The urge to look around the tree was intense, but he didn't move. Soon, the door slammed again.

Charlie looked around the tree.

Nothing.

Taking a few deep breaths, Charlie jogged east towards the Loop. He could cut across the road and through the trees to meet the guys at the river.

He stopped for a moment when he was sure he heard screaming that was suddenly cut off.

It must have been nerves.

Charlie wracked his brain, trying to figure out what it was about the two bound people that touched a nerve.

Then he remembered.

They looked like Mr. and Mrs. Standish.

But they had both died in the fire.

There was another cut off scream.

He ran faster.

Chapter Fifteen

Charlie was stunned to find out that the Friday holiday dinner was more of a day-long celebration that began at ten in the morning. A limo would be at his house at 9:45 to pick him up.

He didn't have a suit.

Although Mayor Mundy had been friendly at the fair, Charlie still worried that he was being drawn into a den of evil. Maybe he was exaggerating, but given the nasty looks he got from Chief Wycliffe and El, both of whom would be at the celebration, he was unsure of exactly how safe he would be. He also worried for Gwen's safety. She might have been the Mayor's granddaughter, but she had defied El and hooked up with Charlie in a very public way. El seemed like the type of guy who would seek revenge.

There was also the matter of what he had seen and perhaps heard at the church.

Charlie thought about bringing the sword or mace hidden in the alcove.

George Bowen was even more excited about the celebration than Charlie. He had tried to get invited to the Mundy mansion; however, the Mayor had ignored him, and the Chief had come between them to keep George well away. Charlie wondered where El had been yesterday. It was a relief that the weasel hadn't been there because Charlie was sure it would have spoiled the day.

The instant Charlie set foot in the living room Friday

morning, his father was all over him. Why wasn't he wearing a suit? Charlie had never needed one. What was wrong with his clean, black jeans, black button-down shirt, formal black Doc Martins, and black velvet Victorian tailcoat? It was practically a suit.

He drew the line at a tie.

No ties.

No way.

Stop asking.

And only white socks—never a color—that no one would see anyway because his Docs were knee-high under his jeans. He'd thought about tucking the jeans in the boots but thought that might have been a little too rock 'n' roll for Coverdale. George relented but was not happy.

Next, George told Charlie all the things he needed to say to help George advance at The Institute. Charlie had to emphasize George's loyalty to The Institute, the work, and Mayor Mundy. Remember how hard George worked and how brilliant he was. Gwen agreeing to go out with Charlie was a positive boon for the Bowen family. If Charlie played his cards right, the Bowens and Blayneys would be joined, and there would be no limit to the heights to which George could rise.

Thanks to George being so adamant about what Charlie was to say, going so far as to make him repeat the praise until he had it memorized, Charlie was determined that, unless someone specifically mentioned it or asked, he would not utter a single word about his family.

Ant got in on the game by suddenly becoming Charlie's best friend, telling him that their arguing and banter was all in familial good fun. She praised Gwen's sense of style and intelligence and assured Charlie that Gwen was supremely fortunate to have picked Charlie. By the way, could he mention that Ant would like to play a more prominent role within the sisterhood?

Nell Bowen sat at the kitchen table reading a gardening magazine. She didn't say a word except to compliment Charlie on his attire. He was so handsome. If he wasn't her son, well ... Charlie shuddered, remembering El's insinuations about mother-son relationships.

He couldn't wait to get the hell out of the house.

Charlie was so startled by a knock at the front door that he farted. It was foul, yet none of his family made their usual complaints.

When he opened the door, Charlie's heart did a flip. Standing there in a black Tuxedo, a black top hat, a gold-tipped cane, and patent-leather shoes that were so shiny Charlie could see his reflection, was El.

That did it.

"Come in, Mr. LaRennes, I'll just be a moment." El stepped into the living room while Charlie dashed upstairs. As quickly as he could, he changed into slender black jeans, also recently cleaned, and tucked them in his boots.

It was time to be rock 'n' roll.

When he returned to the living room, his father sat quietly on the couch while El regaled him with the reasons he should keep his mouth shut. Both men gasped when Charlie jumped down the last three steps and said, "Let's rock 'n' roll." When he got no reaction, he added, "Too much?"

At that moment, Charlie felt supremely confident. He would spend the day with Gwen, and nothing could spoil that.

Without a word, El led Charlie to the limo. As soon as the car moved, El spoke up.

"All right, Charlie. You may think you've gotten away

with something, but you haven't. Gwen is playing with your affections. I know. I've seen her do it before. It's one of her many character flaws. Her grandfather and I have tried to set her on the proper path, but she is defiant. I'm relying on you to get yourself out of this situation gracefully. It would be for the best."

El sat waiting for Charlie's response. Charlie only nodded, waiting.

"I see I'm getting through to you. Look, I know, based on your juvenile actions since you arrived in Coverdale, that you lack maturity. However, I'm relying on your sense of pride to do the right thing. I mean, look at you, dressed like a clown. How could you possibly think a young lady like Gwen Blayney would look upon you as anything more than a passing fancy? A bad choice due to the summer heat.

Charlie shrugged. He listened carefully, though, so he could learn how to recognize gaslighting. It was fascinating.

"I see you understand. Speechless because you know I'm correct."

The limo pulled through the gates of the Mundy estate. There were only a few cars parked in front of the mansion. Charlie wondered how large the celebration crowd would be. He had been hoping for dozens so he could blend in and spend time with Gwen. This looked a little ominous.

"We're here, Charlie. Now, remember your place. Act accordingly and try not to say anything embarrassing or ridiculous if you can help it. You're with the cream of Coverdale society and they do not tolerate ... vulgar, ill-bred, commoners."

Charlie nodded. He wondered what El's pedigree was and how he fit into Coverdale society. Was he nothing more than a sneaky weasel lurking in the background whose only purpose was to ruin someone's day? People, including Charlie's father, deferred to El and almost seemed afraid of him. Today wouldn't only be about being with Gwen. Charlie would learn how to fit into Coverdale society so he could unravel all those mysteries that had him surrounded.

When they exited the limo, Charlie was overjoyed to see Gwen waiting at the front door. Today, she truly was a vision of splendor. Her evening gown was burgundy organza—why did he know that word? —that draped from her shoulders to the floor. It had a plunging neckline that was both revealing and tasteful. It was tied at the waist with a matching sash. Her arms were bare and she wore no jewelry save for a gold charm bracelet around her right wrist. She had left her hair loose, so it flowed over her shoulders and hung to her breasts. He couldn't see her shoes, but whatever they were, they would look magnificent on her perfect feet.

Gwen's only makeup was some red lipstick and matching nail polish. He knew her toenails would also match.

Charlie wanted to drop to one knee and propose right then and there.

With a huge lump in his throat, he managed to say, "Gwen ... wow!"

She smiled. "I love the outfit, Charlie, especially the boots. I bet my Docs would be more comfortable than these heels." She lifted her dress to show Charlie peep-toe pumps that matched her dress. Yes, her toenails matched. And had there ever been more perfect ankles? "I need to get some Victorian clothes. We'd make a good couple." She held her hand out for him to hold. When he took it, she pulled him closer and gave him a peck on the lips.

Charlie felt light-headed.

"Shall we go in? I can't wait to introduce you to

everyone."

A butler opened the door. Before going in, Gwen said, "Oh, hello, Justin. I didn't see you there. When did you arrive?"

El looked furious, so Charlie decided to lighten his mood. With a huge smile, he leaned close to El's ear. "Mr. LaRennes, remember what you said in the limo?" El nodded. "Well, kindly fuck off."

Gwen squeezed his hand and chuckled.

With a tight grip on his hand, as if she were afraid she'd lose him, Gwen led Charlie through a three-story high foyer. Circular staircases went up two sides to a landing leading to a further pair of stairs up to the third floor. What Charlie assumed were family portraits hung on the walls. Judging from the subjects' attire, Gwen's family went back at least five hundred years, so they must have come over from Europe at some point.

The quality of light was a little strange – flickering and colorful. Looking up, Charlie spied a huge chandelier hanging from the center of a high, stained glass, domed roof. Though quite high, he could make out knights and clergymen depicted in the glass. There was writing, but he'd need to be up on the third-floor landing to read it.

Going through the arch created by the two staircases, they emerged into a large room with windows two stories high along the north wall. Through the windows, Charlie could see vast gardens with fountains and statues. There appeared to be a couple of follies way out near the forest.

The room was extremely bright due to huge mirrors opposite the windows that reflected every bit of light that entered. Along the center of the room, covered with red cloth, was a long table with seating for at least twenty or more people. Staff were busy laying out platters of food.

"Through here, Charlie," said Gwen. "Bear with me. This is all new to me." He didn't know what she meant.

They passed through a door at the west end of the room that opened onto a small stone patio. People milled about drinking champagne and talking. Charlie recognized some of them, including the high school Principal, a couple of Councilors, the Chief, and El, who gave him a filthy look. Charlie smiled back and gave a little wave.

"Charlie! So good to see you." Mr. Tyndale came striding over and shook Charlie's hand vigorously.

"I didn't think you'd be here, sir."

Mr. Tyndale laughed. "Protocol, my boy. They couldn't exclude me, no matter how much they desired it. I may be retired, old, and annoying, but I'm part of the fabric of this town, and they can't ignore me." He hugged Gwen. "My dear, you look ravishing. Has this young man made his move yet? Or is he too much of a gentleman for that?"

Charlie blushed when Gwen said, "Oh, he'll make a move, Mr. T., or there'll be hell to pay." She smiled when she saw Charlie's red face. "Charlie is a perfect gentleman. Excuse us, Mr. T., but I have to take my man over to the Mayor and present him."

On their way towards a group of people surrounding the Mayor and trying to catch his ear, Charlie said, "Gwen, what's with all the comments? We barely know each other. It's a little weird."

She stopped and looked into his eyes. "Charlie, I've waited a long time for you. I mean, I didn't know it would be you, just the one who would get me away from all this shit. Don't you feel it, too?" He nodded. "We'll talk later. For now, follow my lead."

"Yes, darling. Or would you prefer, my love?"

"I don't care which, so long as you mean it."

"I do."

"Good. Grandpa!"

Mayor Mundy looked up from the short, round woman speaking to him and smiled at his granddaughter. He moved through the group to hug Gwen.

"Gwen, how marvelous. And Charlie is here. How are you, son?"

"I'm good, sir. Yourself?"

"Never better. Have you met everyone here, Charlie?"

"Most, sir, either at the welcome party, school, or around town. Hello, everyone."

Most nodded at Charlie. Some looked shocked to see him. Above his station? Not dressed well enough? Too handsome to be true?

At the back of the group, El glared at him. Through gritted teeth, he said, "Hello, Charlie."

"Hey, Justin. How are you, sir? I thought more about what you said. My answer is still the same. You still okay with that?"

"Oh, yes, Charlie. We'll have more to discuss later, I'm sure. For now, enjoy yourself." He stalked away.

A gong announced that brunch was served.

Three hours later, Charlie sat with Gwen on a couch in the music room. Gwen rested her head on his shoulder, her right hand on his chest. Rod Stewart sang about a mandolin wind. When she had suggested coming up to see her vinyl collection, Charlie wondered if that was because she had no etchings. Gwen really did have a vinyl collection, and it was massive. An inheritance from her late parents. He was both impressed and jealous. She'd asked him to put on something romantic.

He desperately wanted to talk to Gwen about all the mysteries he had discovered. Plus, he needed to know if the horror that had been brunch would be repeated at dinner. Not being related to the Mayor, Charlie had to sit at the far end of the table, away from Gwen. His seatmates were a woman who would not stop talking and three tramps who stank to high heaven. His stomach growled because he hadn't been able to eat.

The speeches had been interminable and totally confusing. What did the founding of Coverdale have to do with some long-lost kingdom in Europe? And why was the purity of blood so important? Had his family somehow put themselves amidst a town of white supremacists?

Gwen had refused to talk about anything important. She was worried that someone might overhear because El seemed to know everything that was said in the house. He either had the place bugged, or the staff were his personal spies. There was a place they could go after dinner where they'd have all the privacy they needed.

She did answer one important question.

"The tramps. They're venerated. It's part of our religion. On every special occasion, at least three of them are to observe and participate. I've heard rumors that they even ... you know, Louis XIV."

"No way? The wedding night? Are there at least curtains around the bed? We're gonna elope."

"Are you proposing?"

Charlie looked into Gwen's eyes. She smiled. He tried to speak but couldn't get the words out. His face flushed.

"Too shy?" He nodded and Gwen kissed him on the cheek. "But you'd do it?" He nodded again.

Rod stopped singing when the album came to an end. Neither moved to flip it or put something else on the turntable.

Gwen looked up at Charlie, and he looked down at her. The moment their lips met, there was a slight cough behind them. It was a servant announcing that their presence was required for the ceremony.

On the way, Charlie said, "I thought we weren't allowed to participate in anything because we're not nineteen."

"We're not, but we have to watch while the elders go off to do whatever it is they do."

"That sounds really dumb." Realizing what he had said, Charlie tried to apologize. "I'm so sorry, Gwen. I wasn't thinking. Please, pardon me if I've insulted your religion."

She laughed. "You have, Charlie, but I don't care. I think it's all dumb, too. And you haven't even heard the dumbest stuff."

That shocked him. "Being the Mayor's granddaughter, aren't you kind of at the center of all that? You seemed to play a big role with the Sisterhood."

"I am, and I do. Doesn't mean I have to believe in all that bull. And the Sisterhood doesn't do much more than teach girls to be subservient and how to cook."

"What about the tattoo? Ant's got one. So does my mom."

"It's just a sign we belong, that's all. See." She held out her wrist and moved her charm bracelet out of the way to show a tattoo. About an inch around, it was the cross in a circle. "I just have a small one. Some women get them much bigger."

"And Ant wants to play a bigger part. She told me to tell you."

"She can have it. Your sister's as dumb as the rest of them."

On the patio, Mayor Mundy, the councilors, and the Chief

were dressed in white robes with red crosses over the chest. Mr. Tyndale, also enrobed, stood a little to the side, looking uncomfortable. Charlie was certain now that he was in some racist camp—a KKK klavern? —and that he had to get away as soon as possible. He refused to believe that Gwen held any of these beliefs. The tramps stood out on the lawn waiting.

With fanfare, the robed men—only men—marched across the lawn towards one of the follies. When they had all entered and the door was shut, Charlie thought they would be free to get away for a while. He was sadly mistaken.

While the higher-ups did whatever they were doing, the rest had to gather in the library. Drinks were served. Gwen suggested they partake because it was going to be a long afternoon. Charlie decided to try a scotch and water while Gwen stuck to her wine. After one sip, he regretted his choice. So harsh. Next time, he would follow Gwen's lead or ask for root beer.

The people sat down in the many leather chairs scattered about the room. Though their placement looked random, all the chairs faced the center of the room. For the next four hours, Charlie listened to each person in the room go into great detail about why Coverdale was the best place in the world to live and why the residents were the chosen people. He let his eyes wander to the bookshelves as a distraction. His mind drifted, and he almost fell asleep.

He drank far too much and felt no pain. Charlie knew he would have to be careful and not do something stupid or speak his mind.

Gwen's voice jolted him to alertness. It was her turn to speak. Charlie was glad she had told him ahead of time that she thought this was all crap because what she said was scary. She looked forward to her life as a woman in Coverdale, serving her elders and making a family with her husband. All eyes went to him when she said that, and Charlie felt extremely uncomfortable. However, when Gwen mentioned that he was "still to be selected for her," he felt relief and disappointment. He hoped she was faking.

After speaking, Gwen leaned close to Charlie and whispered, "I had my fingers crossed the whole time. You're my man and don't you forget it. Did I slur my words? I had a lot of wine."

"You did fine. I had a lot, too. Too much."

Dinner was another three-hour slog. Charlie was allowed to sit next to Gwen this time, though she wasn't near the Mayor. All those who had been robed occupied the seats at the head of the table. To Charlie's great relief, the tramps were nowhere to be seen. He tucked into the food like he hadn't eaten for days. Gwen kept up with him, which he liked.

After dinner, the men retired to the library for brandy and cigars. The women went into a parlor to gossip while they did needlepoint. Charlie felt like he was in a Jane Austen novel.

El approached them and said, "Charlie, as you might have guessed, you are not welcome to join the men. We are the inner circle of Coverdale society, and outsiders and commoners are banned."

"You can still fuck off, Justin," said Charlie. Els' eyes went wide, but he quickly regained his composure.

"Gwen, my dear, you are not yet of age to join the women. I would be happy to escort you for a walk around the grounds. I'm sure Charlie will wish to leave. He can find his own way home since he feels so bold and independent."

Gwen smiled and said, "Justin, you backstabbing, slimy, little scumbag, please get stuffed."

For an instant, El looked hurt by Gwen's words. He

recovered quickly and smiled. "Gwen, say what you will, but I have your grandfather's ear. You'll be mine, and this," he nodded at Charlie, "will be relegated to the trash heap where he belongs. Where you are concerned, no one will ever get in my way." He walked towards the library.

"What did he mean by that, Gwen?"

"I don't know." Gwen took Charlie's hand. "I need to freshen up. So do you. Meet me here in ten minutes. I know a place we can go."

Chapter Sixteen

Charlie was back in the foyer in five minutes. He was nervous. After what Gwen had implied about the possibility of eavesdroppers in the mansion and El's understandable nastiness a few moments ago, where could they go for privacy? He remembered the guards at The Institute with their machine guns. They probably also had motion detectors, which Charlie guessed was why they found him on that first run. The Institute wasn't far from the Mundy estate; they must meet somewhere along the fence. That might mean more guards and electronic listening devices.

Gwen hurried down the stairs from the third floor. She still wore her formal gown, so Charlie concluded that wherever they were going, it would be clean. His heart thumped while he watched her descent. She was so amazingly beautiful and truly way out of his league. And yet, here she was, eager to spend time with him.

Maybe Coverdale wasn't such a bad place after all. Except for the crazy rules, machine guns, weird religion, lack of access to the outside world, and El.

When she reached Charlie, Gwen took his hand and pulled him down the hall. She put her finger to her mouth for him to be quiet. Halfway down the hall at an alcove, she stopped, looked both ways, then pressed against a panel in the alcove wall. The panel slid to the side, revealing a dark passage. She pulled him through and closed the door.

"This goes to the greenhouse," she said quietly. "I found it years ago when I was playing. I'm sure my grandfather knows about it, but I don't think El does."

"Does it lead anywhere else in the house?"

"No, just to the outside. Why?"

"I found an alcove in my closet back home. I'll explain later."

Gwen took a flashlight from a shelf and lit their way. Steps led down below the level of the cellars, if there were any. The passage straightened, and Charlie figured it went north. It had been cut through bedrock. The chisel and pick marks looked ancient. Perhaps this had been carved out by the natives. But why would they need a passage like this? And who connected it to the house?

Yet more Coverdale mysteries for Charlie to solve.

A few minutes later, they came to a set of steps. The passage continued off into the dark.

"There's a series of caves down there," said Gwen. I've explored them a little, but it feels ... uncomfortable, almost like people aren't welcome. It's hard to explain. Anyway, up here."

She went up the steps. When they reached the top, she shut off the flashlight and slowly opened a door. It was dark out there, wherever there was.

"It's clear."

They exited the tunnel into a small room. It smelled of strawberries and vanilla. Shining the flashlight down at the floor, Gwen crossed the room to a small stool. She stepped up and peered through a little grate. Leaning back, she swung a shutter over the grate and shone the flashlight at a table.

"Light that lamp, Charlie," she said.

Charlie found a box of matches, struck one, and held it to

the wick of the oil lamp. Gwen came over and adjusted it so it put out enough light to reveal most of the room. The area at the top, near the grate, remained in shadow.

Now that he could see, Charlie took note of his surroundings; light blue brick walls adorned with countless children's drawings and paintings. A shelf ran around three walls at about waist height and held dozens of books. Judging by the titles, bright colors, and varying sizes, Charlie concluded they were all children's books. Interspersed were stuffed animals. Gwen's?

A love seat was set against one wall, and a battered coffee table sat in front, on which a vase of fresh flowers sat. There was also a bottle of wine and two glasses. Against the opposite wall was an inflatable mattress with a sheet and blanket neatly folded on top, along with two fluffy pillows. The floor was covered with small carpets which overlapped. Charlie couldn't tell how many there were but could count at least ten.

Beside the table with the oil lamp, a battered dining room chair, its upholstery worn and torn, acted as a clothes horse for a pair of jeans, some socks, and a couple of shirts. On another, even more worn-out chair was a pair of runners.

"This was my hideaway when I was little. I still use it when I need to get away and think. You're the first person other than me to be here since I discovered it." Gwen sat on the loveseat.

"It's wonderful. How did you find it?" Charlie was mesmerized by the drawings. Many showed knights in armor with white surcoats and shields bearing the familiar red cross.

"I was playing in one of the greenhouses. At the back, I crawled under some shelves after a chipmunk and found a small door. This room was on the other side of it. The door is hidden on the other side. I found the cave and secret passage a couple of weeks later. I didn't want anyone coming in the front door, so I filled in the doorway with some bricks and mortar I stole from a work site on the grounds, then nailed some boards to the frame out there."

"And how old were you when you found this?"

"Nine."

He was impressed. "No one can see the room from outside?"

"No. The greenhouse is built against the side of a hill. This room is underground. And its roof is covered with trees and bushes."

"What about that grate?"

"There's a shelf on the other side. You can't see much of the greenhouse, but I set up a mirror by the entrance so I can see if anyone is inside. The gardeners hardly ever use this one anymore. There are newer and better ones on the other side of the garden."

She patted the seat next to her and Charlie joined her. Gwen took Charlie's hand in hers and squeezed.

"Look, Gwen, I know I've only been in Coverdale for about five weeks, but ..."

She put a finger to his lips to quiet him. "I know, Charlie. Me, too. It's ridiculous, and anyone would laugh at us for going too fast, but ... I feel ... silly saying it. I've never said it before."

"I love you, Gwen."

She smacked his arm. "I wanted to say it first, you twit. I love you, Charlie."

Charlie let out a sigh. "Well, I'm glad that's out of the way. I've been holding back since that day in the science lab."

"You must have said it to a girl before. How many girlfriends did you have back in the city? Ten? Twenty?"

"One, and that didn't last long and was a disaster. I'm too tall, I'm too uncoordinated to be any good at sports, and I'm quite the nerd. The girls at my old high school were more interested in the jocks. Anyway, I was too shy to speak to girls. It's a miracle I'm even talking to you."

"I would have been interested if I had been at your old school." She leaned over and kissed his cheek.

"What about you? I know loads of the guys at school are interested in you. Some said they wanted to ask you out, but El threatened them out of it. Still, you must have gone out with some guys."

"No one has ever asked me out, Charlie. Not at school or the theatre or anywhere. You say El interfered?"

"That's what I was told. He did say you belonged to him."

"He's so disgusting. Bad breath, horrible teeth. That shiny head and those beady eyes. How does he get away with so much?"

"Gwen, you've heard him talk. He's a master gaslighter. He had me convinced you hated me and that I was lower than the dirt on the bottom of his shoe. He can talk anyone into anything."

"I hate him so much."

"Let's forget about him for a while. I see you brought wine."

Gwen's face turned red. "Yeah, I thought maybe ... you know ... you and all those girls ... must have ... we could ..."

"What? Are you talking about ..."? She nodded. "But I've never ..."

"I was counting on you to have had ... it. You could guide me."

"I couldn't guide you anywhere, Gwen. I mean, I've seen magazines and all. Watched a couple of movies. But ..."

"Me, too. I thought maybe you could go ..." She looked down. "I freshened up and everything. I've heard it's nice."

Charlie's erection pushed at his jeans and tugged at his hair. It was very uncomfortable. "I'm sorry, Gwen, but I have to adjust. It hurts." He stood, turned away from her, and moved himself around so there was no more pain.

"Let me see." He looked back at her. "No, not everything, just ... that." She pointed at his bulge.

He turned and, for the first time in his life, stood in front of a girl while sporting a boner. He prayed she wouldn't ask him to take it out.

"Wow. I've never seen one up close. I've never seen one, period. In real life."

Charlie sat. "Well, you still haven't. Should I ask you to return the favor? No! Don't! I want to see, but I don't think I could take it right now. You're too ..."

"What, Charlie?"

"Too damned beautiful for words. You're perfect, Gwen. I've been imagining what you look like under that gown the moment I got out of the limo. If you took it off ... I'd have a heart attack ... or I'd make a mess in my ... you know."

Gwen laughed. "Oh, well."

"Anyway, I wasn't expecting ... you know ... I never ever expected or thought ... I don't have any ... Are you on the ... That's too personal. Sorry."

"Too personal. Charlie, I wanted to have ... you know ... with you ... you can ask whatever...Oh, you mean protection? Yes, I am, but not for that. I get bad cramps ... and ... well ..."

"Gwen, do you mind if I giggle uncontrollably? I know that sounds stupid, but right now I'm too happy to contain it. I want to scream. I want to cry. I want ... you."

They spent the next five minutes in each other's arms,

giggling.

"Charlie, can I sit on your lap and we ... kiss for a while?"

"Get up here."

Charlie lost track of time. It felt like hours but was more likely about fifteen minutes.

With their faces barely an inch apart, Charlie said, "Gwen, I love you, and there's nothing I would rather do than ... that. But we've only known each other for a few weeks. I'd feel like I'm taking advantage of you."

"I'm the one that's been making all the suggestions, Charlie. I wanted you to think I was experienced. You know ..."

"Sure, but I thought we'd start slow ... you know ... in a car ... parking and all."

"Oh! You mean, like, a hand up ... or under ..."

"Exactly. The only problem is, I don't have a car."

"And there's no place to go that's private ... except here."

"Let's wait until it's perfect." He looked around Gwen's hideaway. "I mean, this is lovely and all, and I love the scent of strawberries, vanilla, and you. But I've got this picture in my head. We're ..."

"I know, Charlie. I have the same picture in my head." She kissed him. "You look quite nice naked ... in my head."

"Okay, Gwen, we have to stop. I can only control myself so much. And with you being so damned irresistible ... and sitting on my ..."

"But you're resisting ..." She wriggled her backside.

"How about a glass of wine. We need to talk." He tried hard to keep his voice steady.

"Isn't that what we've been doing?"

"I mean about the weird shit that's been happening in Coverdale. And about how I may be incredibly rich."

Gwen got off Charlie. He could not stop himself from watching her backside as she bent over to open the wine and then pour them each a glass. He could see her outline through the thin fabric and thought he was annoying himself by being so focused on the wrong thing.

With a glass of wine each, Charlie began at the beginning with the tale of his run to The Institute.

"Everyone around here gets super-serious whenever The Institute comes up," said Gwen. "Hey, have you ever noticed how, when you say the name of that place, the 'The" is always capitalized?"

"No kidding. Do you know what kind of work they do there? I know my father is an expert on DNA, but that's all I understand."

"To be honest, I've never been interested enough to ask. It's there. I'm not allowed to go near the place. El seems to be in charge or think he is. People who work there shut up about it if someone gets near."

Next, Charlie told her about the problems he had and obstacles he faced when he tried to research the history of Coverdale."

"I'm starting to feel really dumb, Charlie. I've always accepted what they teach at school about the town, which isn't that much. I've not been curious at all. Coverdale is where I live. It's there and that's all I know."

"Don't say that. You're not dumb. Have you been to the city?"

Gwen laughed. "Of course I have, silly. All the time. Well, when Grampa says I can go. And then it's always with an escort because it's dangerous out there. The escort follows me no matter where I go."

"Haven't you ever tried to get away? Ask questions?"

She shook her head. "Not until you came along. I'm expected to be part of the community, Charlie. It builds character and makes you a better citizen. You must join in."

Charlie's jaw dropped. "Did you hear what you just said?" She shrugged. "It's exactly the same as what all the kids say. Be part of the team, build character, better citizen, must join in. You've all been brainwashed."

She glared at him. "That's insulting, Charlie. The people in this town are not evil. They're not bad guys, except maybe for El. You make it sound like we're all a bunch of robots. This isn't a cult."

Knowing he had made an epic mistake and spoken thoughtlessly, he tried to think of a way to make it right. The last thing he wanted was to push Gwen away, now that they were definitely together. But what could he say?

"I'm sorry, Gwen. I wasn't thinking straight. It scares me that some of the bad shit I've seen may affect you. I don't want that."

"This is my life you're upsetting, Charlie. I've lived here all my life. Coverdale is all that I know. Just because we all think the same way about our community doesn't mean we've been brainwashed. That's ridiculous. No one is trying to control us."

"Do you use the post office?"

"I get letters all the time."

"From outside of Coverdale?"

"No. It's always from the school or church. I get a lot of birthday cards. From all over the world."

"Relatives?"

She paused to think. "You know, I don't know any of them. It's almost as if they're sending them because of Grandpa. He's always mentioned in them."

"How's your internet access?"

"Not a problem. I can connect whenever I want and go wherever I want."

"Where can you do it?"

"Here. Only here. The connections at the school and library suck. Other people are on them all the time, so I don't bother trying anymore."

"No hassles?"

Her face turned red. "Grandpa did give me a talking to that one time I searched for ... then watched a couple of ... that's where I ... I didn't do it again. I wanted to, but he was really mad."

"I wonder who told him."

"You think El?"

"Who else? Ever see any tourists? Strangers? Out of towners?"

She shook her head. "Never bothered to look."

"What about your religion? There are no other churches in Coverdale. No other religions. Yours seems a little weird although, because I'm an atheist, all religions seem weird."

"I don't know much about it, Charlie. You saw the way we were excluded today. Yesterday, at the fair, no one under nineteen was included."

"No prayers? Hymns? What's that cross in the circle mean?"

"Maybe, I don't know. Probably because I've heard singing from the church. It's something from the old country. It goes way back."

"What old country? How far back?"

"I don't know. Somewhere in Eastern Europe. I've been told that when we get old enough, we learn the true history of our people."

"Your people?"

"Yes. Those of us of the blood. That's what the symbol means. True blood."

"This is getting weirder by the minute. True blood?" Charlie didn't move. Something forced its way to the front of his mind. "Holy shit. True blood. *Sang real*. The Holy Grail? Templars. No way."

"What are you talking about? Templars? They're knights from the Crusades. The Holy Grail is a myth. King Arthur and the Knights of the Round Table. Anyway, I've overheard Grandpa talking about thousands of years back, the passing of millennia. Longer."

"There's something I have to show you." Charlie reached into his pocket and pulled out some coins from his stash. He held them out to Gwen.

When she looked closely, she gasped. Her face went white.

"Where did you get these?"

"Found them."

"Where?"

"Why?"

"There's a local legend. The Fallen King's treasure. It says that the first people to settle here had a rebel known only as the Fallen King. He had a treasure that belonged to the people, but he hid it away. There's part of the legend that says it was his own treasure and that greedy people wanted to steal it. They tortured him, but he wouldn't tell."

"When is this supposed to have happened?"

"What do you know, Charlie? The coins?"

"I found an old box in my backyard. It was full of coins like that. Thousands of them. They're all at least two thousand years old. Some are a thousand years older. I checked some, and the stash is probably worth millions."

Gwen stood and rushed over to him. She threw her arms around his neck. "Charlie, promise me, no one else knows about this."

"I may have shown Jimmy some of the coins. I trust him."

"Me, too. Where are they?"

"Hidden. I found an alcove in my closet. They're in there with some old weapons."

"A sword, a mace, and a musket?"

"What the hell? How did you know? Did Mr. Tyndale tell you?"

"Another legend, newer." She stepped away, stared at the floor, and then up at Charlie. "Promise me. Nothing that we said or did since I brought you here is ever mentioned again. To anyone. Ever."

"Why, Gwen? What's the big deal?"

"Promise me, Charlie."

"Not until you explain."

"The dome above the hall in the house. You saw it? There's writing around the base. It's hidden behind tapestries. They're anchored to the wall and the dome so no one can look behind them."

"You did?"

She nodded. "When I was about twelve. I was curious. It's in Latin."

"Yeah, about that. If, as Mr. Taverner says, the Romans are totally evil, why is your Grandfather's title Latin? Why would anything be Latin?"

"It doesn't matter. Charlie, the writing. It says that whoever carries a sword, mace, and musket will reveal the truth and end the people. And look." She held up her wrist to show him her charm bracelet. One by one, she pointed out a sword, a mace, a musket, and a circle with a cross.

"Oh, shit."

"Yeah, shit. Not a word, Charlie. Okay? Forget everything we talked about."

"Everything? Even ..."

"No, don't be ridiculous. You can remember ... dwell on it ... let it be the only thing you take away from here. But nothing else."

"Right, because I can't get it ... out of my head. But I'm still going to look for answers. I won't mention anything about the legends."

"Good, because I'm not ready to die yet. We haven't even ... you know ..."

Chapter Seventeen

Charlie yawned. He'd not been able to sleep last night at all.

After their talk in Gwen's secret hideaway, they had returned to the house unsure whether or not they had been missed in the last three hours. She hadn't planned on them being away that long, but the talk and everything else had been so wonderful that neither of them wanted it to end. Back at the house, Gwen used a peephole near the alcove door to see if anyone was in the hall. It had been clear, and they'd hurried out and then up to the music room. They planned to tell anyone who asked that they'd been out on the grounds walking and then in the room listening to albums.

An hour later, when no one had interrupted them, Charlie had reluctantly suggested he head home. The last thing he wanted was to overstay his welcome. And to be honest, it had been getting increasingly difficult to resist Gwen. It had seemed that everything she had said was a double entendre, or that's how Charlie decided to interpret it. She had played along, teasing him and tickling him to no end.

At the front door, they had both expressed relief that the subject of *that* was out of the way. Now they could play it slow and let things happen as they evolved rather than rushing into things.

On the long walk home—Charlie needed the time to clear his head and decide what, if anything, he would tell his parents—he had wondered if he had made a mistake. Gwen had been there and willing. He had scolded himself for almost becoming like some of those guys at his old school. They were always going on about how many times they'd gotten laid and which girls were easy. Charlie never liked their talk, especially when they directed their attention at a girl he knew to be nothing like they hinted at. No, he and Gwen had made the right and proper decision.

But, damn!

The family had been nowhere to be seen when he got home, so he rushed up to his room as quietly as possible. He had decided he would provide as few details as possible about the evening.

Sleep hadn't come. All he could think about was seeing Gwen again tomorrow at school. There was to be another party, this time to celebrate the boys who had recently turned nineteen.

At breakfast this morning, when he had asked his parents how the service went on Thursday, they smiled and said it was fine. Charlie's parents had never taken him to church when they lived in the city, and he wanted to find out why they had taken this sudden interest in religion.

"We're getting old," his mother had replied. "It's comforting, and you feel a real sense of community at church."

Charlie's father had muttered something about everyone at The Institute being a member of the church. It was good for his job to belong.

Charlie wondered again about his father. George Bowen had always worked hard at his old job in some box-like warehouse of a lab in the city, but now he was hardly ever home. He'd heard him coming in after midnight several times over the last few weeks. On at least one occasion that Charlie knew of, his father stayed the night at The Institute. His attitude towards his son had changed even more drastically. Charlie could do nothing right, at least, until yesterday when Gwen showed up.

Charlie's mom didn't seem to notice the change in her husband. She spent all her time in her former studio reading seed catalogs and gardening magazines.

That brought up another curious point. How did his mom get her mail? Charlie had gone to the postal outlet at the Town Hall to check a postal code. The clerk had refused to give Charlie the code book, insisting on checking the code for him. When Charlie asked for the code of an address in Coverdale, Gwen's, he was told he didn't need one: just drop the letter in the box, and it would be delivered. Rather than give rise to suspicions, Charlie commented on how nice it was to live in a small town where you didn't need to worry about such things as postal codes. The clerk had seemed happy with that. When he asked her last night, Gwen hadn't been any help answering questions.

On his way to the school earlier, Charlie had been surprised to see his father drive past with Ant in the car. They didn't stop to offer him a ride. He had a few choice thoughts for them, but in the end he would rather walk anyway.

When he got to the school for the party, he was even more surprised to see Ant in the gym dancing with some older boy. There were lots of couples on the dance floor.

"Had a rough night?"

"What?" Charlie shook the sleepiness out of his head and answered Jimmy. "Restless. Aching muscles. Too much going on in my head."

"So, what exactly did you get up to last night?"

Hoping Jimmy would drop it, Charlie said, "They sure do make a fuss." Cameras flashed. Jimmy's brother, Stan, and several other boys who had turned nineteen were the guests of honor. They were grouped by the stage, having their pictures taken by a reporter from the local paper.

"In Coverdale, turning nineteen is a big deal," said Jimmy. "It means you're a man."

"I bet you'll be relieved when it's your turn," said Gwen.

Jimmy looked shocked by her comment and only replied with a "harrumph."

Charlie sat with Gwen and Jimmy in the front row of the balcony. There was plenty of room downstairs. Two sets of bleachers had been pulled open along the wall below them, but Charlie wanted a little privacy.

Down below, a deejay announced another droning dance tune by a band Charlie didn't recognize. Dancers crowded the center of the gym, another reason to be in the balcony. Charlie was terrified that Gwen would want to dance. Being over six feet tall, Charlie felt like a giant on the dance floor. Being uncoordinated didn't help, either. He couldn't follow the beat of the dance music, and those tunes he might be able to dance to were never played by the deejays.

Ant still danced, now with Jimmy's brother, Stan. It seemed odd.

"So why isn't there a Brotherhood of the Temple for the guys in town?" Charlie asked Gwen and Jimmy.

Jimmy shrugged. "Dunno. Never given it any thought. The guys are usually too busy doing sports to do anything else."

"Can you imagine this guy babysitting?" Gwen reached across Charlie and patted Jimmy's leg. "He'd scare the little kids with that mad grin of his."

"Yeah, besides, he's so short, they'd think he's an elf."

"Hey, anyone would look short next to stretch Bowen."

"Don't forget stretch Blayney here, elf"

"I thought you were supposed to be my friend, Charlie. I see the zit between your eyes has cleared up. What's that on your upper lip?"

Charlie's hand went to the tender spot.

"Look," said Charlie, leaning forward, "there's something weird about this town. Surely you've noticed."

Both Gwen and Jimmy shook their heads. He was relieved when Gwen winked. He had promised to keep quiet about a lot of the mysteries they had discussed last night, but he had told her he would still ask questions. He'd tread carefully.

"I can't find the place on any map, and it's not mentioned in any books or newspapers. The old bat at the library won't let me look at the back issues of the local paper. I've tried a couple of times, and she keeps making new excuses."

"Maybe you're not looking in the right places," suggested Jimmy.

"I know how to look something up at the library. Could be I just need to check a bigger library, possibly at the university in the city." Charlie leaned back and rubbed his eyes. "It's not just the books and the library," he said. "What about the church? It's the only one. Everyone goes, and it looks like the tramps run things. You're not allowed in until you're nineteen. What kind of religion is that?"

"Seems fine to me," said Gwen. Her nostrils flared. He knew he was on sensitive ground.

Jimmy's face remained impassive.

"I thought I saw the Standishes in the church last week. During the service."

"How?" asked Jimmy, a little more interested now.

"I climbed the ivy and looked in. They looked like they were tied up."

"You're crazy, man. They died in the fire. We were there when they brought out the bodies. Remember?"

"And do you remember what I said at the time, Jimmy? The body bags looked empty."

"Charlie," said Gwen, placing a hand on his arm, "there'd have to be a pretty big conspiracy if the Standishes didn't die. All those firemen, the police. Why would they bother?"

"That's what I want to find out. Some kind of coverup? Maybe not everyone in town is in on it? I don't know. But I saw El there and he looked like he was in charge of things. Gwen, have you heard anything strange at your grandfather's place?"

Gwen shook her head, "No, but then again, I haven't really paid attention." He felt a sharp pain in his side. Looking down, he saw that Gwen was pushing her fingers into him. When he looked up, he thought she was going to rip his head off. He'd gone too far.

"Jimmy, could you get us some sodas, please?" Gwen passed him some bills. "And some Milk Duds if they've got them."

"Sure," said Jimmy. He gave them both the stink eye, and Charlie guessed that his friend knew they wanted some alone time.

When Jimmy was at the far end of the balcony near the stairs, Gwen said, "Charlie! What the hell? I thought we agreed. If this is you keeping your promise, I ..." A tear slid down her cheek.

"Damn it," said Charlie. He took out a handkerchief and passed it to her. "Gwen, I'm sorry. As soon as I asked, I knew I'd screwed up. But I don't think Jimmy caught on."

"I know." She wiped her eyes. He wanted to put his arms around her, hold her tightly, and never let her go. "Just be more careful, okay? I don't want to lie in front of Jimmy. He's our friend. But ..."

"You're not entirely sure we can trust him?"

"Am I a terrible person for thinking that? Charlie, after the sword thing, I'm so scared."

"Look, Gwen, I'm still new here. It's strange, but I don't feel too threatened. I can't imagine what you're going through. I show up and turn your world upside down, asking questions and finding stuff that shouldn't be found. I'm accusing your grandfather of nasty things. I almost took advantage of you last night." He sighed. "I just realized. I'm ruining your life. Shit."

She squeezed his hand. "Charlie. Get stuffed. You're not ruining anything. I needed to know about this. I'm sort of on the inside. I can help you and maybe protect you. We need to be very careful, that's all. Besides," she glanced over at the stairs, then slid her hand over his thigh, smiling when she felt him, "I want you to ..." She put her mouth to his ear and said something he never, ever thought he would hear a girl say to him.

Charlie took her hand and reluctantly moved it away. "Gwen, you're the only girl ... woman I want. When the time is right, I'm going to ..."

"Propose?"

He laughed. "At least you changed the subject. But, yes, propose. We're too young, don't know enough, can't support ourselves unless that stash is worth something, and, most of all, have only known each other for a month."

"Do it."

"What?"

"Do it. Now, before Jimmy gets back. We'll be the only ones who know."

Charlie looked around. They were alone in the balcony. He could see Jimmy downstairs at the refreshments table. Everyone else downstairs was too busy dancing or getting their picture taken. He slid off the bench onto one knee. Taking Gwen's right hand in his, he said, "Gwen Blayney, will you do me the honor of marrying me whenever we get things sorted out?"

"Yes, Charlie, I'll marry you. Now get up, Jimmy's heading for the stairs."

He kissed her hand and resumed sitting. "I don't have a ring."

"Your word is good enough for me."

"Damn, Gwen, you're wonderful."

"Hey. Lovebirds, here's your drinks. No Milk Duds, but I got popcorn."

"That's good enough for me, elf," said Gwen.

Jimmy sat staring across the gym as if deep in thought. Charlie and Gwen let him be, enjoying each other's company.

After staring for five minutes, Jimmy said, "Guys, you're my best friends. I need to tell you something. It's important and secret."

"Sure, Jimmy, you can trust us." Charlie felt like a hypocrite the moment he said it.

"Go ahead, Jimmy," said Gwen.

"It's about the thing that El said he helped me with. He didn't help me. He caught me looking at something I shouldn't have. The weasel acted like he was sympathetic, but he was messing with my head, making me think I had done something wrong. That *I* was something wrong."

Charlie guessed what his friend was about to say. "Ant was a smokescreen?"

Jimmy nodded. "Have to keep up appearances, you know.

El thinks I'm over it. He forced me to ... According to him, it was supposed to prove to me that I didn't really think that way and that it was disgusting. Well, it was disgusting and I threw up. I told him it was horrible and I would never, ever do it again. It's true, but only because it was him. He's gross. Let him think I've changed. I haven't. It's not something you get over. It's me, so screw him."

Gwen got up and sat on Jimmy's other side so he was flanked by his two friends. She held his hand. "Jimmy, how old were you?"

He looked at her, then at the floor. "Fifteen."

"I'm taking him down," said Charlie. "I don't know how. Or when, but I'm going to do it. And Jimmy, it doesn't make any difference to me what you are or how you feel. You're still my friend."

"The same goes for me," said Gwen.

Jimmy had tears in his eyes. "Thanks, guys, for sticking by me. I needed to tell someone. It's so damned difficult. I mean, Charlie's got such a fine bum."

"Back off, elf," said Gwen. "Charlie and I are engaged. He's all mine."

That nearly made Charlie fall off the bench. Jimmy looked from one to the other.

"Well, this is a hell of a day. So much for those clowns down there who turned nineteen. My two best friends are engaged, and I came out. You know that's what I meant, right?"

"You ain't heard nothin' yet, elf," said Gwen. She looked over at Charlie, who nodded. "We've got so much to tell you."

"But not here, not yet. I still have some things to sort out."

"For now, act normally, elf," said Gwen. "That is, if you know how. Damn, that doesn't sound right anymore."

"It's okay, you freakish giant lady. Business as usual until you're ready to spill."

"Should we do the 'all for one and one for all' thing?"

Gwen and Jimmy both shook their heads.

"Well, well, look who's here." Jimmy leaned against the balcony rail. He pointed towards the stage where the birthday boys were still having their pictures taken, now with their parents.

Mayor Mundy and several town councilors had arrived. They were all dressed in ceremonial robes, each adorned with the circle and cross symbol. Charlie still thought they looked like the KKK.

They went straight to the stage, and the Mayor addressed the group. After some handshakes, the birthday celebrants were led out of the gym.

"Where do you suppose they're going?" asked Charlie.

"It happens whenever there's a birthday party," said Gwen. The deejay packed up his equipment. "It usually means the party is over," she added, stating the obvious.

The three got up and moved to the balcony stairs. Charlie looked out a window there in time to see the Mayor and his party get into several cars parked in front of the school. Once everyone was in, the cars sped off towards the Loop.

The Institute?

Charlie paused for a moment.

He could have sworn he saw Chief Wycliffe sitting in one of the cars. There was nothing unusual in that, except that the Chief looked like he was dressed all in silver and had a white sheet draped over him. A knight?

What next, wondered Charlie. He followed Gwen and Jimmy down the stairs.

Interlude Three
103 CE

With a hand encased in a heavy leather glove, the silent one brought the glowing sword, fresh from the hot coals, closer to the Fallen King's left thigh. Ever so slowly, he ran it along the bound man's leg, keeping the blade about an inch from his skin. The Fallen King tried to flinch back, but he was bound securely to the blood cross. All he could do was throw back his head and try to howl. The hair on his leg sizzled as the blade passed over it. With the gentlest of movements, the silent one touched the sword to the inside of the Fallen King's right thigh and stabbed.

The skin sizzled, and the wound instantly cauterized. He'd lost count of how many cuts he'd endured.

The Fallen King tried to scream in agony, but his throat was raw, and all that came out was a pathetic whimper. He had resisted answering his inquisitors' questions for hours.

"Where?"

The sword touched the Fallen King's thigh again. He croaked out his pain.

"Where?"

Still, the bound man refused to answer.

Instead, he tried to remember.

He had a name, back before his people had revolted and moved. What was it? The new King had him beaten severely so he would know his new place within the People. Henceforth, he was to be the Fallen King, no longer ... no longer what? Who? The new King, now called Rex Mundi, had allowed the Fallen King to live as an example to the People. This is the fate of those who would rebel against the will of the majority. This is also a sign of the mercy of the People and their new king. The new king had the best interests of the People at heart. He also guarded the secrets of their past and forbade the intermingling with the hated Romans that ... who was he? He had welcomed the Romans and cooperated with them when their legions bore down on the People's ancient capital city in the valley. The Romans provided security, stability, and a sure future for the People. A future endangered by the encroachment of low bloods from the east.

He was Luca! He had been Luca, Rex Populo, King of the People, Guardian of the Sacred Bloodline, leader of the Council. Luca, who was forward-thinking enough to know that the Romans were saviors, not conquerors. The Romans had even adopted their language centuries ago, though they did not realize it and claimed it as their own. Working together, the People and the Romans could have ruled forever. The Romans, once they had served their purpose, of course would become subjugated to the People, for no one could be allowed to rule but the Rex Populo.

But the majority of the Council had resisted Luca's will. They feared the tainting of the blood and knew it would happen no matter how cautious they might be. The hated Romans were to be resisted, not trusted.

He was Luca, and he remembered yesterday.

The sun had beaten down mercilessly, forcing Luca to stop. Sweat poured freely down his chubby face, and his white tunic was drenched. He leaned against a tree to rest for a while, breathing hard in the midday heat. He longed for the cool breezes of home.

Home.

Home that was now a part of the Roman Empire, despite what the Council decreed.

Luca was not happy with his current situation. Since arriving in this cursed place, he had voiced his concerns to the Council many times. He was permitted to be there because of the respect some still held for his previous position as Rex Populo. However, he had been shouted down by his enemies. By Rex Mundi.

What was so bad about Rome? he had asked. Surely, it was better than this new place of horrors. What did it matter that an offshoot of the People had settled here several thousand years ago? That colony had not survived the harsh conditions. What made the Council think things were any different now?

Yet the Council voted against Luca and his dwindling supporters again and again. This was their new home. Though it was thousands of miles from the homeland, it was safe, and the People could work towards reclaiming it from the Romans. The mongrel empire, hardly worthy of the title, would be defeated. The People would regain their homeland. The Scared Bloodline would remain untainted.

Luca remembered with disgust the final Council meeting the night before. Rex Mundi had been particularly threatening. The Fallen King lived at the whim of the People, and the People were becoming weary of the Fallen King's persistent complaints.

Rested a little after the strain of his task, Luca resumed walking.

To maintain secrecy, Luca was forced to do all his work himself, all the harder since he had adopted Roman practices, thus letting himself become overweight and unhealthy.

But at least today, the task was done. His future would be secure once the galley was fully prepared and provisioned. Luca thought about the ocean-going galley lying in wait at the river's bend. She was a beautiful ship, made sturdy for long voyages. She had been like a second home on the voyage eight years ago. Luca had made sure his cabin was luxurious and that he would want for nothing during the journey. If the others had suffered hardship, well, it was their fault for not being as prepared as he had been. He may have been a deposed king, but he had been permitted to retain his wealth.

Rex Mundi had ordered the destruction of their fleet, sure that the People would never leave their new home. Luca had different ideas and had been able to hide his galley in a bay downstream. The face of the Blood-mother watched for danger in the sea ahead while the oarsmen rowed, although the Romans that built her claimed the figurehead represented Juno, a false goddess to the People. Yes, she was a good ship and would soon take Luca back home.

Fools, all of them.

They had learned the wrong lesson from the Jewish revolt. The Romans had crushed the rebels mercilessly. And if what they said about Masada was true, then death was the only outcome for anyone who opposed the might of the Empire.

Death or exile to a hostile land across the vast seas.

The Council had decided to flee. Their forces were weak

and could not continue the fight against the Roman legions. It had been decided that it would be best to hide for a time and build strength. When their might was restored, when the People were ready, they could battle and defeat the legions.

Fools and cowards.

According to Luca and those intelligent enough to listen to him, the revolt taught that it was best to assimilate. Join Rome. Enjoy the benefits and security a strong Empire offered. Enjoy life.

Enjoy life.

That's certainly what Luca expected to do once his plans came to fruition.

A sudden sound to his left had made Luca miss a step, and he had fallen face-first onto a patch of swampy ground. His already dirtied tunic had been torn, and now it had become fouled with evil-smelling swamp mud. Pulling himself to his feet, Luca wiped the stinking muck from his face and again cursed the Council for bringing him to such a place. Carefully, he had picked his way out of the swampy area and found dry land again.

Servants should be doing this work, not one as high-born as Luca. Not the rightful Rex Populo.

Watching where he stepped to avoid further mishaps, Luca had walked out of the woods and onto the riverbank. From far away, he had heard the workmen felling trees and erecting buildings. Scouts had found a good source of granite, and proper homes would be built once it had been quarried.

Proper homes were on the Dalmatian coast, Luca had thought just as he noticed the sword thrust at his substantial belly.

Luca had stopped quickly and stared into the unmoving faceplate of the silent one. Without a sound, more of the silent ones emerged from the trees and surrounded him.

None of them were his friends or supporters.

The Council tried to convince the Fallen King that it would be in the community's best interest for him to cooperate. When he refused to speak, the Council made threats, promising dire consequences if he remained obstinate. Still, the Fallen King stayed silent.

The torture had started this morning.

The Fallen King was bound to the back of the blood cross erected on the riverbank where the road from the temple ended. Symbolically, the Fallen King was faced to the west, faced away from his homeland. The Council and the community were arrayed in front of him. They faced the homeland beyond the traitor.

The priests intoned their prayers.

The whole community gathered to watch the punishment of the Fallen King. It was their custom. The community worked for the benefit of all its members, and all its members were expected to work for the benefit of the community. It had been thus since time immemorial.

It was the way of the People.

The first cut had been made as the sun rose over the eastern hills.

Though he was fat and lazy, Luca did not lack personal courage. He had kept silent through most of the morning.

Soon he could no longer remain silent.

He let his mind drift to his villa on the Dalmatian coast.

Fine wines made from the grapes of his own vineyards were brought to him by servants. Fresh fruit from his orchards was piled high on gold platters. Sweetmeats dripping with honey were stacked within easy reach. Spiced meats and bread, freshly cooked in his own kitchens, were brought out regularly so they were always warm and aromatic.

Then Luca imagined himself reclining on soft cushions, gorging on the food around him. His wife was there, ready to do his bidding. And the four children were also there, being tutored by the Greek slave. The sky above was brilliant blue, and cool sea breezes blew off the Mare Adriaticum, cooling him as the sun burned down from above.

Only now, it was not the sun burning his flesh but the sharp blade of a sword.

Luca tried to scream once more. His raw throat and swollen tongue would not permit it.

"Where? Where? Where?"

He wondered if they would ever cease asking their questions. His mind began to leave his broken and blistered body.

The hot blade kissed his body again and again, but Luca was beyond pain now.

He had returned to his villa. His family was there waiting for him, not sprawled before him, their throats cut, sacred blood oozing into the sand.

He could feel the sun beating down on his brow, soothing him.

Luca was no longer there when the community began to stone him.

Luca was no longer the Fallen King.

Chapter Eighteen

Late Wednesday afternoon, Charlie and Jimmy walked home from practice. Charlie had earned the distinction of being the first Coverdale High student to be tossed off a sports team. However, he had signed up for another team. He had been able to convince the coach to let him sign up early, very early, because he was so good at distance running. The coach had timed Charlie on the half-mile, mile, and five-mile runs, and he had registered excellent times. Charlie was presently the only member of the Coverdale High track team.

"I haven't seen your brother Stan around since the party Saturday night," said Charlie between sucks at the milkshake he had just picked up at the diner. "Did the Mayor and his crowd get him drunk or something?"

Jimmy stuffed some fries in his mouth, chewed them quickly, and said, "I wish it was that simple. I don't know, Charlie, Stan's been acting weird. See for yourself."

He pointed when his brother came around the corner of the library. Stan walked slowly but steadily, staring straight ahead, arms hanging limply at his sides. Charlie and Jimmy stopped on the sidewalk to wait for Stan to reach them. He did but passed them as if he hadn't seen them. It looked to Charlie as if Stan was muttering something to himself, his lips had been moving slightly, but no sound was audible.

Stan stopped at the intersection, didn't bother to check for traffic, not that there was any, and crossed over to the park.

Charlie and Jimmy watched him go through the park, then disappear behind the church.

"See what I mean," said Jimmy. "I'm worried about him. Last night, Dad announced that Stan had changed his mind about university. He's not going to California anymore. Stan's going to the military school that's close to the U. of North Mass."

"What? You're kidding." Charlie couldn't believe it. "No one goes to military school anymore except guys with no necks who can't get football scholarships."

"I kid you not. Lots of the guys from Coverdale end up there. And not just the jocks. Rumor has it they train ninjas. When Dad made the announcement at the dinner table, Stan just sat there. I thought he was going to start drooling. He looked so out of it."

They passed the library, and Charlie happened to look up in time to see the old bat frowning down at him from a second-floor window. She made Charlie shiver.

"God, she should just sit on the roof and be a gargoyle, the ugly old ..."

"Take it easy. Ignore her." Jimmy held onto his friend's shoulder. Charlie felt the tension in his muscles.

"It makes me mad. What in the name of Melvin has she got against me?" Charlie stopped walking and stared back at the librarian. "I ought to ..." He tried to raise his hand, but Jimmy held it down.

"Don't. Whatever you do, don't flip her the bird. It'll only make things worse."

He looked down at Jimmy. "How could she make it any worse? Ban me from the library?"

"She's the Chief's aunt."

"Ye cods."

Charlie stepped back to the curb and bowed graciously to the woman still watching from the window. The side of her mouth wavered ever so slightly, almost creating a grin, and then she backed away from the window. Charlie blew her a kiss.

"Think of it this way, Charlie. She's old. She'll be dead long before you."

He was surprised. "You do have a mean streak in you, elf. I'll make sure I'm nice to you from now on."

"Just tell me what you want me to do."

They walked again.

"You're right. There is something strange about this place. There's no way my brother would have changed his mind about university. He was so excited. He'd already started buying books for his courses. He'd even been corresponding with a professor in California about what he could work on."

"How'd he get the letters?" asked Charlie. He worked over what Jimmy had just told him. "Didn't your parents notice them?"

"He got a post office box in the city last year. He wanted to surprise my folks with his preparations."

Jimmy crumpled up his french fry container and threw it to the ground. He thought momentarily, then picked it up and stuffed it in his knapsack. "Don't want to get nailed for littering."

They walked on.

"So, what *do* you want me to do?"

Charlie thought about it and couldn't come up with anything. "I don't have a definite plan right now. It's all sort of floating around in my head ..."

"Like the grease on the top of a pot of chicken soup?" said

Jimmy.

"Uh, yeah. Look, give me a couple of days to sort things out. I'll come up with a plan."

"A cunning one, I hope."

"For sure."

"By the way, who's Melvin? And ye cods?"

Charlie felt momentary confusion and then realized what Jimmy meant. "I try not to swear, so I substitute silly names and old expressions instead. Since I'm an atheist, I say cods instead of gods."

Jimmy favored Charlie with a blank look. Charlie hitched his shoulders.

"But I heard you swear. You say the F-word and the S-word."

"Yeah, well, it's El. He brings out the worst in me."

"He is an A-word," said Jimmy.

They parted at the corner and went to their respective homes.

Charlie stopped dead when he walked into the house and saw his father sitting in the recliner. George Bowen was hardly ever home now. His work at The Institute had apparently taken an unusual direction that required everyone to work overtime.

To Charlie, it felt like all the time. It wasn't such a bad thing.

His father mumbled something unintelligible at Charlie and got up. He hadn't shaved for a few days, and Charlie could smell sweat. It wasn't like his father to let himself go like this.

"I hear you've joined the track team. Good. Make you a better citizen, part of the team."

Not sure how to respond, Charlie replied, "Er, yes, sir, it's what I'm good at. Might as well use my assets for the benefit of the town."

His father smiled. "Excellent, my boy, excellent." His face abruptly went grim. He waved a finger in Charlie's face. "You watch it with that Blayney girl. Don't try anything funny."

Charlie backed away, annoyed by his father's implication. Whatever he and Gwen may have almost done on Saturday, it was none of his father's business. With a steady but emotionless voice, Charlie said, "I treat her properly. The way *you* taught me. You have nothing to worry about there, *sir*." He hoped this last little barb would get through to his father. They had always had a close relationship, and Charlie was deeply hurt that, in addition to all the other accusations, his father could possibly think he would do anything wrong with a girl.

His father didn't seem to notice the tone of Charlie's words. "Good, good. You just keep it that way. I don't need the trouble at work if you start getting too handy. Besides, if things go well between the two of you, my position at The Institute is sure to improve." He walked to the front door and took his coat off the hook where it was hanging. "I've got to get back to work."

Of all the nerve, thought Charlie. Viewing his relationship with Gwen as a stepping stone to a higher position at his job. Tempted as he was to tell his father to get stuffed, he said, "Work going well, sir?"

His father's eyes popped open and his cheeks turned red. "You keep your nose out of my business! What I do at The Institute is absolutely no concern of yours. Got it?"

George Bowen stormed out of the house without waiting for Charlie's reply. Charlie heard the tires screech when the car sped out of the driveway and down the street.

Charlie wanted to kick himself for opening his mouth and provoking his father, though he hadn't expected such a dramatic response. For the moment, he couldn't find it in himself to care.

Ant bounced down the stairs, gave Charlie a stony look, and left the house. Charlie heard his mother singing in her studio, probably doing more planning for the garden.

He walked into the kitchen. A note on the fridge told him that there was a frozen dinner in the freezer.

"What's happening to this family?" Charlie asked as he removed the dinner from its cardboard box. Frozen dinners. His mom never used to miss making a meal. She had always enjoyed cooking and could have been a chef if she wasn't such a good artist. Plus, she was right there and could have told him in person.

"Everything okay out there?" His mother's voice drifted into the kitchen above the hum of the microwave.

Charlie tried to sound pleasant, but it was difficult. He felt like he had just been thrown out of the family for no good reason. "Fine, Mom," he said without conviction. He wanted to cry.

The frozen dinner was tasteless. But he'd been working over the problems in his head.

It had to be The Institute.

Everything seemed to point in that direction, and no place out in the sticks like this needed *that* much security.

Charlie changed into his running gear and added an accessory he never usually carried: a belly bag. He didn't like to run with things hanging from him, except for his Walkman. He never carried water with him or had any bag bouncing against his stomach or back. This time, however, he made an exception. From his desk, he retrieved a small notebook and pencil, a pen-light, and a pair of opera glasses that he used to use at concerts. They fit easily into the belly bag and didn't weigh too much.

He slipped out the back door, dashed across the yard, and into the woods that separated his backyard from the Loop. He ran slowly along the road until it started curving east towards the Mundy estate and The Institute. Crossing the road, he ran slowly along the verge, keeping his attention focused on the woods to his left.

Then he saw what he was looking for.

A trail.

He checked quickly to see if any cars were coming, then ran into the woods and followed the trail.

Charlie had an excellent sense of direction and could easily picture where he was in relation to the road. The trail paralleled the road for a few hundred yards, then branched north into the hills. When the trail crested one of these hills, Charlie found himself in a small clearing. Directly below him, he saw the Mundy estate. He tried to spot Gwen, knowing the chances were slim that she would happen to be outside when he happened to be running by. But he was in love, and anything, no matter how ridiculous, was possible.

They'd kept a low profile at school, not wanting to draw too much attention to themselves. When the rest of the students found out that Charlie and Gwen were an item, all eyes would be on them and they'd never have a moment's privacy. And privacy was something they desperately needed right now.

He quietly laughed when he remembered the stairs. For the first time in ages, his ears didn't burn with embarrassment. He had confessed his love to his last girlfriend—maybe that was too strong a word. He liked her. She let him take her places and pay. That hardly counts as a girlfriend. They had been standing at the bottom of a flight of stairs that led up to her parents' apartment. When Charlie had spoken the magic words and laughed so hard, she actually sent a gob of spit flying into his eye. He had never spoken to her again or gone out with another girl since.

Until Gwen.

He started running again.

The trail dipped down behind the Mundy estate, then curved around another hill. He guessed that the Institute should be pretty close and was startled when a chain link fence suddenly appeared behind some trees.

The fence was in the middle of the woods, where one didn't belong. Charlie couldn't see the span of lawn surrounding The Institute's buildings. He slowly walked along the trail, following the course of the fence. When he approached a corner, where it turned to the east, something caught his eye.

A flashing red light in the undergrowth.

Trying not to look straight at the light because that seemed to make it harder to see, Charlie moved closer to the source of the flashing.

It was at the base of a maple, under some ferns.

A round black object made of plastic that looked a bit like a light fixture was pointed at the trail. The flashing came from a tiny red light at the object's base. Charlie tried to remember where he had seen something similar.

Then it hit him.

The security lights outside their house in the city. The motion sensor below the flood lamps.

Charlie stumbled back across the trail into the bushes on the other side. The ground gave way beneath him, and he rolled down a steep incline, coming to a hard stop against a fallen tree.

He was in a narrow cut between the hills. At its bottom, a small stream babbled along. He brushed leaves and mud from himself, then heard voices from the trail above. He dove over the fallen tree and hid on the other side. Through a slit between the trunk and the ground, he could see the top of the slope.

Two men in uniform appeared.

Institute guards. With machine guns.

"The detectors indicated something came this way," said one of the guards.

"There's no sign of anything now. It could have been a fox or a deer," said the second guard. "Those sensors are pretty sensitive. A mosquito fart could set them off."

"Yeah," said the first guard.

Charlie thanked nothing in particular for the sunny weather the last few days. The trail had been dry, so he had left no tell-tale tracks.

The guards moved away.

He stayed hidden for at least ten minutes.

Not wanting to alert the guards again, he set out along the cut. The going was easy because the canopy of trees kept the undergrowth down there to a minimum.

After about fifteen minutes, Charlie saw a break in the trees. Moving cautiously to the top of the slope, he found that he was at the northeast corner of The Institute grounds. The trail he had followed earlier passed a few feet in front of him.

There, by the fence, was another motion detector.

Charlie slid back down the slope and continued along the cut. It curved to the southeast, heading towards the river.

Knowing that he wasn't too far from the stone circle

where he and Jimmy spent a lot of time talking and insulting each other, Charlie scrambled up the opposite side of the cut and ran through the woods. There was no trail, but it should not be too far.

He soon realized that he had missed the circle and doubled back to find it. He heard more voices ahead of him, cursed his bad luck, and swung back to the east.

He stopped running and leaned against a tree to catch his breath.

Silence.

Whoever had been in the woods hadn't heard him running.

A twig snapped to his left.

As quietly as he could, Charlie backed away from the sound. He wasn't paying enough attention to where he stepped and had time to think *not again* when the ground fell away beneath him.

This time there was no gentle slope. Charlie fell straight down into blackness. He landed on dirt, bounced, rolled, went over an edge, slid down gravel, landed on a flat area, but couldn't stop his roll and went over another edge. For a moment, he thought he might have fallen into a bottomless pit. At last, he landed in soft sand.

His whole body hurt. He'd bitten the inside of his lower lip and could taste the blood. Nothing seemed broken, though he was sure there would be scrapes and bruises. A lot of bruises. Feeling his nose to be certain, Charlie was relieved it wasn't damaged. He had a great fear of breaking his nose, perhaps because a kid at his last school had broken his nose at least three times. That kid's nose was huge, bent, and bumpy, and the other kids were heartless with their jibes.

Sitting in the darkness, Charlie cursed himself for being

careless. Nonetheless, he kept alert for more sounds.

There were none.

He fished the pen-light out of his belly bag. Luck for him, the bag hadn't been torn off in the journey into darkness.

The narrow beam revealed that he was in a cave. When he moved to stand up, his hand brushed against something hard on the ground next to him.

Charlie gasped when the pen-light beam settled on a Viking helmet sticking out of the sand. His backside clenched when he realized how close he had come to landing on the object. There weren't any horns, which was only a Hollywood myth, but they were sharp and rusted enough to have done serious damage.

Next to the helmet was a skeleton. It was a jumble of bones. A few feet further on lay a larger pile of bones, helmets, swords, and decayed clothing.

Where had he gotten himself? He shone the flashlight around and saw a couple of dark passages leading who knows where.

Charlie backed away from the remains and hit something hard, causing him to bite down on his damaged lip. He spat blood.

He turned and shone the light at it.

A large woman looked down at him, her once painted wooden face now a dull grey.

Charlie stared at the figurehead of a Roman galley.

Chapter Nineteen

Charlie stood in the dim light, staring at something that should not be there. After checking his head for wounds or bumps in case he had a concussion, there was only one conclusion that could be reached.

The bow of a Roman galley should not be sticking out of a cave wall on the outskirts of a small town, let alone in North America.

He put out a hand to touch the thing to make sure he wasn't seeing things. The wood felt real. There was still some trace of paint on the sides where eyes were usually located. The figurehead, a woman which Charlie found unusual, was grey. If it had any paint or pigment, that was long gone.

Why a woman? Some Roman goddess? Hera? No, she was Greek. Who was the wife of Jupiter? Juno! Could this be Juno or perhaps Minerva, Neptune's wife? She would make more sense for a ship. Maybe she was Cybele. His head was starting to hurt from trying to remember his Roman gods. Looking into her face, he could see she was exquisitely carved, so life-like, he expected her to breathe. Images from *Jason and the Argonauts* flashed through his mind.

"Get your act together, dummy. She's Roman, not Greek. I know. Since you're so lovely, I'll just call you Gwen."

He walked around to the port side, where it protruded from the wall. A couple of oars lay rotted and broken on the cave floor, their shafts sticking out of the cave wall. From their configuration, Charlie guessed this might be a bireme and was probably about one hundred and eighty feet long. His idea was confirmed when he checked the starboard side. The cave wall was further towards the stern here, though only by a few feet. But it was enough to show the two banks of holes where the oars came out of the hull. The deck was too high for him to get a look.

Charlie stepped back, stared at the galley, then said, "What the hell is a galley doing in Coverdale?"

As far-fetched as it seemed, could this be why Mr. Taverner was adamant that the Romans were bad guys in history class.

Ridiculous, yet here it was.

Charlie's head wanted to explode.

He remembered what else he had found. Turning back towards the hole he had fallen through, he shone his flashlight over the mass of Viking bones. Now, Vikings here made more sense. It was well-known that they had reached at least as far as Newfoundland and perhaps part-way into the interior. Charlie remembered seeing some old archaeology show that supposedly had a Viking sword found in the Midwest.

Vikings in Coverdale. What next? Egyptians? Ancient Chinese? Aliens?

Charlie counted the skulls in the pile. With the one he almost landed on, there were five. Hardly enough to man a longboat. A raiding party, perhaps? Scouts?

Letting out a long sigh, Charlie said, "No more mysteries, please. I've got enough on my plate."

Where exactly was he? He had been running away from The Institute – had passed by the circle of standing stones. How long had he been running? A few minutes? Ten? Usually, Charlie had an excellent sense of direction. But he'd fallen down the hole, bounced a few times—his ribs hurt from that—and possibly rolled when he hit the cave floor. He needed to get out and take his bearings.

There was a noise coming from his right. Charlie froze and waited. It was voices. He couldn't understand what they were saying; they were still far away, and the echo in the cave muddled their words.

He had to hide. Where?

Not daring to wave the flashlight around, Charlie ran across the cave to the galley and looked for a side cave or niche to hide in. He thought about climbing up the side and hiding on the deck but doubted the wood would be strong enough to hold his weight. It was two thousand years old.

About five feet from the hull, a pile of dirt and rock had fallen from the cave wall. Charlie dove for it and pulled himself as tightly as possible behind it. He didn't know if the pile was high enough for him to remain out of sight. Without his flashlight, he couldn't see very far in the dim light filtering through the hole. He hoped that whoever it was wouldn't look his way or notice anything out of the ordinary. His pack was on the ground next to him.

Footprints! Did he leave any in the sand? It was too late to do anything about that now.

Keeping his eyes closed because that would help him become invisible, Charlie listened.

As the people got closer, Charlie was able to distinguish at least three voices, all male. They were complaining about something that was too heavy and messy. Why should they be the ones to clean up his mess?

"Careful, you idiot. He might hear you," said number one.

"Down here? Don't be stupid. He wouldn't have this place bugged. Relax," said number two.

"I wouldn't put it past him. You know cameras have been found all over the place," number one again.

"Yeah, even bathrooms. Pig," number three.

Charlie guessed they were talking about El.

"Anyway, it's not far. Just up here a ways," number two.

The men shut up. In the dark, Charlie didn't know which way they went, so he opted to stay hidden for a while longer. It was lucky he did because the men returned about fifteen minutes later.

"That was disgusting," said one.

"Will you shut it," said two.

"Why? I'm entitled to my own opinion," said one.

"Wrong. You're entitled to *his* opinion," said three.

They were definitely referring to El. Cameras in the bathrooms. He'd have to warn Gwen. And Ant, though she probably wouldn't believe him anyway and would report him for spreading rumors.

Charlie waited another fifteen minutes. When no further sounds came from any direction, he climbed out of his hiding spot. He figured he had three choices now. Go left and explore the cave. Go right and explore the cave the other way. Get the hell out of the cave.

He looked right, looked left, looked right again.

"I'm not crossing the road," he said quietly. "Get it together."

Throwing caution to the wind, he went left, towards where the men had been. The further down the cavern he went, the worse the stench got. Charlie pulled a handkerchief from his pocket and held it over his nose. He went slowly, sweeping the flashlight across the ground to avoid traps or sudden holes.

He came to another passage that went to his left. The stink was coming from there. With his stomach doing nervous flips,

Charlie stepped towards the reek.

Immediately, he wished he'd gotten himself out of the cave as fast as possible. He turned tail and fast-walked back to the larger cavern where he'd first fallen in. With a last look at Gwen on the galley, Charlie started to climb up the hole to the surface. By now, whoever had been up there should be gone.

At the entrance to the hole, he waited and then cautiously stuck his head out. There was nothing around him but weeds and trees. Birds sang in the canopy. He could hear running water and thought he might be closer to the river than he realized.

Climbing the rest of the way through the hole, Charlie took his bearings now that he could see the sky and some landmarks. There was the trail with the gnarly oak about twenty feet back in the woods. The oak was on the east side of the trail. That meant the galley in the cave below faced west. The three men came from the north and returned that way. The horrible stench—he shuddered remembering what he saw—lay to the south.

Walking east, Charlie took note of the lay of the land. There was a definite dip as he walked over what he calculated would be the stern of the galley. In about three hundred yards, he arrived at the shore of the Pannon River. At this point, the western shore ran almost straight north to south. He could see up the river where it curved west around the peninsula. After that, he remembered from his runs that the river ran past a small bay then curved south for a mile before it went west and past Coverdale.

The galley would be located almost at the furthest end of the bay. What was it doing in the middle of the land, hundreds of yards from water? Had it been under construction? Or perhaps it had been on the old shoreline of the river. If the galley had truly been there nearly two thousand years, it likely acted as a small barrier to the flowing water. Silt and debris would have built up until the galley was buried and the peninsula formed.

The peninsula was quite large. Could it have grown that much in two thousand years? Charlie smiled. He had another reason to do some research. No one could suspect anything if he looked up rivers and how deltas and peninsulas were formed.

Did he have time?

Charlie pulled his pocket watch from the belly bag. It was a family heirloom that no one seemed to want. There was an odd inscription inside the case front that he'd never been able to decipher. He was relieved that the watch hadn't suffered any damage in his fall.

8 p.m. What time did the library close, and could he make it there in time?

No. He'd have to go in the morning. But first, he had a couple of things to prepare.

He'd wanted to run all the way, but it turned out he had hurt his ankle in the fall. It wasn't swollen or sprained, only banged up and tender to the touch. The extra pressure of thumping his foot down in a run made it worse. He needn't have worried. Everyone ignored Charlie when he walked into the house an hour and a half later.

Alone in his room, Charlie thought about what he had discovered in the cave. The galley was fantastic enough. The Viking bones and weapons made the mystery more interesting and confusing.

It was the other discovery, the last thing he had found when he had gone where the men had been. Charlie had tried to forget what he had seen and smelled. He couldn't.

The question now was, who could he tell about the mutilated corpses? They were fresh, the blood still wet. He didn't recognize them, but the backpacks and sleeping bags told him they might have been hikers.

The men had been talking about El. Charlie realized he had to be extra careful now that he knew that El was a killer or at least ordered killings. He would have to weigh the possible consequences if he was going to cross El again.

He had to warn Gwen and Jimmy.

Chapter Twenty

Jimmy stayed away from school Thursday with a bad stomach, and Gwen had a couple of tests for which she needed to study. Charlie felt frustrated all day because he had no one to talk to about his discoveries from the night before. He still wasn't entirely sure he should share the information about the fresh corpses and their implications. The less Gwen and Jimmy knew, the safer they would be.

Maybe.

Then there was the Roman galley. Nowhere that Charlie could remember had any book or document suggested that the Romans had crossed the Atlantic.

No teacher or lecturer Charlie could remember suggested that the Romans had ever crossed the Atlantic.

Charlie paid closer attention during Ancient History to see if Mr. Taverner referenced the Romans. Hadn't he said, at the beginning of the year, that the Celts had established trade connections with North America? Thinking the Romans might have done the same thing wasn't too farfetched.

Charlie thought about asking his history teacher about it but vetoed the idea. It would not be a good thing to arouse suspicions.

At least this explained the source of the coins Charlie had found in the backyard.

Another maybe.

The moment school let out, Charlie ran over to the library. Logging into the computer catalog, he quickly found several books on geology, geography, rivers, and one on naval history. If anyone asked, he would tell them that he wanted to study how rivers change over time because he had a great interest in the Amazon River and how it was being affected by climate change. The naval book was because he was a history buff and was reading about dreadnoughts.

It was close enough to the truth to be plausible, he thought.

When Charlie turned off Sevres Street onto his own, he spotted a white car turning onto Hugues at the far end of the street. El used a white limo. His heart sank. He must have been seen last night near The Institute. Either that or El was there to cause trouble for the fun of it.

Stepping into the house, he was surprised to see his father again. He was tempted to make some bitter comment about being grateful that his father had graced the house with his presence two days in a row. The look on George Bowen's face kept Charlie's comments from being uttered.

He looked furious, his face red as the T-shirt Charlie wore today. Before Charlie could say a thing, his father was at him.

"You were at The Institute again. The Chief told me this afternoon. And Mr. LaRennes was just here about it as well. Don't deny it."

Charlie was sure the guards hadn't spotted him last night, but with all the high-tech security stuff out there, he might have been caught by a hidden camera. Rather than get caught in a lie, Charlie decided to tell the whole truth. Sort of.

"Yes, sir, I was out running and got turned around in the woods. I got disoriented and ended up out by The Institute. As soon as I saw where I was, I bolted back to town."

This seemed to calm his father a little.

"Do you know how much harm your stupidity is doing? You're putting my job at risk, you idiot."

Charlie calmly took in what his father was saying.

"Because of your carelessness and thoughtlessness, I am being confronted in my own house. My own house! How dare you bring that here."

He wanted to ask about the family. Didn't his father care about the family? He kept quiet.

"The only thing that's saving you from worse trouble right now is that Blayney girl." This surprised Charlie. How could Gwen be helping him with his father? Then he remembered.

"I understand Mayor Mundy approves of you, though I can't understand why." Charlie's eyes narrowed. "But if the Mayor approves of you, that must mean he approves of me. So, my job is safe. If or when you see the Mayor again, be sure to let him know that you are the cause of all the trouble, not me. You might want to have a talk with Mr. LaRennes about it, too. He, at least, is willing to help you."

At that moment, Charlie lost any remaining respect he had for his father. It was a hard blow to take because they had been so close. But having his father use him to secure his position at work…that was just intolerable. There was no sign of support or understanding. All that mattered was George Bowen's job security.

He wanted to shut out, "Fuck you," and leave, but he knew he wasn't ready for that. Yet.

It suddenly became easier to lie.

"I'll make sure I don't go anywhere near The Institute again, sir. I'll confine my running to town and the track at school, sir. I want you to be a success at work, and anything I can do to help, just tell me."

It was all Charlie could do to hold back the tears when he saw the satisfied smile on George Bowen's face. He didn't utter another word to his son.

That put Charlie over the top.

Once George Bowen had gone out the door on his way back to The Institute, Charlie ran upstairs to the bathroom and threw up. Though his stomach was emptied, he kept heaving until he grew dizzy and collapsed beside the bathtub. He lay there for several minutes, gathering his strength while his head spun.

Ant pounding at the door, demanding to be let in, woke Charlie up. He hurriedly rinsed his face, looked at his red and puffy eyes in the mirror, and pushed past his sister without a word.

He had to get out of the house. It no longer felt like home. He paused at his closet and thought about the coins hidden in the alcove. It would be so easy to pack some of them in his knapsack and leave town. He wouldn't have to pack any clothes. With the coins, he would have enough money to buy whatever he needed.

Gwen.

He couldn't leave her behind. He knew she was in danger from El. Charlie had to get to the bottom of what was happening in Coverdale.

And he couldn't forget Jimmy, either. He was a good friend who was probably in as much danger as anyone, judging by what had happened to Stan.

And what El had done to him. He wanted to take that sword out of the alcove and skewer the bald-headed bastard with it.

Charlie would save them both.

He just had to figure out how.

Back on the streets running an hour later, Charlie kept to his word and went in the opposite direction from The Institute. Moving briskly along the river, Charlie turned to cross the bridge before he hit the downtown area. He had never run on the south side of the Pannon before and thought it might be a safe, inoffensive place.

On the other side of the bridge, Charlie chose to run west. Ten miles down the road lay the freeway that led to the city. The road followed the river for a few miles before the Pannon turned north and disappeared into the hills and its source. The road now ran through dense forest.

He had been running for about twenty minutes when it struck him that no cars had passed in either direction. Surely someone must have been coming back from work in the city or passing to or from one of the towns further up the river.

Approaching the bend in the river, Charlie saw something flashing through a break in the trees.

"Great," he said, out of breath, "more motion detectors."

He slowed and trotted closer to the bend. When he heard the crackle of a police radio, he ducked into the trees beside the road.

Moving as quietly as he could, Charlie cut through the trees to better see the activity ahead.

A Coverdale police cruiser sat on the shoulder. Two barriers had been set up across the road, blocking both lanes. It was the cruiser's lights Charlie had seen through the trees. A car from the freeway pulled up, and the driver got out. Before the driver could take more than two steps, one of the policemen who had been sitting in the cruiser intercepted him.

Waving the driver back to his car, the officer said, "Sorry, sir, there's been a bad accident further up the road. There's no way through. You'll have to return to the freeway and take the next exit."

The driver thanked the officer, returned to his car, and sped away. The officer remained standing in the middle of the road until the car had disappeared around a bend a mile down the road. Then he returned to the cruiser to finish eating the doughnut he had left on the cruiser's dashboard.

Charlie ran through the trees to rejoin the road and head back to Coverdale.

It was then that it struck him that he hadn't encountered an accident on the way here.

He came to the bridge and stopped when he spied Jimmy riding along the Loop. Jimmy skidded to a halt at the far end of the bridge and waited for Charlie.

"My man, what're you doing out here?" Jimmy bit down on a piece of licorice.

"I need you ..." said Charlie, still breathing hard.

"I didn't know you cared," said Jimmy.

"... to lend me your bike. I have somewhere to go, and my ankle is killing me." This wasn't exactly the truth. The ankle he'd hurt falling into the cave still ached a little, but it no longer affected his running. But he wasn't yet ready to tell Jimmy his ideas. He hadn't finished formulating them.

As he dismounted, Jimmy complained. "I hope you realize how much of a sacrifice this is, me walking home. I have this huge bag of goodies to carry." He held up the candy bag he must have purchased at the shops.

"You're a pal," said Charlie as he climbed on the mountain bike. He grabbed a couple of pieces of licorice from the bag. "I owe you one. Hey, I thought you missed school today because of a wonky stomach. What's with the junk food?"

"A man has to replenish his strength after an illness. This

is my way."

Charlie laughed as he rode off, at first wobbly because he hadn't ridden a bike in years.

"Don't break her. She means a lot to me," Jimmy shouted after Charlie.

Back over the bridge, Charlie turned east and rode off into the night. He turned off the headlamp on the handlebars. No point in alerting anyone to his presence.

This part of the road was new to Charlie, and he had no idea where it led. From what he could remember of the maps he had checked at the city library a few weeks ago, there might be a town about fifteen or twenty miles up the road. He couldn't be sure.

Charlie saw Coverdale across the river. The town looked peaceful. He spotted the remains of the old dock and, on the high bank above, the theatre marquee.

He thought the bottom of such a steep and high bank was a strange location for a dock. Surely, there was a place elsewhere that provided easier access to the town.

Further along, some boys threw rocks at the old bridge pilings. Across the river from the pilings, about a mile away, Charlie saw where the old road from town cut into the woods going due east.

Charlie kept pedaling. The sun had gone down, and the woods on either side of the highway were pitch black. He wasn't worried about being hit by a car. Certainly, the cruiser would keep anyone from sneaking up behind him, and he had a hunch that there would be no traffic from ahead.

The new road wound its way between the hills. The sky was clear, and the moon and stars gave off enough light for Charlie to see the spot where the old road from town connected with the new highway.

He wondered how old the old road actually was.

Charlie wanted to check it out, but there wasn't enough light to see what he needed to see.

About a mile past the old road, Charlie came upon the familiar flashing lights. He pulled over to the side, dismounted, and rolled the bike to the edge of the woods. He left it resting against a tree and crept through the bush as quietly as possible. Sure enough, a cruiser was next to the barriers blocking the road. Silhouettes revealed the policemen inside the cruiser.

Not seeing any point in going further, Charlie returned to town.

The next night, Charlie followed the same route out of town. The police were still guarding the road. This time, though, a driver who was stopped put up some resistance to the detour.

"If I have to go back to the freeway," he said, "it'll add another hour onto my trip." To Charlie, it sounded like the man was about to cry.

The officer standing at the barrier shook his head in sympathy. The second officer from the cruiser approached the two men at the barrier.

"What's the problem?" he asked, his hand on his holstered gun.

"I need to get to Anderton, and I don't want to go back. This is the shortest route." The driver had a hand on the barrier, and Charlie thought he would try to push it out of his way.

The second officer calmly but firmly said, "No one is allowed through. The freeway is open now, and this road is closed. The bridge is being dismantled because it's unsafe. Move on."

The driver stood his ground, but when the second officer eased his pistol out of its holster, he hurried back to his car and sped away.

No one was being allowed into Coverdale or along the road that passed the town. That also meant anyone trying to leave town would have to pass the roadblocks.

Coverdale and the people in it were cut off from the outside world.

Chapter Twenty-one

Friday afternoon, when school let out, Charlie walked Gwen home. Both were frustrated because it was difficult for them to be together. When they were out in public, people stared. He didn't want to have her over to his house because he wished to keep his relationship with Gwen private. He didn't think his family deserved to know anything, especially his father. They couldn't go to Gwen's for fear of running into El. It was too difficult to get to Gwen's hideaway when there wasn't a party going on. Staff were everywhere, and they couldn't get a moment to access the secret door. Charlie wondered if there might be a way to go through the tunnel past the hideaway. They'd check that out at some time.

Before getting to the Mundy estate, they agreed to meet the next morning on the Loop, close to his house. He didn't tell her why or anything about what he had found in the cave.

Jimmy had missed school again. When Charlie returned Jimmy's mountain bike Friday night, he still didn't explain why he needed to use it. Jimmy agreed to meet Charlie at the stone circle as early as possible the next morning. Charlie thought Jimmy was going to start asking all kinds of awkward questions when Charlie asked him to bring the biggest flashlight he could find. But Jimmy had paused for only a moment then promised to rouse himself early, despite it being a Saturday morning when he could sleep in.

Charlie looked hard at Jimmy and could see the trust that

Jimmy had for him.

Sleep that night was fitful. He kept waking up with nightmares about knights chasing him through the woods. The knights always turned into Chief Wycliffe. By seven the next morning, Charlie's sheets were drenched with sweat.

He rummaged through the garage and found two large flashlights and a couple of road flares. He didn't think the flares would be of use, but he crammed them into his knapsack with the flashlights.

At eight o'clock, Charlie went through his backyard into the trees, then crossed the Loop to the trail. A few minutes later, he was surprised when Gwen came striding down the trail. She was dressed all in denim, and her feet were clad in hiking boots. She carried a knapsack on her back.

"What's with the outfit?" Charlie asked after they had kissed hello.

"Knowing you, a long day together meant a hike in the woods. I packed us a lunch, too."

"You really are perfect."

"Maybe, but why did you want to meet here? And where are we going?"

"We're meeting Jimmy at the standing stones ..."

"Stone circle."

"Stone circle, whatever. We're meeting Jimmy there, and I didn't want to walk through town carrying a knapsack. I thought we could take the trail back past your place."

"But that will take us past The Institute. Chances are good we'd be seen."

"Yeah, that's where my plan fell through. Any ideas?"

"I know a way." Taking Charlie's hand, Gwen led him north along the trail towards her home. When they were up near where Charlie had first looked out over Coverdale, she found a small gap in the bushes leading to another trail.

"This goes down the hill, then turns and runs all the way to the river trail on the other side of town. We have to cross the Loop again, but it's at that tunnel of trees where no one should see us."

"Brilliant."

It took them about an hour to reach the stone circle. Jimmy was there, sitting on his favorite stone, eating a doughnut. He didn't seem surprised to see Gwen.

"Arfgh glumph wagga foo," he said, indicating the opened box of doughnuts resting on the stone beside him.

Charlie shook his head in disgust when he realized he knew exactly what Jimmy had said. Between bites of a maple iced with peanuts, he told Gwen, "Jimmy figured we'd be hungry and stopped on the way to get us some breakfast."

Gwen found two pint cartons of chocolate milk in a bag next to the doughnut box. She took one and sipped the milk through a straw. "I like your idea of a healthy breakfast," she said, picking up a Boston cream. She sat next to Jimmy.

When he had finished eating his doughnut, Jimmy finally spoke clearly. "What's up, doc? Why'd you make me interrupt my beauty sleep?"

"A hundred years of sleep wouldn't help you, Elf," said Gwen. "And thanks for the doughnuts."

"If you weren't my best friend's girlfriend, I'd say something nasty about Amazons." Jimmy feigned anger. Charlie knew Jimmy and Gwen had been friends for a long time. They'd kept quiet about it to avoid any complications. Gwen didn't have any friends, boys or girls.

"Amazons beat up elves." Gwen flexed her biceps.

"Promise?" replied Jimmy, a look of anticipation on his face.

"Children," said Charlie.

Arming themselves with more doughnuts, Gwen and Jimmy listened while Charlie spoke. Pacing in front of them, he explained what he had discovered along the highway the last two nights and what he thought that meant.

"But why haven't I ever seen these roadblocks when I've gone to the city?" said Jimmy.

"Me, either?" said Gwen.

Charlie stopped pacing and shrugged. "Maybe they're only on at night. No," he corrected himself quickly, "that wouldn't make any sense. They must pull them back when someone they know is going to pass?"

"They're a figment of your imagination," said Jimmy. A swat to the back of the head from Gwen silenced him.

Resuming his pacing, Charlie reviewed everything else strange that had happened since he moved to Coverdale: the fire at the Standish house, the church, The Institute, the tramps, the odd stuff being taught in history, the absence of Coverdale from any maps.

"There could be logical explanations for all of that, Charlie," said Gwen softly. "Are you sure about this?" She seemed genuinely concerned about Charlie. They had already spoken about some of this stuff. He decided she was prompting him so he wouldn't forget anything.

"The coins," said Charlie, and pulled a small piece of silver from his pocket. Holding up the coin for Gwen and Jimmy to see, he continued, "This comes from sometime between 14 and 37 CE, the reign of Emperor Tiberius. He was particularly nasty and perverted."

"So," said Jimmy, staring in fascination at the coin. "It came from someone's collection."

"I don't think so." Charlie put the coin back in his pocket.

"I found something. Follow me."

With quick glances at each other and shrugs, Gwen and Jimmy jumped down from the stone and followed Charlie along the trail back to the river. Jimmy had made sure to stuff the leftover doughnuts in his knapsack.

Where the trail curved back towards Coverdale, Charlie paused and pulled aside some bushes to reveal a small arrow made of rocks.

"I left markers the other night," he said, walking into the woods.

Charlie found several more rock arrows and then came to a small cairn of rocks.

"We're here," he said.

"We're where?" asked Jimmy.

"That's what I found." Charlie pointed to a hole in the ground next to a large oak.

Jimmy didn't look amused. "You found a hole in the ground." He feigned enthusiasm. "Can you tell it from your ..." Gwen cuffed the back of his head and wagged her finger at him.

"Come on." Charlie got on his knees and went into the hole, careful to avoid slipping and rolling in again. "You can support yourself by holding onto the roots. It's safe."

Jimmy and Gwen hesitated.

"It's dark and dirty," said Gwen.

"And there could be spiders and centipedes and beetles," added Jimmy.

"Yeah, yeah, yeah," said Charlie. "I've been down here before. It's perfectly ..."

Charlie yelped and disappeared down the hole.

Jimmy dove for the hole and stuck his head inside. "Charlie!" he cried. "Charlie! Are you okay?"

"Hurry, Jimmy, he might be hurt." Gwen knelt next to Jimmy and tried to see into the hole.

Light flashed into Jimmy's eyes, blinding him.

"Just kidding," said Charlie calmly.

"I knew that," said Jimmy quickly.

"Out of my way," said Gwen, pulling at Jimmy's jacket. "I have to break his face."

After he had helped the others down, suffered a fake-out knee to the groin from Jimmy and a painful sideburn grab from Gwen, Charlie passed Gwen one of the big flashlights he had brought. Jimmy fished into his own knapsack and produced a Fisher Price light.

"It's all I could find," Jimmy said sheepishly. His light gave off a surprisingly powerful beam.

Charlie shone his light on the floor, and the others both said "yuck" when they saw the skeleton. They said it again when she lit up the pile of bones further in.

"Owe me a coke," said Jimmy, trying to hide his nervousness.

"Not now," whispered Gwen.

Charlie led them further into the cave.

"Lady and gentleman, I present ..." said Charlie as he swung his light up.

Gwen and Jimmy were silent. They automatically added their light to Charlie's to illuminate the galley. Jimmy's mouth hung open while he took in the sight.

It looked like the ship was sailing out of the cave wall. The grey wooden face of the figurehead stared down at the three with blind eyes.

"I called her Gwen. I hope you don't mind."

"Not at all," said Jimmy.

Charlie looked at his friends. Gwen moved forward and

ran her hand over the ship. Jimmy stayed rooted, his face full of wonder. A single tear rolled down his cheek.

"Why am I reacting this way?" Jimmy's voice was shaky.

"Because everything you've believed in has been torn apart." Charlie placed his hand gently on Jimmy's shoulder. "Think about it. A Roman galley, here, in Coverdale. The Romans weren't supposed to have crossed the Atlantic. This changes everything." Charlie's voice rose, getting more excited. "Just think about it."

"But what's it doing in a cave?" asked Gwen.

Charlie thought about what he had read in the library books, but before he could answer, Jimmy spoke up.

"Silt," he said. "The ship probably got left here, on the riverbank, and blocked the river's flow. Silt was deposited and built up around the ship until it was covered."

"But where'd the cave come from?" asked Charlie.

"Got me on that one," said Jimmy.

Gwen moved back from the remains of the ship.

"Guys," she called, "the cave goes further in."

"Towards the end of the peninsula," said Charlie. "Don't go any farther. Please."

"What's that smell?"

"Please, Gwen, stay here. I'll explain."

Charlie and Jimmy were still debating how the galley was buried when they heard Gwen scream. She hadn't waited.

They charged in the direction of the scream, beams of light bouncing wildly over the cave walls. They found Gwen staring at the corpses.

"The other night, when I was down here, three guys brought them here. From what I heard, it was under El's orders."

"But why?" Gwen put her arms around Charlie and held

on tightly.

"I don't know, Gwen," he said while he stroked her hair.

"Did you explore down there?" Jimmy shone his light further down the cave.

"No. The moment I saw these guys, I bolted."

"Then let's go," said Jimmy.

"I suppose we should try to be quiet," said Gwen. "If there were men down here the other night, they may be back."

"Maybe," said Charlie. "When I first got down by the galley, I didn't notice any footprints in the sand. I don't think they come here very often. It might have been a one-off."

"Still, caution," said Gwen.

Ten nervous minutes later, the cavern began to get lighter. Charlie noticed dark spots on the cave wall. They looked like other passages. A few feet further on, they looked up. Overhead was another hole in the cave's ceiling.

Directly below the hole was another skeleton. Some cloth still covered part of the skeleton; its feet were clad in the remains of a pair of leather shoes with large buckles.

"Poor guy," said Jimmy, pointing at the skeletal hand and arm bones that rested a few feet away from the body. "That had to hurt."

Charlie examined the hole. It seemed very smooth and regular to him. At the top, he thought he could see bricks or large stones.

"It's the well," said Jimmy. "We must be under the oak grove."

"You've been here?" said Gwen, holding on tightly to Charlie's arm.

"Not down here, I never saw this guy before. But I've been up there." Jimmy looked up. "I was out exploring and found it a couple of years ago. There's this ring of oak trees, massive things, must be a thousand years old. Their limbs are all tangled, and you can climb all over the place. In the middle of the grove is this well. It was odd, but I didn't think much about it. I suppose I should have."

"You weren't to know," said Gwen. She walked a little way along the cave. "Oh, fuck me. Another one. Sorry, took me by surprise." Her flashlight illuminated the far wall of the cave. A grey dragon looked as if it was trying to claw its way out of the cave wall.

"A Viking longship!" Charlie ran over to the ship and ran his hands across the relic. He was excited. "Back there, in front of the galley, those are Vikings. I almost sat on a helmet." He waited for a goofy remark from Jimmy, but none was forthcoming. Charlie continued his examination of the longship. "It looks burned. The same thing must have happened to this as the galley."

Gwen cut in, "The wreck of the longship changed the flow of the river."

"Yeah," said Jimmy, "we're in the middle of this big peninsula that sticks out into the river. You can see it from town."

"Come on," said Charlie, "I saw some places where the cave branched off. I want to check them out."

Charlie led the way, and the others followed. The first branch turned out to be a small cavern. A mound of bones was at its center, with weapons piled along the walls. They appeared to be Viking in origin. It was almost completely buried in the dirt of the cave floor.

"The crew of the longship?" said Charlie.

The next branch was also a cavern, larger than the other. Most of its space was taken up by a huge mound of bones. Bits of leather and hair were mixed in. Spears, axes, knives, and bows and arrows were thrown around the floor. Upon closer examination of the bones, they appeared to have been cut. The natives, probably Iroquois, guessed Charlie, had been hacked to bits.

The third cavern was the most gruesome. Cloth had not rotted away from the bones as much as in the other caverns, leading Charlie to assume that these bones were of more recent origin.

"They look like soldiers, probably French," said Charlie.

Jimmy hefted a musket from the pile near the cavern entrance. "Wow, is that a cannon?"

In the far corner, there was indeed a rusted cannon, its iron-clad wheels rotted and broken.

There were no other caverns.

"It's like some kind of grave," Charlie speculated, "each from a different time in history."

"Not a grave," said Gwen, "a garbage dump."

Charlie pondered this. "Where'd you get that idea?"

Gwen shrugged. "It's just the way the bodies have been tossed into piles in the caverns. Then their stuff, their equipment, was thrown in after them. Whoever put them in here didn't care about them. They didn't keep the weapons. That cannon ..." Her voice trailed off.

"Something's been going on here for a deuce of a long time," said Charlie.

"But what?" asked Jimmy. "And just how long do you think a deuce is?"

Charlie scratched his chin. "Those French soldiers were probably from about three hundred years ago. The Vikings would have to be about a thousand years old, give or take a few hundred years. The galley, I'm guessing is almost two thousand years old."

Jimmy whistled. "This is too much. It's unbelievable."

"You touched the galley," said Gwen, "and the weapons." Turning to Charlie, she asked, "What about the natives?"

"The natives were most likely local. Iroquois. Hurons. Abenaki. Other Algonquians. There are so many because they probably come from all times since whoever is doing this started whatever it is."

Jimmy paced about. "I'm still confused. Anybody hungry?"

Gwen looked disgusted. "How can you think about food with all these corpses around? You're sick."

Jimmy waved her off and pulled a doughnut out of his knapsack. "What next, boss?" he asked around bites.

Charlie looked back towards the galley. "The men came from down that way. It goes on for quite a bit. Shall we?"

Jimmy and Gwen looked at each other and then back at Charlie.

"It could be dangerous. Those men were killers. We're just teenagers," said Charlie.

"I want to get to the bottom of this," said Gwen, her tone determined.

Jimmy sighed. "I guess I do, too. I just wish I'd had the chance to ... you know ... live a little."

Gwen patted his shoulder. "If ... no, *when* we get out of this, go see Emile the florist. He's a good guy and he knows stuff. He's also ... you know ..."

"I guess you're not so bad for a freakish Amazon after all, Gwen."

"I'm always kind to elves, Jimmy."

Looking ahead, Jimmy said, "In for a penny. Any idea where it goes?"

Charlie shone his flashlight into the darkness. "Roughly

northwest. Straight towards The Institute, I'd guess."

"Fuck," said Gwen.

All three shivered.

Chapter Twenty-two

Charlie estimated they had walked nearly three miles. At one point, a large stone protruded from the ceiling. He surmised they were under the stone circle.

It was now well past noon, and all three of them were sweaty and dirty.

At first, the cave had been narrow and low. A few hundred yards along, they had come to a blockage where the walls had collapsed. Dirt and debris were mounded almost to the roof. It looked fresh.

"Maybe it was those guys you heard, Charlie," said Jimmy.

"But why cave it in?" Gwen threw aside some rocks.

"Could they have known I was there? Could be they blocked it off so I couldn't follow."

They had spent half an hour digging through the barrier and found themselves in a much larger cave. The walls were no longer of earth but rock.

Charlie could sense they were steadily going upward into the hills that ringed Coverdale. Twice they stopped to rest and have something to eat and drink. Gwen had packed enough sandwiches for all three of them as if she had known in advance that Jimmy would be there. Jimmy's knapsack seemed to be a cornucopia of junk food and soda. He brushed off their comments as if having large quantities of food about his person was an everyday occurrence.

Just as they rounded a bend, they were assaulted by a terrible smell. The stench hit them like a wall. Charlie had been aware of something odd about the air for a few minutes but dismissed it as cavern stink, perhaps bat droppings. Now, he wondered if there were more bodies.

The three advanced through the miasma, trying not to gag and covering their faces with handkerchiefs. The reek seemed strongest outside a cavern that branched off to the right. Jimmy indicated that the others should wait while he had a look.

His face was pale when he staggered back. Jimmy leaned against the cave wall and emptied his stomach. Charlie fought back the urge to join his friend when the odor of the vomit, mixed with whatever was coming from the cavern, assailed his nostrils. Gwen held Jimmy, seemingly immune to the fumes until he was able to stand by himself.

Without a word, Jimmy moved along the cave, eager to escape the cavern. They walked in silence until the air cleared, and they could breathe without needing the buffer provided by the handkerchiefs.

"More bodies?" asked Charlie, taking hold of Jimmy's arms.

Jimmy still looked sick and swallowed hard before answering. "Yes. Very fresh, like a couple of days. Newer than those ones back at the galley."

Charlie's mind flashed back to the cruiser he had seen on his bike ride.

"They were thrown in a corner like garbage. I think their throats had been cut." Jimmy ran into the shadows, and the retching sounds floated back to Gwen and Charlie.

"Wait a sec," said Charlie. He ran back to the branch, hoping he was wrong. He wasn't. He returned to the others and said, "I recognized one of them. Saw him at the roadblock Thursday night. He was arguing about not being able to get through. The last thing I saw, one of the cops was pulling his gun."

"The cops are involved?" Jimmy was shocked.

Gwen remained silent. Charlie guessed she was thinking about Uncle Willy and perhaps her grandfather. She looked at him, tears flowing down her face. He put his arms around her and held on while she sobbed into his shirt. When she stopped, they looked into each other's eyes. She mouthed, "I love you." So did he.

Charlie asked, "Do you want to go on? This is getting pretty serious."

Jimmy shuddered. "Gotta find out what's happening, man. This is my home town. I don't like this crap."

Gwen concurred. "I don't want to think my grandfather is involved, but he's the Mayor. If something's going on, and he knows about it, I want to know." She took a deep breath. "Or at least, I want to know he isn't involved. He can't be, Charlie. He can't be!"

Charlie wanted to say something to ease his friends' discomfort but couldn't think of anything. He had a lot less to lose in this. He was new to town and had no roots here. Charlie's world wouldn't fall apart if they uncovered something especially nasty.

Charlie became even more determined to protect Gwen. And Jimmy.

When they were about to move on, Jimmy held them back.

"If those bodies are that fresh, that means someone's been down here in the last day or two."

Charlie caught Jimmy's meaning. "And they may still be

here, or around somewhere."

"We'll be very quiet and careful," whispered Gwen. She gave Charlie's arm a squeeze of encouragement, and they set off again.

Soon, they came to a set of massive steel doors. The cave had gradually widened and grown higher without their noticing. The doors filled the end of the cave, rising at least twenty feet to the ceiling. Together, the doors were about twenty feet across. At the center of each door was the cross in a circle symbol. There appeared to be no latch on this side – no way to open the doors.

They looked at each other as if to say, "Now what?"

Jimmy found the solution when he shone his flashlight along the walls on either side of the doors. There was a break in the wall on the left side that you could only notice if you held a light pointed away from the doors. When the doors were opened, judging from the scrape marks they made in the floor of the cave, the break was hidden behind the left one.

They squeezed into the break, which went ahead for about six feet, then jogged sharply to the right.

Moving ahead without making a sound, the three found themselves behind a heavy cloth barrier. Light filtered in from underneath. When Charlie snapped off his flashlight, the others followed suit.

Getting down flat on his stomach, Charlie crawled to the light. He peered out and saw a smooth tiled floor immediately on the other side of the barrier and a glass wall about ten feet away. Seeing no feet or any sign of movement, Charlie carefully raised the cloth and stuck his head out.

He saw right away that he was looking along a gallery that curved away from him to the left and right. The gallery's outside wall was covered with immense tapestries; Charlie was peering out from the bottom of one. The inner wall, about twenty feet high, was glass.

Through the glass, Charlie saw rooms. More accurately, he saw laboratories.

No one was around. Charlie crawled out, followed in short order by Gwen and Jimmy. They remained silent. Charlie looked along the walls for any indication that there might be motion detectors or cameras watching them, but he could discern nothing.

Stepping up to the glass wall, they looked up. They could see the floors above, at least four, before the angle got too awkward.

"The core of The Institute," Charlie said into Gwen's ear. She repeated it to Jimmy.

They slowly walked around the gallery. While Jimmy and Gwen looked through the glass, Charlie examined the tapestries. They appeared medieval and older, covered with knights and damsels, strange symbols and signs. In every corner was the cross and circle symbol. Around the edges was a description of what the tapestry was about in Latin, mostly references to battles. Charlie was able to translate some of it, but he had trouble concentrating.

A sharp hiss and a muffled scream drew his attention.

Farther along the gallery, Gwen and Jimmy were standing, transfixed by whatever they had seen through the glass.

Charlie joined them and nearly fainted at the sight that met him.

It was a lab with three hospital beds arranged at its center. Monitors, connected to the beds' occupants by dozens of wires, flashed and spat out tapes with jagged lines in red ink. Above each bed were odd machines that Charlie didn't understand. Thick tubes ran from the devices down to each patient – if that's what the three were. Something red pulsed through the tubes.

Blood.

Bottles attached to the sides of the machines were filled with the red stuff. If it was blood, there was far more than came from the average human body, Charlie was sure. The blood in the bottles bubbled and swirled like the juice in the dispensers at the diner.

It was a ghoulish sight, made all the worse by the occupants in the beds.

The three Standish boys.

"We've got to get out of here," said Gwen. She could barely get the words out.

Charlie nodded in agreement, then paused.

"I don't remember which tapestry it was," said Charlie.

"Down from the big doors," said Gwen. Her hope faded when she saw at least four sets of large steel doors along the gallery's outer wall.

"It doesn't matter," said Jimmy. "I can't go back into that cave. Not with those corpses in there."

Charlie was about to argue, but the look on Jimmy's face told him they'd have to leave his friend behind if they took the same route.

"What then?" asked Charlie.

Jimmy made a circling motion with his hand. They'd have to go around the gallery and see if there were any other exits.

They found one in no time.

An ordinary-looking door led into a cinder block stairwell. Metal stairs went up and down. They tried to decide which way to go when the door clicked shut behind them. It was locked.

"Now what? Up or down?" Gwen looked at Charlie for guidance.

Before Charlie could answer, Jimmy said, "I'll go up and have a look."

Jimmy bounded up the stairs two at a time, his sneakers hardly making a sound.

"Where do you suppose everyone is, Charlie?" Gwen leaned back against the wall.

"It's Saturday, their day off?"

"But someone must be here to check on the patients."

"Staff meeting?"

Jimmy came bouncing down the stairs. He did not look happy.

"We're locked in the stairwell," he said hoarsely. "I went to the top. The stairs end at a door that opens into the middle of The Institute grounds. Nothing but grass for hundreds of feet. We'd be spotted before we could reach the woods, even if we could get out that way."

Gwen pointed down.

The stairs only went down one flight and led to a corridor. At the end of the corridor was a smaller version of the steel doors they had seen in the gallery.

The door opened easily.

"I don't like this," said Jimmy. "It's too easy. *This* is the only open door?"

"Jimmy's right, Charlie. It's almost like we're being guided."

"No one knew we'd be going to the stone circle or that we'd find the cave. Anyway, we don't have much choice, do we?"

They went through the door and entered a brightly lit tunnel. The walls were covered with white tiles decorated at twenty-foot intervals with the red cross in a circle. Florescent lights were centered along the curved ceiling.

The tunnel seemed to go on forever. The white expanse of the walls was occasionally broken by heavy steel doors, all of which were locked. Charlie guessed they had traveled about a mile and a half when the tunnel forked. The left fork ended at a wooden door about a hundred yards away. The center fork sloped up to another steel door. The right fork was blocked by rusted steel bars. About five feet into the fork were heavy oak doors, barred and chained, with a huge padlock.

Quietly, Charlie said, "I think this goes towards your hideaway. That tunnel you were uncomfortable in."

"I wish we could go there now." She grabbed the bars and tried to shake them, but they didn't move.

But the steel door opened without a sound, and they found themselves in a large meeting room. The walls were paneled with dark wood. The only adornment was a ragged white banner with a red cross hung from the ceiling at the other end of the room. Ornately carved chairs were set around a circular solid wood table. There was a door in the wall to the right.

"Wait here and keep this door open, just in case that other one is locked and we're trapped in here," Charlie said to Jimmy.

Charlie and Gwen went to the other door and were about to try the handle when they heard a voice from the other side. They couldn't understand what was said, but the tone was unmistakable.

Fury.

Gwen's eyes widened. "That's my grandfather," she whispered. Another voice spoke up, steady and calmer. "Uncle Willy."

"Let's get out of here," said Charlie, pulling Gwen along.

They heard the men enter the meeting room as the steel door closed behind them.

"We'll have to kill them," said the Chief matter-of-factly.

There was a scrape of chairs on the wooden floor. More than two chairs.

Charlie indicated they should wait. Putting his mouth to Gwen's ear, he said, "They're not coming through. We might learn something."

With her mouth on Charlie's ear, she said, "Not too long. This place scares the crap out of me." She placed her mouth against Jimmy's ear. Charlie figured she was repeating what they'd said.

With their ears pressed against the steel door, they listened.

"Are you really sure that's necessary?" That was the Mayor.

"They've broken our laws. They have to pay," said the Chief.

"Let's not be too hasty, Chief. They are of use to us. Isn't that right, Mr. Bowen?"

El!

"Absolutely." Charlie recognized his father's voice. "Charlie is especially important. So is your granddaughter." The bastard.

"What about the other one?" said El.

"He can be trained. Anyone can be trained. But he needs to be strong," said the Chief.

"He's strong enough, despite his mental weakness," said El!

Charlie saw Jimmy shudder and ball up his fists.

"He's of no use to me," said George Bowen. "Except

maybe as a source for some experiments I'd like to carry out. You see ..."

"There's no need to bother our Rex Mundi with the details, Mr Bowen," said El. "I'm sure he'll ask you if he's interested."

"We could just kill them. Drain them and be done with it," said the Chief.

This time, it was Gwen who clenched her fists.

"Are we done here?" It sounded like the Mayor had had enough.

With that warning, Charlie, Gwen, and Jimmy tip-toed down the tunnel to the fork, turned left, and ran to the wooden door.

Gwen asked, "Why were they talking about us like that? What do they mean?"

"I don't know," said Charlie. He could feel the blood pounding through his veins as his heart raced. He tried to slow his breathing and calm down. "But we've got to get the hell out of here. And fast."

"They were talking about killing the other one. Or experimenting," said Jimmy. "I think I'm the other one? I don't have a mental weakness. Fuck them."

"I think we are in or under the Mundy mansion," Charlie said. "We've gotta get out of here."

Gwen sang, "We've gotta get out of here. Right now." Charlie squeezed her hand.

"Oh boy, oh boy, oh boy." Jimmy looked all around as if trying to find a quick way out. "Oh boy, oh boy, oh boy."

Charlie yanked open the wooden door. "There's nowhere else to go."

The solid oak door was covered with carvings, the most prominent of which was the cross and circle at the center. It opened on a dark tunnel. They pulled out their flashlights and turned them on. The walls were of large stone blocks, so tightly fitted together that they required no mortar. The roof was mammoth stone slabs. The stone floor was worn smooth by the passage of thousands of feet. The tunnel seemed to go on for an eternity.

Jimmy pulled the door closed behind them. There was the click of a lock engaging.

Every ten feet, the walls were broken by low arches. Carved into the capstones were words, the second of which were names. Shining his light around, Charlie recognized the names of some people in town: Roger, Caxton, Young, Goodspeed. The first word on each capstone was in Latin, though Charlie didn't know what the words meant. *Promiscuum. Contagionis.*

They were forced to crouch to pass through the arch closest to them. It opened into a small room that looked as if it had been carved out of solid rock. Along the walls, in tiers, were niches. In each niche was a body wrapped like a mummy. Below each niche was a small inscribed metal plate bearing the name and dates of the person within.

"I think we've found the Coverdale cemetery," said Charlie.

"Oh please," said Jimmy, "not more dead people."

They left the room, which belonged to the Youngs, and stood in silence for a while.

Charlie looked at the capstone again and pondered the mystery of the Latin words.

It was almost like promiscuous and contagious. What on earth could they have to do with people's names?

Charlie eventually spoke up. "I think you know what we have to do." Gwen and Jimmy nodded their agreement. "I think this tunnel will take us into town. It's going to be a long walk. Are you ready to pass through the halls of the dead?"

Gwen took his hand and squeezed it. She smiled at him.

Jimmy looked sick but tried a smile, too.

They set off, not knowing what they'd find at the end of the tunnel.

Chapter Twenty-three

They walked in the semi-darkness for an hour. The tunnel was cool and dry, but the massive stone blocks made the atmosphere oppressive. Jimmy was shocked to see a crypt with KNOX CONTAMINATUS carved into the capstone.

"Hey, Knox. This is my family." Jimmy stood staring up at the capstone. "Does *contaminatus* mean what I think it means?"

"My Latin is rusty," said Charlie, "but I think it means contaminated."

"Contaminated with what? Handsomeness? Awesomeness? A big ..."

"Elf!" Gwen swatted the back of Jimmy's head.

He turned swiftly and faced her. "Lady, I'm getting pretty sick of you hitting me and calling me elf. Okay?"

Gwen's eyes popped open. She stuttered, then said, "Jimmy. I'm sorry. It was all in fun. I didn't mean ..."

"People never mean, but they still do. Enough!"

Her eyes watered up. "Jimmy, I'm so sorry. Please, you're the only person in this damned town that I've ever thought of as a friend."

"Sure. A friend. One you had to hide in case you got in trouble with Grandpa Mayor."

"No, Jimmy, it wasn't like that. I didn't want to attract attention to you. You've seen what these people can do. I didn't know it was this bad. And El, what that piece of shit did to you. I *tried* to keep you out of his line of sight."

"Yeah, and look how that worked out. Before he made me ... he bent me over and ..."

Gwen fell to her knees in front of Jimmy and threw her arms around his waist. She cried quietly. He glared down at her. Gradually, his face softened. He put a hand on her shoulder and used the other to stroke her hair.

"I'm sorry, Gwen. I just found out I'm even more worthless than I thought. I shouldn't have taken it out on you."

"Don't apologize, Jimmy. I shouldn't have treated you that way, even if my intentions were supposed to be good. But it was my family that did this to you. I should be begging for your forgiveness."

Still stroking Gwen's hair, Jimmy said, "What you should apologize for is being only slightly shorter than me even though you're on your knees. Damned freak."

"That chocolate bar in your shirt pocket. My body heat is melting it."

He pushed her away and then frantically pulled the bar out. It was incredibly limp. "Bitch!" He tore open the wrapper and stuffed the contents in his mouth. When he had swallowed, he licked the melted chocolate from the inside of the wrapper.

Looking at Gwen, Jimmy said, "I love you, Gwen. But not in that way. That's Chuckie's job. You can still call me elf, Amazon."

"Are you two done?" Charlie stood waiting with his arms crossed. "There could be mad killers down here."

"We were having a moment, Charlie," said Gwen.

"Yeah, back off," said Jimmy. "So, am I contaminated?"

"I don't think it means anything bad to a normal person," said Gwen. "All this crap seems to have something to do with blood. Maybe your family has the wrong blood or has something in it that they, whoever they are, don't like."

"That makes a lot of sense," said Charlie. "So, some blood could be contagious or maybe a bit dangerous. I don't know what promiscuous blood is."

"We should probably discuss this later," said Gwen. "Like you said, there could be mad killers down here."

Jimmy cursed mildly, then moved swiftly to escape his dead relatives.

About ten yards along the passage, Charlie went cold and squeezed Gwen's hand so hard she gave a short screech. He pointed at a capstone bearing his family name. He stood for several long minutes staring at the arch, trying to decide whether or not to go in. Charlie had been interested in his family history, but his parents had never been forthcoming with information. He only knew about his grandparents and a paternal uncle who was supposed to live in southern France. This meant that his family had been involved in all this long before his father brought them to Coverdale. Was the whole new job thing a scam?

There was a new word by the Bowen name that gave Charlie pause.

PURUM.

Pure?

"What is it, Charlie?" Gwen removed her hand from his. He hadn't realized he was still squeezing and hurting her.

"*Purum.* I think it means I'm in deeper shit than we thought. It might explain why they said I was important. Pure blood?"

Steeling his nerves, Charlie passed through the arch. The crypt went back farther than the beam of his flashlight could penetrate. The niches closest to the arch had nameplates that were covered with verdigris. Charlie assumed these were the oldest precisely because they were near the front. Charlie tried to rub some of the green rust away but failed to make the plates more readable. The earliest date he could read might have been 25, but the implications made Charlie's mind reel back in fear.

He walked as far as he could into the crypt. There were dozens, maybe a couple of hundred niches carved into the rock, each containing the mummified body of a dead Bowen or whatever the family had been. The name seemed to change sometime around 1750. At the farthest end of the crypt, Charlie found his grandparents. He clearly remembered the funeral service after his last grandparent, his father's father, had died. There had been no graveside ceremony because the man was to be cremated, or so Charlie had been told. Here was Grandfather John, wrapped like a mummy and lying in a niche in the rock under a town Charlie had never heard of until a few months ago.

Charlie was so overpowered by the implications of what he was seeing it took him a few minutes to figure out what was wrong.

The dates were incorrect. Grandfather John had died in 2006, but the copper plate under his niche gave his death year as 1894. The numbers weren't merely transposed because his birth date was listed as 1806. It didn't make sense.

Charlie said nothing when he re-joined Gwen and Jimmy, who had waited for him inside the crypt.

A quick check of his pocket watch told Charlie they had been in the tunnel of the dead for almost two hours. He stopped his companions and whispered to them, "We should almost be there."

"Where?" asked Jimmy.

"Haven't you figured it out yet? We're under the town. Up ahead, there should be a staircase or something leading up to the ..."

"Tomb outside the church," Gwen finished the sentence for him.

"Right. With any luck, the door won't be locked, and we can get out of here."

Jimmy didn't seem convinced. "The way our luck's been going, there'll probably be a welcoming committee on the lawn."

"Cheer up, Jimmy, we'll be out of here soon." Gwen tried to sound cheerful for Jimmy, but the lightness of her tone was forced. Jimmy walked away. "Charlie, why haven't we found a Blayney crypt?" Now Gwen sounded worried.

"I think I've found it, sort of," said Jimmy's voice from the darkness ahead.

Gwen and Charlie saw the beam of Jimmy's flashlight move as it illuminated the capstone of a massive arch. This arch was easily twice the size of all the other arches in the tunnel and was surrounded by intricate reliefs.

The only name on the capstone was REX MVNDI.

In a low voice, Charlie said, "The King of the World. I think they really mean it."

Charlie entered the crypt and quickly scanned the first few niches. All of them had nameplates free of verdigris and dirt; in fact, they looked as if they had been polished recently. The only name on the plates was "Rex Mundi."

"Someone takes care of this crypt," said Gwen from near the arch. She seemed reluctant to go any further into the enclosure.

Charlie reached out to touch one of the nameplates. "If this really is the burial place of the King of the World, then that makes sense."

"Who's Regina Mundi?" Jimmy was examining one of the nameplates.

"That's Queen of the World."

Jimmy went further into the crypt. "There don't seem to be any Princes or Princesses of the World. I guess they don't count."

"Maybe they get buried with whatever family they marry into," said Charlie. "Or each Rex only has one son."

"The Mayor is my maternal grandfather," said Gwen with a shaky voice. "Where is my family? Where are the Blayneys? Where are my parents?"

Charlie took Gwen in his arms. He hugged her, trying to comfort her. She shivered a little but hugged him back, holding on tightly as if she didn't want to let Charlie go, ever. He remembered what Mr. Tyndale had said about being Gwen's great-grandfather. Should He tell her? No, it wasn't his place to reveal something that important. Mr. Tyndale would do it when the time was right.

"There aren't any other Blayneys in town," said Jimmy. "I checked the phone book."

Gwen and Charlie regarded Jimmy with puzzlement. He shrugged. "All this crap with El and the Chief trying to keep you two apart. I got curious and wondered if you had any cousins I didn't know about. Someone who might not get Charlie in so much trouble. But there wasn't anyone."

Charlie was touched by his friend's desire to help him with Gwen and had to force down a lump in his throat. "Thanks," he managed to croak. "You hoped to set me up with someone other than Gwen."

Gwen almost swatted the back of Jimmy's head but pulled back.

"No, go ahead. I deserve it for thinking you two weren't destined to be together," said Jimmy. "Will you name your firstborn after me?"

She sighed, then swatted the back of his head.

"Your family must be from out of town, Gwen," said Jimmy. "Maybe from down south, where that university is that everyone seems to go to."

"The University of North Massachusetts," she said.

"Yeah," said Jimmy. "We could check it out later," he added confidently.

"On that note," said Charlie, "we should get moving. We've been underground for too long. Jimmy's starting to look like a mole." He reluctantly released Gwen.

"Better than looking like a zit," said Jimmy.

Charlie's hand went to the tender spot below his nose.

Shining his flashlight down the tunnel, they could see a set of steps leading up. The tunnel continued into the darkness. Before they got there, they found one final arch. This one was different in that it didn't lead into a crypt but was carved out of the rock with a shelf for a single corpse. Now, on the shelf, only some decayed cloth and broken bones remained. To Charlie, it looked as if someone had taken a hammer to the bones and smashed them.

Above the arch, carved into the bare rock, was REX POPULO.

"King of the People?" said Charlie.

"Only one," said Gwen. "I wonder why they changed the name. Or maybe he was something different altogether."

"We'll probably never know," said Charlie.

They moved on.

The wide stone steps that they assumed led up to the tomb in the churchyard were only twenty feet past the Mundy crypt.

Snapping off their flashlights, the three cautiously went up. They were met by a massive stone door that opened onto a small landing. The tomb had no windows, but they could hear the wind howling outside. Rain splattered on the roof.

"Must be a heck of a storm out there," said Jimmy.

The stone door had no handle. Charlie tried pressing and pulling the stones and carvings around the door, hoping to find a secret latch or spring that would release it. He found nothing.

"I guess we keep going along the tunnel," said Jimmy.

Two minutes later, they were standing at the top of another broad flight of stairs, this time, Charlie guessed, leading into the church.

"If it's locked, I'm going to kick it down," said Jimmy through clenched teeth. He eyed the wooden door that blocked their progress.

Charlie hesitated for a few moments before trying the door. He didn't want to be disappointed again. On either side of the door, sconces held candles melted to almost nothing. They might help Jimmy hack at the door.

Taking a deep breath, Charlie grasped the latch and pulled. The door opened easily and quietly.

Stepping through the doorway with Gwen and Jimmy, Charlie saw they were behind a thick lattice screen that backed the altar.

When they stepped around the screen, Mayor Mundy said, "I thought you'd never get here. We've been waiting."

El stood next to the Mayor, a smug smile on his weasel face.

Chapter Twenty-four

At the sound of the Mayor's voice, Charlie grabbed Gwen's hand and pulled her back. The three of them turned to run back into the tunnel. What blocked their way was a sight that froze them in mid-step.

Chief Wycliffe stood in the doorway. That was enough to stop them, but what did the trick was the way he was dressed. He wore a suit of chain mail, over which was draped a white tabard emblazoned with a red cross. The tabard was cinched at the waist by a wide leather belt. From the belt hung an empty scabbard.

The Chief held a broadsword out towards them. His eyes sparkled, but his face was grim. To Charlie, it looked like the Chief wanted them to make a move so he could use his weapon.

Jimmy dropped his knapsack and raised his arms in surrender. Charlie and Gwen raised their arms, still holding hands.

"Please come all the way in," said the Mayor calmly. "And put your arms down. No one's going to hurt you unless you force them to."

The three moved to the front of the altar, closely followed by the Chief, who pointed his sword straight at their backs, particularly Charlie. Seated before them in the right-hand set of pews were the members of the Town Council he had seen at various functions since arriving in Coverdale. They were dressed in their full ceremonial garb. In the left-hand pews were the twenty or so tramps from around town.

Behind the Council, Charlie saw his parents and Jimmy's father. George Bowen looked at his son. Charlie thought his father was having an argument with himself. It was as if he couldn't decide whether to be angry or afraid. One second, he scowled at Charlie as if he wanted to kill his son; the next, he looked sheepishly at the Mayor like he wanted to hide. Charlie's mother's eyes flitted around the church.

Charlie thought she might be admiring the architecture, oblivious to what was happening to her son. He felt momentary guilt for being unkind to his mother.

For his father, he felt nothing. Maybe not entirely nothing; there was some contempt.

"Sit," said the Mayor. He indicated three chairs that had been arranged in front of the altar.

On the way to the chairs, he had a good look at the altar. Atop it was a gigantic stone circle with a cross inside. It sat on another stone circle that had wooden posts sticking out. Did it rotate? In front of the circle sat a pile of shackles.

That did not look promising.

Charlie, Gwen, and Jimmy sat, facing the Council with their backs to the altar. Everyone stared at them, though Charlie saw that now his father would not look him in the eyes. His mother seemed more interested in everything about the church but the front.

The Mayor paced the space between the pews and the seated captives, for it was apparent now the three were captives. The Chief stood next to the seat Jimmy had taken and another policeman, also dressed as a knight, stood next to Gwen.

Charlie, sitting in the middle, watched the Mayor

nervously, trying to sort out what he was seeing:

The Chief and one of his men dressed like knights.

The Mayor wore robes and a golden crown that Charlie hadn't noticed before.

The Council, the tramps, his parents, everyone looking infuriated with them.

Charlie's knee began to jerk with a nervous twitch.

The silence was broken only by the sound of the Mayor's pacing.

Finally, Gwen spoke up. "Grandpa, what's going on? Why are these people here?"

The Mayor stopped pacing in front of his granddaughter. He looked down at her, his face full of sorrow. "You've caused us a lot of grief, my dear. I don't blame you." He glowered at Charlie. "But you should have known better, even if you did achieve our goal on your own."

Goal?

"Hey, Charlie," said Jimmy, "is this the part where the bad guys reveal their evil plans to the good guys?"

The Chief cuffed the back of Jimmy's head, almost knocking him out of his seat. "Quiet, boy!" he shouted. "Show respect for your betters."

Jimmy shook his head, trying to clear it. "Careful, Jimmy, the crusader doesn't have much of a sense of humor," said Charlie.

"Where's his cape, To the Bat ..." This time, the power of the Chief's blow knocked Jimmy to the floor. Charlie moved to help Jimmy back into his seat. The Chief stood by impassively, his eyes never leaving Charlie.

Before sitting, Jimmy faced the Chief and said, "No one gets to smack the back of my head except the Amazon here." He indicated Gwen then took his seat.

"Grandfather, why are you being so mean?" She turned to the Chief. "Uncle Willy? Don't hit my friend again."

The Chief bowed his head as if in respect.

"We're not being mean, my dear," said the Mayor calmly. "It's just the way things are. And thank you for your help."

Charlie spun in his seat and gaped at Gwen. She looked surprised.

"I'm glad you decided to speak to me about your plans for today. It made everything so much simpler to arrange."

Charlie felt his heart break. Betrayed by someone he loved. Yes, he was sure of it now. He loved Gwen, but there was a searing pain across his chest.

It was clear that Gwen could understand Charlie's feelings of betrayal. She tried to explain. "Charlie, I was so confused by what's been happening. Last night, I confided in grandfather and sought his advice. I'm sorry, I didn't know. I only told him I was seeing you today."

Charlie said nothing, not wanting to let out words he might later regret. Gulping in air, he looked at the Mayor.

"You've been here for almost two thousand years, haven't you?"

The Mayor smiled but remained silent.

"You might as well tell him," said someone from the choir box. "He's been more determined to get at the truth than any of the other sheep in this town. He deserves that much."

Mr. Tyndale got up slowly from his seat and, leaning heavily on his cane, hobbled over to the Mayor.

"You've got no business being here, David," said the Mayor. "This is the Council's concern."

"I'm the eldest member of this community. I have every right to be here. And she's ..."

The old man waved his cane in the Mayor's face. The

Chief made a move, but the Mayor motioned him back.

The Mayor stood his ground for a few seconds, then backed down. "Alright, David, I'll give the boy what he wants."

Charlie bristled at being called boy but didn't let that stop him. "*Have* you been here that long?"

The Mayor leaned against the railing in front of the pews. "We arrived here in 95 CE by your reckoning. We have our own calendar to measure time. You found the remains of one of our galleys in the cave. Some of our ancestors arrived much earlier but with less success. They built the stone circle."

"And nobody knows about you?"

"As you saw, we take care of intruders." The Mayor smiled.

The Chief stepped forward. "Sire, I don't think you should be telling this boy our secrets. He should be killed for the violations he has committed. As should the others."

The Mayor waved him off. "You must excuse the Chief," he said to Charlie, "he has a tendency to take his job too seriously at times. He also tends to forget his place and who you are," he added for the Chief's benefit. "They're not going anywhere."

"How have you been able to stay hidden for so long?"

"Our soldiers are particularly efficient, and we've got people in certain places who look out for us. They deflect prying eyes. They even divert nosy satellites."

Charlie turned to look at the Chief. "You look like a Templar." A grin crossed the Chief's otherwise impassive face.

"Excellent, son," said Mr. Tyndale. "You've studied your history."

Charlie nodded thanks at the old man and continued, "But

I thought the order was founded sometime around the crusades, in the eleven hundreds or so."

"That's what we want the world to believe, boy," said the Chief. "The Knights of the Temple were founded more than four thousand years ago to protect our homeland and our King." He bowed towards the Mayor and proudly said, "We have acted with honor ever since."

"So why show up for the crusades?" asked Jimmy, fully recovered from the blows to his head.

"It was a ploy," said the Mayor, "a way for our troops to gather strength in an attempt to regain our homeland. It failed, but not through any fault of ours. We had poor allies who could not be trusted."

"Where was your homeland? Hungary?" asked Charlie, still unable to believe what he was hearing. It so radically changed what he had learned of history.

The Mayor nodded at him. "Impressive. We once ruled a significant part of the area you call the Balkans. The part now called Hungary was the center. The People became weak and decadent. We were finally driven out by the savages of Rome."

He could see now why they hated the Romans so much. That explained his history class and the trouble he caused by his questions.

"But your name is Latin," said Charlie. "Roman."

A shadow crossed the Mayor's face. "They all stole our language from us, claimed it as their own. We can use whatever we want. It's ours."

Charlie decided not to ask any more questions. Things were getting too weird.

"Ask him about the Fallen King's treasure," said one of the councilors. Charlie didn't know the man, though he remembered being introduced to him at the welcome-to-town party.

"Yes, boy," said the Mayor, at which point Charlie resolved that the next person to call him boy would pay dearly, "What did you do with the treasure? Your father was unable to find it in your room."

Charlie felt another blow to his heart. He knew his father was only out for himself, which was clear early on, but to hear it confirmed by the mayor hurt. Now, to turn on his own son? He looked at the man he could no longer think of as his father. George Bowen smiled as if nothing was wrong. Position before family. Charlie wanted to spit in the man's eye.

But what had happened to the coins? Mr Tyndale knew about the alcove. Did he tell?

"I don't know what you're talking about," said Charlie. "Who's the Fallen King, and what is his treasure? By the way, what am I supposed to call you? Mr. Mayor? Mr. Mundy? Rex? Your Highness? Maybe a proper name like Sid or Ben? You look like a Ben to me. What do you think, Jimmy?"

This time, it was Charlie's turn to be cuffed by the Chief. "Don't be smart, boy. Answer the question."

Charlie smiled and looked the Chief square in the eyes. "Thanks, Uncle Willy."

Confusion filled the Chief's face for an instant, and then he punched Charlie in the jaw. Charlie went crashing into Gwen, who was knocked to the floor.

A collective gasp rose from the Council and the tramps. The Chief looked horrified. The Mayor's face was a mask of fury. The policeman beside Gwen helped her to her feet and righted her chair. "My lady," he said.

The Chief fell to his knees, hands clasped before him. "I beg forgiveness, Rex Mundi. I did not mean to strike a person of the Blood." To Charlie, he sounded terrified.

Through clenched teeth, the Mayor said, "We'll discuss it later, Chief. For now, try to curb your natural instincts to kill anything that moves before it gets *you* killed."

The Chief bowed his head and rose. He gave Charlie a look so filled with hate and venom; Charlie was sure he was doomed if the Chief ever got any say in the matter.

"He is the most loyal of followers, but he tends to get carried away defending our interests," the Mayor said, the anger gone.

"Damned maniac, if you ask me," said Mr. Tyndale.

The Mayor ignored the comment and said, "You may call me sire, though I suppose my proper name is the Rex Mundi. Now, the treasure?" He stared down at Charlie, who had remained on the floor, trying not to cry from the pain of the Chief's punch.

Charlie spat a glob of bloody saliva in the Chief's direction and got to his feet. His head spun from the blow and he swayed a little. Without hesitation, Charlie said, "There isn't any treasure. I found a few Roman coins in the garden. I made out like there were lots to impress Gwen." He hoped she would see through the lie. "Who was this Fallen King anyway?"

"He was one of the original exiles, a deposed king," said Mr Tyndale. "He supposedly had a hoard of gold and silver coins that he brought from the old world. It was said that he grew angry with the Council shortly after their arrival in this place and hid his hoard against a time when he would return to the old world."

"Rex Populo?" said Charlie.

"Impressive. He was tortured, but never revealed where he had hidden it," added the Rex Mundi. He nodded to his left.

Charlie looked and nearly fainted. He hadn't noticed the smell of fire with all the excitement, but there, next to the altar, stood a brazier. Its coals glowed bright red and orange. Sticking out from the coals was a large sword, its blade glowing from the heat.

"Is that for me?"

"I would hope not, but one never knows," said the Rex Mundi.

"If I may, sire," said El, who until now had remained silent in the background. "I know this boy better than he knows himself. Likewise, young James."

The Rex Mundi looked at his henchman with disdain. It was obvious the man had as much respect for El as Charlie. "All right, Justin. But be careful."

"Sire," said El with a bow. He moved to stand in front of the captives. "Now, while I must agree with the Chief that the three of you deserve punishment for your, shall we say, misdemeanors, you all have flaws that have caused you to act foolishly."

"Flaws your imagination created," said Charlie.

"Now, now, let's not get ahead of ourselves, Charlie. There are things I know that, perhaps, you don't want others to know?" He smiled and looked over at Jimmy. "Cooperation assures discretion."

"I'm gay. He raped me. Screw you, El Baldo."

There was a gasp from the crowd.

El's composure slipped for a moment, but he regained it quickly. "James, you know that's not true. I tried to help you in a time of great confusion. I am a small man. It was you who committed the ... wrong. Lies will get us nowhere."

Jimmy spat at El but missed.

El moved on to Gwen. "Dear Gwen, so loyal to me and

helpful. You kept me informed about everything, didn't you? I know you have deep feelings for me, and we've discussed that we must wait until you are of age. No, don't deny it. You've persisted for years and I've remained a gentleman despite your offers of ... shall we say, mutual pleasure. We can sort things out after we've dealt with the issues at hand."

He turned to face the Rex Mundi.

"Sire, your granddaughter has been the strongest among us. Despite this boy's attempts to seduce her and at one time assault her to steal her virtue, Gwen has been brave enough to tolerate his advances for the benefit of the People."

Charlie felt everyone's eyes on him. El was painting him as some kind of abuser. He turned to look at Gwen, knowing that if she had said anything, it was in innocence and not a betrayal. He wished he could tell her how he felt and that he was sorry for ever doubting her. Gwen looked back at him and smiled. He knew she knew how he felt. She winked.

"And now you, Charlie, who has harbored secret and unhealthy desires for both his mother and sister." There was a gasp from somewhere in the crowd. "Look at your mother now. She's had to be put on medication because she's so worried about you. See what you've done."

He looked over at his mother, who was still looking all over the church as if unable to focus on anything. Was she drugged? Was that why she had changed so drastically since the move? Were drugs dampening the free spirit in his mother that he had so admired? George Bowen didn't show the slightest bit of surprise at this news. Charlie had no trouble believing his father would go that far to protect his job. No, he didn't have a father anymore.

"Despite being told time and again that Gwen was not interested in you, you have persisted to the point of attempted

... I shan't repeat the word. I've tried so hard to be kind and help you, Charlie, but you insisted on pursuing your misguided attempts to soil this lovely girl."

Charlie took a deep breath. "Justin, El Baldo as we call you, or you back-stabbing, slimy, little scumbag, shut the hell up. I'm tired, as I'm sure everyone else is, of your constant attempts to gaslight everyone. You're worthless, have nothing to offer, set people against each other by making up ridiculous shit and spreading lies." He looked over at the Rex Mundi. "Sir, if you have any mercy in that cold heart of yours, torture me now so I don't have to listen to this asshole anymore. Please."

Still appearing calm, El said, "Now, Charlie ..."

"That's enough, Justin," said the Rex Mundi. "I think we can take things from here. It seems, incredible as it may be, that this young man has the measure of you and can outtalk you at every turn."

"But ... I ..." El looked defeated.

"Sit down, Justin, and remain silent," said the Rex Mundi. While El returned to his seat, the Rex Mundi stepped in front of Charlie just as he spat out another bloody glob of saliva. The Rex Mundi handed him a handkerchief. "Please, Charlie, stop desecrating our church. Use that for your mess."

"Thank you." Charlie blew his nose loudly. His jaw throbbed. "So, what now, Rex Mundi?" He felt Gwen take his hand and squeeze. Instantly, Charlie was prepared to do whatever he could to protect her.

"Yeah. How about you let us go and we forget any of this ever happened?" Jimmy said, still grinning. "I'm quite prepared to forgive and forget. Maybe not El, but fuck him anyway. How 'bout you, Charlie? Gwen?"

Before they could answer, the Chief lifted Jimmy by his

jacket collar and tossed him into the air. Jimmy crashed to the floor and rolled into the railing in front of the pews. As he tried to pick himself up, the Chief strode over and kicked him in the stomach.

"Chief!" the Rex Mundi shouted.

The Chief ignored him and picked Jimmy up. He threw him against the choir box. Jimmy grunted when he struck the wooden railing and fell in a heap to the floor.

"Jimmy!" His father jumped up to go to his son's aid, but was held back by Charlie's father.

"Chief!" the Rex Mundi shouted again, louder.

Distracted by the shout and Gwen's anguished cry of alarm when she finally saw what was happening, the Chief didn't see Jimmy rise. The boy reached out, grabbed a large candlestick that stood by the choir box, and raised it over his head, ready to bring it down across the Chief's back.

Charlie didn't see what happened next; it was all a blur, but he pieced it together later.

Apparently aware of his attacker, the Chief pulled his sword free of its scabbard. Just as Jimmy lunged, the Chief spun and thrust his sword forward. He must have realized that Jimmy was no real danger to him because he turned the blade at the last moment. However, Jimmy's momentum carried him onto the Chief's sword, and the blade pierced his left side, just below his ribs.

The Chief staggered back, unbalanced by Jimmy's weight. Charlie saw the tip of the sword emerge in a shower of blood from Jimmy's back. Jimmy coughed once, spewing blood into the Chief's face, then crumpled to the floor.

Jimmy's father screamed and tried to run to his fallen son but was now held back by several councilors.

The Chief stood, impassive, over Jimmy's bleeding body.

Five of the tramps dashed to Jimmy. One held his hands over Jimmy's wound while the other four lifted the boy. They swiftly carried him out a door at the end of the west transept, leaving a trail of blood as they went.

Charlie stood, overwhelmed with rage by what he had seen. He wanted to strangle the Chief but felt totally helpless. The other knight had drawn his sword and stood behind Charlie, ready to run him through if he tried anything.

"Don't worry," said the Rex Mundi, trying to calm Jimmy's father. The councilors still held him. "The priests will take care of him."

Jimmy's father broke away from the councilors and ran after his son. The councilors started to follow but were called back.

The Rex Mundi turned to regard Charlie, his face stern. "You've seen what can happen. The choice is yours. You've already caused one person to suffer. Do you want to inflict more harm?"

Charlie noticed George Bowen do a double-take at the Rex Mundi's words. "You're threatening my family now?" Charlie said as calmly as he could. "Brave of you." He gave the man what he hoped was a withering look of contempt and sat down.

The Rex Mundi gave Charlie a formidable look. "We could get your cousin here, but he's busy undermining the regimes that pretend to rule our homeland."

A cousin! Charlie wondered if there were any more surprises in store for him today?

"We don't know exactly where he is, and we don't have the time to search for him. We need your bloodline, boy," the Rex Mundi went on, "and you're the one that can help us the most."

"Purum?" Charlie thought for a second, then said, "I don't know what you're talking about, but no way am I ever going to help you."

The Rex Mundi snapped his fingers, and a door by the church aisle opened. Ant stumbled in, followed by another policeman dressed like a knight. Her wrists were bound, and her hair was tied back. When she reached the railing and halted, the Rex Mundi nodded to the Chief, who stepped over the railing and stood behind Ant. He grabbed Ant's hair and pulled her head back sharply. Ant let out a choked scream.

The Chief held a dagger to Ant's throat.

"Ant!" cried Charlie. "No!"

"You should feel privileged, boy," said the Rex Mundi, smiling. "Most boys must wait until their nineteenth birthday for the ritual of initiation. Say the word, and you will be admitted to our community."

Charlie saw the pleading in his sister's eyes. Tears rolled down her cheeks. A trickle of blood ran down her neck from where the Chief had nicked the skin with his dagger.

"Do it, Charlie," said his sister. "Please!"

Mr. Tyndale stepped forward.

"Think, my lad, think. Even Galileo had to admit when he was wrong. Think." The old man stared at Charlie.

He stared back, trying to understand what was going on. "But Galileo ..." he began. Then it hit him. "But it still moves." He stopped speaking and looked over at Gwen. She was so beautiful. He thought about Jimmy, his best friend, probably dead thanks to the thug now holding his sister.

Ant screamed again.

"Okay," said Charlie, sure of what he had to do now. "Where do I sign up."

Chapter Twenty-five

Charlie sat quietly in a small room off the chancel with Mr. Tyndale. The old man had insisted on accompanying Charlie while preparations were made for the ritual of initiation. Gwen had been taken to another room where she was being prepared for another ritual that Charlie could only guess about.

After a quick wash, Charlie was presented with a ceremonial outfit. He didn't think much of it: a short white tabard made of rough cloth with a red cross across the chest. He pulled it over his head after removing his jacket and T-shirt. His hair was tied back with a red headband. They replaced his black and dirty jeans with loose-fitting wool trousers that itched. He had to wear sandals. He felt foolish in the clothes.

Word reached him that Jimmy was in serious condition but would live. He was being cared for at The Institute. Charlie had shuddered when he thought about the Standish boys hooked up to the machines in The Institute. He hoped Jimmy wouldn't suffer the same fate.

He still marveled that a little guy like Jimmy had been bold enough to attack the Chief. There was a brave heart in that elfish body.

"Tell me," Charlie finally said to Mr. Tyndale. The fury of the storm outside unnerved him. It seemed to be directly overhead now, ear-shattering claps of thunder followed immediately by blinding lightning flashes.

Mr. Tyndale leaned forward on his cane, sighed, and said, "The Rex Mundi can only be passed on through the male bloodline. Our present King had only one son who was killed with Gwen's parents in an accident."

He looked away for a moment and quietly said, "If it was an accident. Damn you, Justin."

"You said Gwen is your great-granddaughter. Does that mean you're part of the Mundi line? And when are you going to tell her about your connection? She feels so alone. There are no Blayneys in the crypts."

"I can't tell her yet. In time, son. As for the missing Blayneys, they always presented a bit of a problem for the Rex Mundi."

"How? What's it got to do with Gwen? This is such a load of ..."

Mr. Tyndale took Charlie's hand. "Although Gwen is a direct descendent of the Blood, she cannot inherit. Not only is she female, it's the wrong line of the Blood."

"He said they need my bloodline. I don't understand. How can hers be the wrong line?"

"Your great-great-great grandmother was a member of the Mundi line. You are the closest male to the Blood through your mother. The tests on you were ... positive, astounding at 90 percent purity. That's higher than our current King. Thanks to your father's work at The Institute, the Blood will continue. And become more pure."

Charlie felt confused. "What exactly is my father's work? How does it make me anything special?"

"You are compatible with the present Rex Mundi. You can continue the Blood from his line."

"I still don't understand. Why not Gwen?"

"She's 90 percent as well. But her line is not as, shall we

say, popular with the hierarchy." The old man smiled kindly at Charlie. "You'll figure it out, I'm sure. You're smart enough. It's nothing for you to worry about right now. There are more pressing matters at hand."

"Why are you being so nice to me? I thought I'd caused all kinds of trouble for you lot."

"My lot," the old man chuckled, "not really anymore. Though he owes much for my loyalty, the current Rex Mundi does not have respect for me or my line. He has turned from the old ways and wants too much power. And as for Chief Wycliffe," he shuddered, "when I was Chief, we did things with less relish for shedding blood."

Charlie was astounded. "You were once Chief of Police here?"

Mr. Tyndale straightened a little in his chair. "I once commanded the whole of the Order," he said proudly, "though I always had time for my films."

"How did you find the time?"

"Mine were more administrative duties. That was a time when the war was in a quiet phase. I fear it might be gearing up again."

"What war?"

"The world war that has raged since Napoleon first took his army out of France. It's all connected. Over two hundred years of non-stop conflict. Men like the Chief want to heat things up. Provoke. Attack. Idiots." He sighed. "Still, it's not for you to worry about yet. Perhaps in a few years, perhaps not. A lot depends on you and Gwen."

Charlie's head was ready to explode. "Why are you telling me this?"

"I hoped you would understand."

"I've read about Galileo," said Charlie, taking a chance

and trusting Mr. Tyndale.

"I thought you might have," the old man said. "You're curious about the town. We used to receive ships from the Old World. No doubt you've seen the docks."

Charlie nodded. "I wondered about them. They seem to be in an odd location, at the bottom of a steep river bank."

"Before the town was rebuilt in 1878, there was a fortified wall around it. The only way into the town from the river was through a tunnel just above the docks. The tunnel connected to the old commercial building, now my theatre, and thence to the church."

"What about other ships coming up the river?"

"There's a series of sandbars downriver that make it appear unnavigable. But if you had a chart or were plain unlucky, you could find your way through."

"Why was the town rebuilt?" asked Charlie, taking in everything the old man said.

"To disguise its age. A town built almost two thousand years ago would stick out like a sore thumb around here."

"But you kept people out or killed any that got through."

"There was always the chance someone would see something and escape our guards. Why take the risk?"

"And you sanctioned it?"

"I actively participated in it, Charlie. I suppose, from your point of view, there are no good guys and bad guys in this. We all have innocent blood on our hands. In the old days, the Rex Mundi only ruled our own small world. Nowadays, they take the title too literally. It's a shame."

The implications of what Mr. Tyndale had told him scared the crap out of Charlie. He wanted to run away and not be involved in this anymore.

Charlie thought for a moment. Gwen. He couldn't forget

Gwen.

There was a knock at the door, and then a knight stuck his head in the room.

Mr. Tyndale rose and stuck out his hand. Charlie took it and shook it. "It's always good to meet another old movie fan," said the old man. He hobbled out the door. Before he exited, Mr. Tyndale turned back to Charlie and said, "When I was young, the theatre was a place I could go to escape the realities of life for a little while. Those old movies tell us a lot of things, Charlie. Resist the temptation to ignore them." He left the room.

Charlie followed and was surprised to see the pews were full. It looked as if most of the townspeople had turned out to see the ritual of initiation. The Rex Mundi walked over to Charlie.

"This is a special day," he beamed. "Not only will you be joined with the community, but the Blood will be doubly ensured when you are joined with Gwen."

Charlie gaped at him. If that meant what he thought it meant, Charlie was about to get married. He was speechless, his mind a mass of confusion. Sure, he loved Gwen and wanted a future with her. They were engaged, but he wanted them to sort things out themselves. He did not want some megalomaniac to do it for them.

The Rex Mundi led Charlie to the choir box and passed him to one of the waiting tramps. Perfect Ones, Charlie corrected himself. He had finally remembered something he had read in one of his history books. The Cathars, a sect of heretics in medieval France, had called their priests Perfect Ones, and the Cathars were supposed to have come from somewhere in the Balkans. The Perfect Ones took vows of poverty and roamed the countryside, spreading the word.

They were highly respected by their followers.

He was living in an historical nightmare. Charlie's rational mind wanted to stop everything, talk to these people, and find out the truth behind a lot of historical speculation.

Charlie's emotional mind just wanted to run screaming out of there and hide for a few dozen years.

He looked around the church. The Perfect Ones all sat to one side, deep in prayer. The Council was arrayed across the front pew. The choir box was filled with knights: musical soldiers? The Chief sat in the center, staring straight at him. He did not look amused. Charlie's parents sat in the second pew, a significant move forward now that Charlie was about to be honored, he guessed.

He wondered if his father was satisfied now. He didn't care.

A door in the eastern transept creaked open, and Gwen entered the church. She was a vision, dressed in a white gown with red trim and red ribbons woven into her hair. She looked nervous, and when she saw Charlie, she blushed.

Charlie guessed she must have been told what was to happen.

A knight led Gwen over to stand next to Charlie at the altar.

Charlie's legs shook. The choir began singing a hymn. He didn't recognize the tune, but the words were in Latin and told the story of the rightful King and his new bride. Staring straight ahead, Charlie tried to formulate a plan.

Behind the altar was the lattice screen. Through the carving in the screen, he could see the door that led to the tunnel.

Charlie took Gwen's hand and casually looked around. The closest people to them were the Perfect Ones, about ten feet away.

"Gwen," said Charlie, looking ahead and trying not to move his lips, "can you hear me?"

"Yes," came a husky reply.

"Do you want to get out of this? Do you trust me?"

"I want to be with you, Charlie, if you can forgive me for betraying you." Gwen sounded so sorry. Charlie wanted to take her in his arms and hug the doubt right out of her.

"There was never anything to forgive." Charlie glanced at Gwen, and the radiant smile that greeted him made him doubly sure of his desire to get her away from this. And to marry her.

"Open the door to the tunnel when I give the signal. You'll know when." He gave her hand a reassuring squeeze then let go.

The choir continued to sing, the Perfect Ones kept up their prayers. The congregation had their heads bowed.

Quietly, Charlie said, "Now."

Gwen darted to the side of the altar and around behind the screen. Charlie leaped onto the altar and threw candlesticks and chalices into the congregation. He tried to push over the stone cross, but it was too heavy to move on his own.

The sound of the storm had masked Gwen's exit. The first noise to get anyone's attention was the cry of someone upon whom Charlie scored a direct hit to the head with a candlestick.

Everyone turned in the direction of the cry. Everyone except the Chief. He was on his feet immediately, trying to shove his way to the front of the choir box.

Charlie saw the Chief moving, looked through the screen, and saw Gwen waiting for him inside the tunnel door.

Charlie took a few quick steps and leaped at the screen,

hoping he was heavy enough to do what he had planned.

When his feet collided with the wood, it was enough to start the screen toppling backward against the wall behind the altar. When the screen hit the wall, Charlie's momentum carried him straight through the lattice and into the open doorway. The screen shattered, raining chunks of wood behind the altar and blocking the door.

He slammed the door shut, yanked one of the sconces from the wall, and jammed it into the latch. Charlie pulled the second sconce from the other side of the door and smashed it into the first. The door wouldn't hold for long, but it might give them enough time to escape. Charlie picked up Jimmy's discarded knapsack and fished out the child's flashlight. He snapped it on and gasped.

While Charlie had been jamming the door, Gwen had removed the white dress. Charlie's jaw dropped when he saw her wearing only an embroidered cotton undershirt, silk panties, and satin slippers. Despite the seriousness of the situation, he couldn't stop his physical reaction to the sight.

"No time to gawk, twit. We've got to run, and I couldn't move very quickly in that thing. But thank you. Now get that silly thing off."

He quickly removed the tabard and tossed it aside. Gwen raised an eyebrow when she saw his bare chest. She took Charlie's hand, and they ran down the steps. At the bottom, he stopped her when she turned to run towards the crypts.

"This way," he said and pulled her behind him.

The beam from the flashlight flickered as they ran. Charlie figured the batteries must be wearing out. From behind came the sound of someone pounding on the door.

They came to a heavy iron door in another twenty yards. It was covered with rust and didn't look like it had been opened in years. Charlie ran the fading light beam around the edge of the door, looking for a latch or handle. He found it. He also noticed what looked like fresh oil on the hinges, some of which had dripped down the door. Letting go of Gwen's hand, Charlie grabbed a few handfuls of dirt and threw them over the oil. He pulled on the handle, and the door opened easily and silently.

"Thank you, Mr. Tyndale," he whispered.

"What do you mean?" asked Gwen.

"I'll tell you later," he said, then cursed under his breath when he heard voices in the tunnel behind them.

He tugged Gwen through the door and gently closed it. He heard the latch click shut.

The tunnel took a few unexpected twists, but Charlie's sense of direction told him they were headed the right way. There were no sounds of pursuit behind them. Twenty minutes later, they came to another flight of steps.

"That'll lead up to the theatre," he said, and they ran past the stairs.

The dim light of the storm flashed from far up the tunnel. Charlie was tempted to toss away the almost useless flashlight but kept it because the last thing he wanted was for one of them to slip and get hurt. Not when they were this close to getting away.

They walked carefully until the sound of the storm met them when they neared the end of the tunnel. Lightning flashed and showed tree roots draped across an opening.

Pushing aside the roots, Charlie looked out into the night. Rain poured down, making visibility almost nil. He could hear water splashing.

A flash of lightning revealed they were about twenty feet from the river's shore, under the old docks. A motorboat was moored to one of the rotting pilings.

Charlie and Gwen slid down the muddy riverbank to the docks. Though it was dark and raining heavily, Charlie feared Gwen's fancy undershirt might attract attention. He need not have worried because she was soon covered with muck when they both lost their footing and tumbled the last few feet to the river's edge.

They remained still, momentarily listening for any sounds of someone coming after them. Between the thunder crashes, he heard distant shouting and perhaps the baying of dogs. Would they take them into the tunnels and follow their scent?

The darkness and the heavy rain made it almost impossible to see anything beyond the cover of the bridge. That should also mean their pursuers wouldn't be able to see them.

They carefully waded out to the motorboat. Luckily for both of them, it was August, and the water was not too cold. After helping Gwen climb into the boat, Charlie joined her.

Gwen reached over, untied the rope from the piling, then sat in one of the seats.

Attached to the steering wheel was a plastic bag. He opened it and found a note.

G & C. Go west, inland. They'll expect you to go downriver towards the city. There's a small channel on the opposite shore where the roadblock is set up. Row through it quietly. They will probably be on the alert. Once past the bend, go full throttle for half an hour, then look for the duck blind on the western shore. Just inland is a shack. You'll know what to do. Good luck. Maybe we'll meet again. G, have C tell you about my family. D.

They looked at each other. "No time to wonder now," said Gwen.

Charlie stared at the boat's controls. He had never driven a motorboat.

"Ever driven one of these before?" he asked Gwen.

"I've never even driven a car. So, no. What about that?" She pointed at a key in the dashboard, so Charlie turned it.

The motor roared to life while thunder crashed overhead and muffled the sound. Once it had started, the motor settled down to a low rumble.

Charlie gripped what he assumed was a throttle and pushed it forward.

The boat surged ahead, throwing Charlie back into his seat. Unprepared for the sudden move, Gwen yelped as she was thrown out of her seat onto the boat floor. He was tempted to pull up and help her back into her chair but decided to get them out of there as fast as possible. He grabbed the wheel and twisted it to steer the boat downriver.

No one followed them.

Gwen scrambled back into her seat, rubbing her left knee. "I'm okay," she shouted above the storm when Charlie looked over at her. "Drive this thing."

Charlie took one last look back just before the boat passed under what remained of the new bridge. In a flash of lightning, he saw the silhouette of a man standing on the bank above the old docks.

He was leaning on a cane.

Epilogue

The motorboat had taken them up the Pannon River, the driving rain and thunder concealing them and the sound of their vessel. A force of habit had made the policemen at the roadblock turn on their cruiser's lightbar. The flashing red had created an easy-to-see warning that they needed to shut off the motor. The current through the narrow channel had been too fast for them to row, so Charlie jumped in the water to pull the boat close to shore. The channel was only about four feet deep, and Charlie and Gwen were able to tow the boat using the mooring lines.

The temperature had dropped quite a lot. When they were through the channel and back on the boat, both were shivering uncontrollably. Huddled together for warmth, they found the duck blind and, beyond it, the shack. There were fresh clothes for both of them, somehow removed from their own closets back home.

Coverdale was not home anymore. It was now a strange place of threats and danger.

A most welcome gift was a thermos of hot tea. It was clear that whoever had left their things had been at the shack within a few hours of their arrival, perhaps only minutes. Someone had known what the Council had planned for the pair. That someone—Mr. Tyndale? —had gone to great pains to ensure their escape. But he was old and frail.

There had to be others in Coverdale, perhaps friends and

allies, who hated the direction the Rex Mundi was steering them as much as Mr. Tyndale. A single blue rose in a vase gave them a hint as to the identity of one of them.

An overnight bag held some toiletries and a surprise. Crammed in an envelope were hundred-dollar bills. Another envelope held several thousand dollars in smaller bills.

A final gift was a set of car keys.

Outside, they found a minivan, fully gassed up. The interior was done up like a small home with twin beds, a mini stove and microwave, and a fully stocked refrigerator. Cupboards contained more food and necessities. It was cramped but looked comfortable.

In a storage unit under one of the beds were the sword, mace, and musket from the hidden alcove in his room. There was also a bag of coins from the Fallen King's treasure. Gwen shook with fear because of the old legend when she saw them. He told her what he learned from Mr. Tyndale about how they were for him to use. Neither knew what it meant.

A map on the driver's seat had a route laid out that would take them north through the forest to a series of backroads and old highways leading west, far from Coverdale.

They drove off immediately. Gwen watched Charlie closely, anticipating the time she could share driving duty. They only stopped for gas, to use the bathroom, and to let Charlie grab some sleep for a few hours.

On the third day, Gwen drove. She was much better at it than Charlie.

Four days later, they were in a mall parking lot on the outskirts of Santa Fe.

They hadn't spoken more than a few words to each other the whole time.

"Why did he help us?" Gwen asked at last between

mouthfuls of fast-food burgers.

Charlie's haggard face looked back at her from the driver's seat, where he kept watch for anything suspicious. "Because of you, Gwen. In the note, he wrote for you to ask me about his family. He took me into his confidence one day when I was looking for you. He's your great-grandfather. On your mother's side. He said something about the Blayneys always causing trouble."

"I don't understand."

"Neither do I. He said something about you being in direct line with the Blood, like me, but that your line was the wrong one. It's not as popular, whatever that means."

"But he was one of them."

Charlie put down his burger and took Gwen's hand. "He didn't seem to like what your grandfather was doing – what his aims were. Maybe he just wanted to go back to the old ways, the old ideals, and saw helping us as a start."

"The old ways didn't sound much better, Charlie. They still killed people who found them. There must be something else. Those things going on at The Institute, maybe?"

"Until we get a chance to talk to him, we'll never know."

Gwen jumped back, eyes wide. "You can't possibly think of going back there. They'll kill you the moment they see you. Me, too."

"I have to find out what's going on. And I have to make sure Ant's okay. Even if she is a pain, she's still my sister. Mom, too. Fuck my father."

"No way, it's too dangerous."

Charlie looked her straight in the eyes. "I have to find out."

Gwen didn't look convinced. "Absolutely not, Charlie. If you really love me, you'll stay with me, far away from those maniacs."

"I do love you, Gwen, more than anything. But ..."

"But what about me? Where do I stay while you risk your life? I want to go with you."

They had argued for hours. Charlie refused to allow Gwen to endanger herself. In the end, they kept going west.

The next day, in Albuquerque, while Gwen was in a store getting supplies, a man showed too much interest in her, asking many pointed questions. Though Charlie thought it might have been someone trying to pick her up, she was frightened, sure she had been recognized.

They left town immediately.

Over the next four months, they became intimately familiar with each other. They kept on the move, traveling only at night, spending the daylight hours hiding in plain sight in mall parking lots, sleeping in shifts. They quickly got used to using a bucket instead of gas station bathrooms to minimize contact with others and lessen the time required to be out of the van. Fear overcame Charlie's disgust, but their dignity trumped fear the fourth time the bucket tipped over while they were driving. The stink lasted for weeks.

Gwen had suggested they find an isolated cabin somewhere in the mountains to hunker down. However, they both became spooked by the slightest scrutiny from strangers. Charlie saw signs in graffiti, shop windows, and newspapers that hinted the hunt for them was still on.

Paranoia ruled their lives: they trusted no person, no hiding place.

The enemy could be anywhere, anyone.

They kept moving.

With the onset of winter, they went to California and roamed there until the following spring.

For two years, they wandered, never staying in one area for more than a week.

When their cash ran out, they dipped into the stash of coins. That had been a learning experience. Dealers were suspicious of a young kid selling such valuable items. Charlie had been forced to sell many of the coins for far less than a reputable dealer would have paid. Still, selling a single coin covered their expenses for a couple of months. As time passed, though, and Charlie began to look more mature and become wiser to dealers' ways, he got a fairer price.

One day in a coin shop, while waiting for the owner to assess the Greek coin Charlie was selling, he noticed a newsletter. The main story was about a series of rare coins appearing on the market over the last few months. The writer speculated on their origin. The writer's name, a collector, was Knox. Charlie took the store owner's first offer, five thousand in cash, and beat a hasty retreat.

That was the last one they sold.

Whenever possible, they did research on the Temple. Gwen's gift for lateral thinking enabled her to ferret out obscure facts and follow leads Charlie would have missed. They scoured libraries, starting with the most obvious items first. They learned everything that was known about the Knights Templar, Balkan history, and anything that might help. Charlie created a database of names and places to aid in their research. All of it on file cards so as not to leave a digital trail. The names of Coverdale families were researched, but not surprisingly, there was little information about them.

The mother lode turned out to be the University of North Massachusetts. Though closely allied with the Temple, the university was open to the public. Gwen concluded it was a source of not only extra income for the Temple but also knowledge and possible recruits. Heavily disguised—Charlie had grown a long beard and shaved his head; Gwen had cut her hair short, dyed it a dark brown, and had given herself a perm—they had gone to the university library and archives. Still, they only stayed a couple of days.

Charlie and Gwen were determined to bring the Temple down. It might take years, but they had nothing else to do and nothing to lose. They had laughed at the audacity of two young people fighting an institution that had lasted for twenty-five hundred years or more, but someone had to do it.

Two pieces of information proved to be both perplexing and terrifying.

"The Institute is searching for the Holy Grail," said Gwen one day while sitting in a library carrel in Gainesville, Florida.

Charlie leaned over to Gwen from the next carrel. "It's *Sang Real*. True Blood. No, not like the TV show. They want the bloodline to be pure from something too far back in the past to figure out. They're nuts. They'll do anything to achieve their goal."

Three weeks later, in New Orleans, Charlie left Gwen in a used record store while he went to check a few things at a local library. An hour later, he hurried her out. He looked panicked.

"Drop everything and follow me." When Gwen protested, he gave her a steely look and said, "No questions. We've got to get out of here fast."

They jumped in their van and were outside the city limits within half an hour, on their way to Baton Rouge.

"What was that all about?" Gwen asked, keeping her eyes on the road ahead. It turned out she was a much more cautious driver than Charlie, less prone to panic in tense situations.

He looked at the road map on his lap, trying to figure out where to go next. "West at Baton Rouge. We'll go to Mexico for a while," then looked in the van's side mirror.

"Nobody is following us," Gwen said, trying not to sound anxious.

"I was searching the military academy records back at the library."

Gwen looked shocked. "Charlie! We're supposed to stay away from computers. What were you thinking?"

"I'm sorry. It was stupid, but I was following a lead."

"Did you get far?"

"Nothing too deep, just trying to find out what was going on. I found their training manual. They teach their men to walk on air."

Gwen snorted.

"I'm serious," Charlie said. "They walk so quietly, they can move through a forest without disturbing the birds or bugs. You'd never know they're there. Carpets are nothing to these guys."

"What are you getting at, Charlie? You're not making much sense."

"They're coming after us, and we'll never know when they're around."

"I know they're after us. They have been ever since we left Coverdale. But they don't know where we are."

Charlie started to cough, hacking so much his eyes watered. He quickly loosened his seat belt, rolled down the window, and leaned out, retching. Gwen pulled the van over to the shoulder, but Charlie gasped that she should keep going.

He would be alright.

"Sorry," he said when he seemed recovered, "nerves. You know, I threw up before our first date."

"Good times," they said in unison and laughed.

Gwen squeezed his hand.

"While I was reading the training manual," Charlie continued, "the screen suddenly went blank. Then a message came up, 'Hello, Charlie.' I nearly wet myself and got out of there as fast as I could."

Realizing they couldn't cross the border without any ID, they stopped in Houston, where Charlie searched the dark web for some way for them to get new identities. It was surprisingly easy. However, it was expensive. Using some fancy computer work, they were able to acquire what they needed by trading the remaining coins from the stash through a convoluted route that maintained their anonymity.

Armed with untraceable passports, credit cards, and personal documents, Charlie and Gwen went to Mexico.

They drove through Mexico quickly, stopping to see some Aztec and Mayan ruins. Charlie couldn't resist.

South America had seemed like a good idea. It was about as far from Coverdale as they could get without leaving the Americas. Their enemies were connected with Europe, and so might not have contacts down south. The Andes and the Amazon jungle provided a wealth of places to disappear.

Gwen stood out like a sore thumb: a six-foot white woman with long blonde hair, but she kept herself wrapped in whatever passed for native dress and walked with a stoop. Charlie was relieved that she had let her hair grow and return to its natural state. He'd stopped shaving his head, and his beard was too hot for southern climes. Silly, maybe, but it was a small bit of vanity for both of them. They learned to speak Spanish and Portuguese, and eventually, no one took much notice of them.

In the fifth year of their exile, they were in a small town high in the Chilean Andes. It was market day. Passing a cemetery wall, they were stunned to see a red a cross in a circle. The paint was still wet. Like deer in the headlights, they froze for an instant, then turned and ran into the crowd-filled streets. Taking a circuitous route, they got back to their hotel by the river in about an hour.

Charlie regretted the moment of weakness that had led him to talk Gwen into staying in a small hotel rather than the van. It was only for a few nights, and the queen-sized bed was a luxury he thought they deserved.

"How did they find us, and why aren't we already dead?" Charlie wanted to hit something.

Gwen said nothing but began to pack their simple belongings. Most of their research notes were locked in the van.

Charlie carefully unscrewed the light bulbs from the fixtures in their room, then went into the hallway and removed the ones from the fixtures there, too. He put all the bulbs in a pillowcase and then stomped on it, crushing them.

"I saw this in a movie," he said, spreading broken glass along the hallway leading to their room door.

He closed the door and looked at Gwen. She stopped packing and sighed.

"There's not much chance of us getting out of here, is

there?" She walked over to Charlie and put her arms around him.

"The broken glass might give us some warning. Even silent assassins can't walk silently over that much glass."

There was the sound of a crunch from the other side of the door. They looked at each other and moved over to the window. It was too far to jump down to the roof of the next building.

"I love you," they said together. "Owe me a coke."

The door burst open, and the assassin strode in, broadsword thrust out ahead of him.

"Charlie and Gwen," said the assassin.

"Jimmy!"

www.ingramcontent.com/pod-product-compliance
Lightning Source LLC
Chambersburg PA
CBHW051124300726

48981CB00023B/538/J